MindField

A Novel

John F. Egbert

iUniverse, Inc.
New York Lincoln Shanghai

MindField

Copyright © 2006 by John F. Egbert

iUniverse books may be ordered through booksellers or by contacting:

iUniverse
2021 Pine Lake Road, Suite 100
Lincoln, NE 68512
www.iuniverse.com
1-800-Authors (1-800-288-4677)

This is a work of fiction. All of the characters, names, incidents, organizations, and dialogue in this novel are either the products of the author's imagination or are used fictitiously.

ISBN-13: 978-0-595-42158-9 (pbk)
ISBN-13: 978-0-595-86498-0 (ebk)
ISBN-10: 0-595-42158-X (pbk)
ISBN-10: 0-595-86498-8 (ebk)

Printed in the United States of America

WITHDRAWN

30/04/24

MindField

I dedicate this book to my daughter, Stella, for the knowledge she continues to share with me; knowledge gleaned from all her contributions and experiences as a Deaf person in the field of education.

A tipping point is the best way to understand the emergence of fashion trends, the ebb and flow of crime waves, or, for that matter, the transformation of unknown books into bestsellers, or the rise of teenage smoking, or the phenomena of word of mouth, or any number of the other mysterious changes that mark everyday life. Think of them as epidemics. Ideas and products and messages and behaviors spread just like viruses do.

—Malcolm Gladwell
The Tipping Point
How Little Things Can Make A Big Difference

Acknowledgements

I would like to thank my wife, Shirley, for being patient and for understanding who I am, and all that I wanted to achieve in life. I also thank my two wonderful children, Clyde and Stella, who grew up adventurously as I have. I have learned many things from them about life. I am sincerely speechless about how fortunate I am for having such a wonderful family.

I would also like to thank my special friend, Robert Woodcox. He has been my mentor, coach, and advisor throughout the collaboration of writing this book.

Prologue

Stella Bannister leaned forward in her chair at the kitchen table and read the article from *New Scientist Magazine* out loud.

"It says here that scientists have broken down Mona Lisa's smile into four basic human emotions. It's '83% happy, 9% disgusted, 6% fearful, and 2% angry,' according to a University of Amsterdam computer that applied 'emotion recognition software' to Leonardo da Vinci's masterpiece."

Paying only half attention as his wife read the article, Nathan Bannister watched as the coffeemaker dripped the last of the fresh ground coffee into the pot. "Yeah? That's interesting," he replied vacantly and poured himself a cup.

Undeterred by his groggy lack of interest, Stella continued. "The computer algorithm they used assesses human moods by examining key features such as the curvature of the lips and crinkles around the eyes. It then creates a score based on a selection of basic emotions."

"They can tell all that from a simple expression?" Nathan asked and pulled up a chair.

"Yes, and I've told you this before. According to one of Charles Darwin's oldest theories, humankind has only six basic emotions, and now a lot of psychologists are saying that they agree with his findings."

"So, what are these emotions? No, wait, let me guess. Let's see," Nathan said before giving his wife a chance to answer: "There's happiness, sadness … and, uh, that's all I can come up with right now."

"Not bad," Stella replied, thinking, *how so like a man. Everything distilled down to black and white.* "But then there's anger, fear, disgust, and surprise. Of course, there are many subtleties within those six, but basically that's it," Stella replied as she watched Nathan pour an exorbitant amount of sugar into his coffee.

"And the most interesting thing about this is that everyone in the world, regardless of whether they're from Bora Bora, Istanbul, or New York recognizes these emotions instantly. It's a universally shared dialect, no matter what language you speak. A man who's lived in China his entire life can tell when a woman from Brazil is angry. Even a three-month-old baby recognizes these emotions.

"By the way, would you mind pouring me a cup?" she said as she turned the page of the magazine.

"Oops. Sorry, honey," Nathan said before getting up and heading back over to the coffeemaker on the counter.

"Well, of course everyone recognizes these emotions," he added as he handed her the cup. "I mean, I can always tell when *you're* disgusted, honey. Like now, you're thinking *what an insensitive clod. Didn't even ask me if I wanted some coffee.*"

Stella turned her mouth slightly; giving her husband one of her more subtle expressions—a knowing look—part smile, part resignation.

"It's like I'm the Mona Lisa and you're the recognition program. You picked up on the subtle differences in the shape of my mouth and eyes—tiny little nuances—and intuitively processed them in your brain in less than a second.

"Now, of course, we've been married for ten years, so it's not that big of a deal. What intrigues me is that people who have never met pick up these same things just as quickly. They just aren't aware of it on a conscious level. But can you imagine what it would be like if everybody *did* consciously use this universal language?"

"You think that'd actually work?" Nathan asked, already knowing the answer.

"Absolutely!"

"Hmm. Since when did you add Behaviorist to your credentials?"

"Since you started working with the people over in Troy—since they all started getting sick." Stella replied. "Can I have a little sugar, too?"

PART

I

1

Termez, Uzbekistan. Formerly U.S.S.R.

July 13, 2010

A small, one-bedroom stone house is nestled at the base of a soaring black mountain range. Inside, a family of three sleeps, sharing one room. The embers of a fire smolder in the rock fireplace, the burned, smoky odor hanging in the air.

A baby wakes in the middle of the night. She has had a nightmare. She stands up in her crib but loses her balance. Her legs slip through the slats and her body falls like dead weight, her jaw crashing down on the top rail, throwing her head back violently.

She screams as blood trickles down her chin.

Her parents are sound asleep in the bed next to the crib. Her father is caught up in a dream; her mother slumbers peacefully, exhausted from a hard day's work.

Eventually, the child tires of crying and falls back to sleep as well.

When the sun rises and pours through the lone window in the room, the mother awakens to see that her child's cheek is stained with dried blood. She screams and reaches out for the girl, brushing her hair back to reveal the bruised and swollen neck.

"Vlad," she says to her husband. "Wake up."

Her husband does not stir.

"Vlad, get up. What is the matter with you?"

No response.

The mother runs to the phone to call a doctor.

There is no dial tone.

She dials frantically anyway—no ring. No answer. She thinks the phone is dead.

2

"It starts with nausea and vomiting. And it's much worse than the food poisoning I had a few years back," the frail man said.

"Then what happens?" Nathan asked, lifting the stethoscope from the right side of the man's chest and placing it nearer to his heart.

"It gets worse, much worse. The migraines are unbearable. Then more nausea, flashes of brilliant white lights, and squiggles racing through my vision. Can't stand the light. Can't stand any sounds. I just want to go crawl in a dark hole someplace and die."

"How long before the vertigo sets in?"

"A day or two, maybe longer."

"Do you have it now?"

"Oh, hell no. I wouldn't be here if I did. Can't get off the floor when that happens. Everything just spins around. You feel like you're about to be flung off the face of the planet."

"Anything else?"

"The ringing. Nonstop ringing. It's like I'm standing next to a giant church bell, or maybe right inside it. It's awful; I can hardly describe it. Then, after a few minutes, it goes away. But it always comes back. And of course, you can't hear a damn thing for hours afterward."

"Does everyone in town go through the same thing?" Nate asked, making another notation on his pad.

"Pretty much. Some of them have had seizures. I've seen people fall down in the store and just start flopping around like a bass out of water. We've only got the one clinic in town, so it's hard for them to get to everyone. It's been going on now for a week, and you know what?"

"What?"

"It's gettin' a lot worse. The doctors from Spokane, the ones who said they were specialists, came and went and were totally baffled. No one knows what it is. They said someone would come from the CDC, but we haven't seen them yet.

"That's when I decided to call the EPA. We had nothin' to lose."

*   *   *

Watching the wide-open evening sky shift from dark blue to violet over the town of Troy, Montana, Nathan Bannister sat at a desk in the town's only medical clinic—a small, sparse, gray room—and rubbed the soft stubble of beard on his chin.

He was a rugged man: tall, with big shoulders and thick forearms toned by years spent digging fence-post holes at his parents' ranch. He wore a flannel long-sleeve shirt, a pair of faded Levi's and heavy Justin cowboy boots; uncommon clothing for someone working for the Environmental Protection Agency. Combing his fingers through his thick mahogany hair, he realized that he was long overdue for a shower.

At the end of that first day in July, he had interviewed ten people on his list, and each time the story was identical. As far as he could tell, more than half of the citizens shared the same confounding symptoms.

He was one of a handful of scientists with the EPA that specialized in the monitoring and research of airborne contaminants, and after the Homeland Security Agency had become the umbrella agency for infectious disasters, it seemed that airborne threats were becoming more and more common.

In fact, hardly a week passed anymore without some sort of threat to the nation's security: bomb scares or chemical disbursements—tainted water supplies, plagues, diseases—anything to kill, maim, or at least scare people and ultimately shut down infrastructure and the economy.

Today, he was in Troy, about twenty-five miles north of the last disaster he'd investigated—the asbestos poisoning in Libby, Montana. *Thank God,* Nathan thought, *most of these things don't pan out to be anything as serious as that.*

But the Libby incident had been a different situation. It involved the asbestos that came from the mines. First it killed miners. Then it killed their wives and children, slipping into their homes on the sooty clothing of the hard-working men. Eventually, the mine was closed, but the dying went on.

The fatal symptom of the asbestos poisoning was the coughing up of blood. It was a slow, painful, and ugly death where each individual literally drowned in his own blood or simply stopped breathing.

That was ten years ago in 2000, and Nathan's investigation was the reason a national scandal was uncovered—the government had tried to sweep it all away—hide it as if it had just been a minor misunderstanding. *As if it wasn't enough to deal with potential terrorism,* Nathan thought, *we also have to deal with fraud and cover-ups from our own government—cover-ups that cost lives.*

3

*P*aris, France. Amarante Hotel. July 28, 2010.

"Ladies and gentlemen. Can we have order? Will the members of the summit please come to order?" the chairman asked, pounding a heavy wood and brass gavel on the podium in front of him.

Seated in a large oval auditorium in the five-star hotel were thirty of the world's leading biochemists representing the U.S., France, Germany, Spain, Britain, Canada, and twenty-four other countries.

The room was filled with the chatter of anticipation as the chairman continued to bang the podium.

One notable representative—the Russian delegate—was not yet in his seat. His name was Dr. Sergi Revchenko, a specialist in biochemistry, and he had been invited to the summit to discuss environmental issues, emerging technologies and, in particular, breakthroughs in the hot-button topic of personalized medicine and the use of nano-technologies in chemistry.

Revchenko was the eastern counterpart to the three American scientists, Robert Fleishman, Craig Venter, and Francis Collins who had nearly simultaneously published the first full genome (map) of a living organism in 1995—an obscure bacteria that can transmit meningitis. That had begun the revolution in research to map the human genome.

Revchenko's tardiness was not unusual the chairman thought. *Though brilliant, he'd always been a little scattered. Besides, he was now over eighty years old.*

The chairman decided to start the meeting without Revchenko's participation, inviting the first delegate to the podium.

The British delegate rose to his feet, approached, and tapped the microphone to ensure it was working and then began to speak to the group.

"Fellow chemists, as you know, we are here for two days to discuss a variety of issues. However, I think we all agree that personalized medicine is one of the most fascinating topics we face.

"Unfortunately, Dr. Revchenko has apparently been delayed, so I will give you a brief description of what he'll be talking about."

He cleared his throat.

"Ladies and gentlemen, consider what's coming soon: Your entire genetic code will soon be imprinted on an ID card, very much like your ATM card. Everything that is known about your health, your body, will be contained on that magnetic strip across the back of the card.

"A healthcare official or doctor will simply swipe the card into a portable reader and they will have everything they need to know to begin personalized treatment—treatment that is designed specifically for you and your particular problem.

"Personalized medicine is literally just around the corner. Very soon, a simple test will allow doctors to predict with great accuracy whether a given medication will work for you, or be highly toxic to you.

"Currently, as you are all aware, most of our medical expenditures are for doctors and interventions; in other words, treatment *after* the fact, after you get sick.

"Treatments will shift from emergencies to specific, deliberate personalized actions prior to the 'event,' before there is an emergency. Once scientists know what you are predisposed to because of your genetic structure, then a specific preventative treatment will be 'designed' for you.

"These medicines won't necessarily be more pills or injections, they might wind up being the food you eat, or the soap you use, a patch on your skin or something you simply inhale ... or, it could be almost science fiction—medicines could be contained on a microchip smaller than a grain of rice that is permanently implanted under your skin.

"Ladies and gentlemen, this brings us into the realm of nano-technology, the science of building things at the atomic level. As Dr. Revchenko will tell you, it's quite possible right now, in today's laboratories, to write a person's name using single atoms. But, of course, you all know that. What you may be interested to hear is that recently, in America, Cornell University scientists have built 'nano-submarines.' These devices are equal parts organic and inorganic. They run on the same bioelectric energy that powers our cells. Some of these submarines even have actual propellers."

At that point, the British scientist paused for dramatic effect: "That's right, propellers. They can run for two-and-a-half hours on a single charge; and they are about as large as a virus, which we all know is only visible under electron microscopes.

"We believe, along with Dr. Revchenko, that sometime in the near future, 'nano-nurses' or 'nano-doctors,' meaning a minute amount of medicine, will ride in these molecular-sized subs to the specific diseased cells within your body and eliminate them with molecular doses of medicine—medicine that does not affect any other part of your system.

"Just imagine the potential of that kind of personalized medical care. Something the size of a few atoms in your bloodstream playing a very high tech medical version of a video arcade game, shooting down only those individual and specific bad cells, which were about to make you very, very sick."

The speaker paused, took a sip of his glass of water, and then continued.

"In addition, for the first time, we will be able to see a complete map of how life was programmed—no mean feat.

"It literally means that in the not-so-distant future, we will be able to control our own evolution. We will completely understand our heredity and the biological transmission of traits. We could stop disease dead in its tracks and reengineer our own immune systems. We could personalize medicine. The possibilities are limitless, ladies and gentlemen."

The British delegate paused and looked to the door. There was still no sign of Dr. Revchenko. He'd been scheduled to speak after the British delegate's introduction.

The chairman stood up as the British delegate sat down.

"Ladies and gentlemen, it appears that our keynote speaker has been detained. Let us continue with the delegate from the United States," he said, gesturing to the far side of the auditorium.

*   *   *

In the heart of the city at Two Avenue Gabriel, on the northwest corner of the historic Place de la Concorde, stood the United States Embassy—a majestic, baroque building whose architecture dated back to 1768.

The building faced the gardens of the Champs-Elysees and off to one side was the famous Hotel de Crillion, perhaps the most beautiful example of eighteenth century French architecture in the country.

Inside the staid and quiet embassy, just down the hall from the Ambassador's office, sat a small, nervous man. Though it was a sweltering July day in the city, the man with thin graying hair and thick bifocals wore a heavy, full-length camel's hair coat. With his left hand, he twiddled the brim of a fedora hat. In his right hand, he held a legal size manila folder that was bulging with paperwork.

He sat on the hard marble bench, which faced the Ambassador's outer office door. A larger than life bronze statue of Benjamin Franklin, one of the earliest ambassadors to France, stood nearby, glaring down at the small man, scrutinizing him.

President Bush had nominated Craig Roberts Stapleton as Ambassador to France. When the new President, Robert Jordan, was elected and George W. Bush left, Stapleton was asked to remain.

A half hour had passed since the small man had been asked to sit in the foyer. He sat patiently, but his eyes were continually scanning his surroundings. They would dart from the doorways to the folder in his lap, and then back down the hall.

When another fifteen minutes passed, a young man appeared in the Ambassador's doorway and strode across the floor, his footsteps echoing off the hard marble and up through the rococo building.

"Dr. Revchenko," the man said as he extended his hand and smiled. "I am Wes Baker, Ambassador Stapleton's assistant. I'm sorry we've kept you waiting so long."

The slight man, not 5 feet 7 inches tall, rose to greet the assistant.

"That is quite alright, young man. What I have to say to the Ambassador is extremely important. I will wait as long as I need."

"Well, that is what I'm here to help you with. Before you can see Ambassador Stapleton, you will need to be interviewed by a few other people here—our security staff."

"That is quite all right, Mr. Baker. This matter *is* one of security—national security for your country. I'm sure they will want to hear what I have to say."

"I'm sure they will, doctor. Come. Come with me."

As the doctor followed alongside, he added, "Mr. Baker, did I tell you I would be asking for asylum?"

Baker turned back abruptly, "Uh, no, no, doctor, you didn't. That will complicate things a little."

"I have no intention of complicating things for you, Mr. Baker. We must take care of this matter as soon as possible. I will need to be granted asylum before I can reveal the, how do you say, parameters of the virus," the diminutive man said, as if he'd just simply ordered a ham sandwich for lunch.

"Virus?"

"Yes, extremely contagious and often deadly. And quite an ugly demise as well," he added.

4

$\mathcal{N}$athan had never been political and didn't much care for all the bureaucracy that was so much a weave of the fabric of his job, but he was a dedicated scientist who was genuinely concerned about the environment. He wanted to help people, and the EPA was his best opportunity to do what he felt he was chosen in life to do.

He was raised on a cattle ranch outside Billings, the one his parents still owned. They had instilled in him a love of the outdoors and a respect for every living thing, which seemed inevitable given the part of the country where he was raised.

In the summers, Montana seemed endless: larger, bluer, more infinite than any other part of America he'd ever seen.

He was an avid fisherman and hiker. During the summer, if he had the time, and he wasn't working on the ranch, he volunteered with the forestry service to clear firebreaks.

Had he not gone to the University of Western Montana on a chemistry scholarship, he knew he would have been an M.D., or even a veterinarian. He'd graduated with a Masters in Environmental Sciences in 1997 and immediately applied to the EPA.

Working with the agency gave him an opportunity to do everything that was important to him. He believed deep in his soul that he could make a difference in people's lives as one of the roughly 4,000 EPA employees that were actually engaged in science and medicine. The other 14,000 worked in legal affairs, management, or as engineers.

After the Libby asbestos scandal, his superiors, the administrators in Washington D.C., tried to force him to leave—they knew they couldn't fire him, so they tried intimidation and peer pressure, but his whistle-blowing had been far too loud and too well publicized.

When he'd first heard about the new situation in Troy, it had occurred to him that maybe there was still some fatal dust from Libby blowing north.

For years, the local and state governments had done nothing to clean up the mountains of pinkish-tan waste, rock, soil, and asbestos dust that had been dumped after the ore was removed.

The tailing piles—mounds that could be as tall as twenty feet high—weren't even covered. They were just allowed to sit there in the open, exposed to every breeze, wind, or storm that blew through Libby—and there were plenty of winds that came through that area from Troy.

The state had been confident that no asbestos was blowing off the hills, they'd said, but Nathan knew better. *How could it not? That was just common sense, but common sense was often in short supply in Washington.*

Eventually, 192 people died horrible deaths and another 375 were diagnosed with incurable lung disease, which, in some cases, dragged the anguish on for years.

Troy was different, though. Once Nathan had interviewed some of the residents, it became apparent that this was not the same, slow-onset condition. This was immediate, striking its victims like lightning.

It could have come from just about anywhere—from the water, from food—but he felt comfortable ruling out the few mines, which were now mostly closed.

Nathan knew this area well. Each winter, his father would bring him here to hunt and in the spring to fish. The landscape was stunning. It appeared that the town, a mere five square miles, had been carved out of the forest and framed by several crystal-blue lakes.

There wasn't much manufacturing in Troy, where the small population of around 900 survived by working in the agriculture, forestry, and fishing industries, or worked at the school, one of the motels, or in the restaurants that catered to the tourists: the hunters, fishermen, or campers.

Troy was a quiet, unpretentious town. In the previous year there had been no murders, no rapes, and no robberies.

Nathan was intent on interviewing as many people as he could before he had to leave. The brass in Washington wanted a full report within the week.

It was six o'clock, and though he'd spoken with nearly thirty people that day, he wanted to turn in earlier and get an even earlier start tomorrow. With his feet dragging, he checked in at a Motel Six out on Highway 56, where he planned to call Stella and check up on his three-year-old daughter, Jennifer.

Nathan fell asleep that night having no idea that in a town of similar size—a sleepy village about 14,000 miles away in Termez, Uzbekistan—many of the residents were experiencing the same vertigo and nausea.

*   *   *

Early the next morning, the 1960s' style rotary phone clanged in Nathan's ear. He jerked his head and instinctively reached to the table. Next to the phone was the silver-framed picture of Stella and Jennifer that he always took with him on trips.

"Nate, I thought you said you were coming home today. Jennifer is so disappointed. I also thought you were going to call me last night. You promised you'd only be up there for two days. You know I worry about you when you're investigating these unknown health hazards."

Nathan sighed. He'd forgotten to call. Exhausted, he'd simply fallen across the motel bed and slept in his clothes.

"Sweetie, I'm sorry. I was dead tired last night and I've got to get the results of these tests completed. I can't just leave here without some answers."

"Well, you missed Jennifer's play at school."

"Stella. Honey. Please. I already feel guilty. You know I'll be home by tomorrow night. I promise I'll make it up to both of you. I love you very much."

There was a pause.

"Okay, but this time please call me when you're headed home."

The phone went dead and Nathan put the receiver down gingerly, as if not to antagonize his wife any further. This had been his fifth trip away from home this year, each one more extended than the last. *At least he was only a few hours away,* he thought, as if that somehow made the separation a little more palatable.

His work had taken him to seven states in his district and he knew it was hard on his family. What made matters worse was the fact that Stella's teaching job at the University only went from September through June. July and August were the only two months they had to spend some real time together.

Nathan resolved that when he got home, he wouldn't take another assignment for at least two weeks. Nothing would stand in his way this time. His marriage had been stretched a bit already. Nathan could feel it when he returned each time. *Sure, she said she wanted him home, but the receptions had gone from ambivalent to outright cold in the last couple of months.*

He began to roll out of bed when the heavy plastic phone on the nightstand clanged once again. It was the lab in Washington calling. Nathan glanced at the clock. It wasn't even six o'clock.

"Mr. Bannister?"

"Yes."

"This is Avery Beckman in Washington."

"Do you have the results?" Nathan asked directly.

"Yes and no."

"What does that mean?"

"Well, we know that it is either a virus or a bacteria," Beckman said.

"And ...?"

Nathan paced from one side of the room to the other as he listened.

"It's very strange. We did the tests three times to confirm and each time it came out the same. It has a lot of the same properties as spinal meningitis, which can be deadly. At a minimum, it appears to be able to cause major problems in the brain and spinal cord."

"Definitely not what I was wanting to hear."

"We're just hoping it's the viral version, not the bacteria."

"What does that mean?" Nathan said, as he retrieved the small memo pad that he always carried in his back pocket, braced the phone between his shoulder and neck, and began to write.

"If it *is* meningitis, there are two forms—bacterial and viral. The bacterium is far nastier. It causes an infection, which covers the brain and spinal cord, as well as septicemia. There is a vaccine for meningitis group A, the virus, but not for group B, the bacteria.

"You do realize that this needs to go to Homeland Security tonight," Beckman said. "I mean, even though it doesn't seem to cause death at this point, it could manifest as any number of nervous system problems. You should alert the hospital there as well.

"The best places to do serious testing on this are at the CDC and the Army Medical Research Institute for Infectious Diseases."

"Jesus Christ," Nathan gasped and collapsed onto the bed. "Can't you give me another day or two before you call Homeland? Those bastards will muck this thing up before we even know what we're dealing with."

"I'm afraid I can't do that, Mr. Bannister."

"Yes you can. Imagine what will happen in this country if word gets out that spinal meningitis is spreading. We've got to make sure we know what's happening here first. If this turns out *not* to be life threatening, then starting a nationwide panic will do more harm than the disease."

There was a long, silent pause on the line.

"I suppose you're right, but I don't see any way to keep a lid on this for more than a day. Seventy-two hours at the most."

"Thanks, doc."

After hanging up, Nathan's first thought was to call his wife and break a promise he'd made to her less than ten minutes ago. She would not be happy and he didn't blame her.

*D*r. Revchenko was escorted down a maze of corridors in the embassy building. He'd never seen so much marble in his entire life. Though the building was a U.S. Embassy, the rococo paintings, statues, banisters, ornate cornices, and complicated crown moldings reminded him more of a museum.

He was a renowned biochemist, but he was no stranger to politics. During the early 1980s, when President Reagan was calling his country The Evil Empire and the KGB was torturing its own countrymen, he had been forced to work for them under the guise of research. In that capacity, he'd traveled to many of the U.S. Embassies and was always presented as an expert on research into nuclear fallout, its impact on the environment and human body.

The Russians were trying to convince the Americans that they had no intention of using nuclear weapons; but, of course, they did. They were scared that Reagan's plans for a giant offensive nuclear missile shield were a reality. Reagan dubbed it Star Wars. They were so scared they went bankrupt trying to fight it.

Following Brezhnev's death in 1982, the Soviet Union began to crumble. After the succession of Andropov and Chernenko, Mikhail Gorbachev took over party leadership, but by the late 1980s the constituent republics of the Soviet Union began to secede.

The result of all the successions left the country splintered into new countries such as Uzbekistan, Belarus, Latvia, Kazakhstan, and others, each with its own government. On December 25, 1991, Gorbachev resigned and the USSR as it had been known was officially dissolved. But in Russia, suppression and the KGB lived on.

*   *   *

Revchenko had done his homework over the years. There was the Secretary of State, every diplomat's boss. Then there were Under Secretaries, Foreign Affairs Specialists, Assistant Secretaries, and even Coordinators for Combating Terrorism.

What it really all came down to was that eighty percent of the employees of any given embassy, whether that was American or Russian, Chinese or Brits, were really nothing more than spies in diplomats clothing, hiding behind diplomatic immunity, able to carry valises and briefcases that no one could look into, not even at an airport by the TSA after 9-11.

Each embassy, no matter how ornate or simple, was also a high tech listening post—rooms and rooms filled with the most sophisticated "eyes and ears" technology conceivable—things most people didn't know existed.

Sergi Revchenko knew where Mr. Baker was taking him. He would be going down into the bowels of the stately building for interrogation. There would be a safe room, one with a heavy steel and lead door, one where the walls were made of five-inch-thick concrete with a sheet of lead embedded within. No sounds ever left that room.

He also knew it wasn't going to be easy to defect. There would be a thousand questions; but, of course, if he had something with enough value to trade, it would go easier.

As predicted, one of the men pushed a key into a large steel door, slowly opened it and gestured, without speaking, for the doctor to go inside.

"Sit over there," another man said.

The doctor took a chair and placed his fedora and briefcase on the table in front of him.

"Okay, doctor. Where shall we begin?" one of the men asked.

Dr. Revchenko said, "Gentlemen. Before I tell you my story, it is important for you to know that I was forced into all this. The KGB threatened to kill my family if I didn't do the work.

"And then, when I did finish working on the virus …," The doctor began to choke up, slowed down, took a deep breath, and continued, "they had my wife and daughter executed anyway. They were hanged separately; they didn't even allow them the dignity of dying together."

He brought his hands up to cover his eyes.

"That was in 1981, but they never used the virus. I made sure of that."

"Wait a minute. Slow down," the man said. "What virus?"

"Yes, sir. So sorry," Revchenko said, and then he began to relate his entire story.

Each of the three men questioning Dr. Revchenko wore a plain gray suit and black tie. As he sat on a hard metal chair behind a steel table, they paced around him, throwing out questions as he talked, making notes, and tape recording it all.

He'd been in the small windowless room in the basement now for more than an hour, but he was calm. His outward frailty masked a hardened inner strength.

One of the men stopped, pulled up another chair, faced Revchenko, and said, "And just how did you make sure they never used the virus, doctor?"

"Simple. I stole it. I also took the vaccine we developed."

"All right. But if that was the case, then how did it get to Uzbekistan? Why are those people getting sick? And further, why are the Russians poisoning their own people?"

"It's not the Russians who are doing it," Revchenko said ominously.

"Who then?"

Revchenko squirmed a little in his chair.

"Well, let's put it this way—some of them wear checkered scarves around their heads and necks."

"Arabs?

"No, not technically. Two fundamentalist Iranians stole it from me. You know, many still call themselves 'Persians,' not Arabs."

"I don't get it. Why would Iran want to poison a small Russian village?"

"You gentlemen obviously missed the history course at Langley," Revchenko said.

"Before Uzbekistan was ever part of the USSR, it was originally conquered by Muslim Arabs. They didn't join the Russian Federation willingly. Now that they are an independent country ... well ..."

Revchenko began to stand.

"Sit down, doctor. We can hear you just fine," one of the men said.

"Three years ago, protests broke out in Andijan in Northern Uzbekistan over the imprisonment of twenty-three Muslims accused of being Islamic extremists. The protestors took thirty hostages. Soldiers started to fire on the protestors, leaving many of them dead—about 1,000 people, though the government said it was more like 175. That was a lie, of course.

"It was payback time for the Muslims, and that was when they decided to test it for the first time."

The three inquisitors looked at each other as if each was searching the others for validation or believability.

"What are they testing?"

"Whether the virus will work as an aerosol and if it will work in that climate. The virus is more than twenty-five years old, and viruses can mutate or become irrelevant over time; more importantly, though, they want to know if it will kill large numbers of people quickly. It can be deadly, but again, it's very old," Revchnko said in a voice giving out from the explanation.

"Why that climate?"

The doctor thought for a moment before speaking, making sure he didn't give away too much too soon.

"Because there is a small town in America with roughly the same climate and about the same population—small, contained, primarily by forest and lakes—same as Termez—and the two cities are on the same latitude. That is where they'll be bringing it into the country; easier to get into the Midwest from Canada, than into New York.

"There's a lot of lonely border out there. And even if they were stopped somewhere, in all likelihood, they would be allowed to cross with simply a driver's license."

The two men nodded in agreement from behind Revchnko to the inquisitor sitting across the table. It was common knowledge that the Canadian border was a sieve.

"In both towns, they can keep things quiet and then wait to see what develops. If it works there, God knows where else they'll try to use it. And, in case you also missed the geography class at Langley as well, Uzbekistan shares a border with Afghanistan," Revchenko said, becoming increasingly more sarcastic.

"Oh Jesus. So what town in the Midwest and when?"

"Well, that's what we have to talk about."

"How did they get the virus?" the man asked.

"After the KGB murdered my family, I was sent to a research lab in what is now Belarus. That's where I took the virus and the vaccine. It's been in a liquid nitrogen suspension for more than two decades."

"Why? Why would you keep something like that unless you intended to use it?"

"To keep it out of their hands and as a bargaining chip. By the late eighties, I was working with the human genome projects in Moscow. Several years later, in 1995, three Americans who were working on similar projects discovered and mapped the first genome of a living organism. That organism, oddly enough, was a bacteria that causes meningitis—ironically, the very virus I had been working on.

"Instead of having us work with the genome information for the good of mankind, the KGB saw it as an opportunity to develop another weapon.

"I knew then that I had to defect and come to share my work in nano-technology. It was a perfect fit with what they were doing, and I also never lost site of getting even with Colonel Gravchinko, the man who had my family killed. He tortured them for days before he had them both killed."

The doctor could see he'd lost his inquisitors, who probably didn't know a genome from a gnome.

"So, what has the virus got to do with all that?" one of the men asked.

"I still have the vaccine, or at least enough to start replicating it."

*   *   *

In the Dark Ages, it was religious fanaticism. Then came the Nazis and the Fascists, followed sharply by Communism—and now we had come full circle. We were back to Uzbekistan and God knows where else in the U.S., and religious fanaticism. Threats. Always the threats, Baker thought as he closed the heavy steel door behind him.

Regardless of the politics, whether it was just some demented mind, a grab for power, or a my-God-is-better-than-yours zealot, to Baker, a career diplomat and a man who truly had ethics, it came down to one simple problem—ignorance, which breeds prejudice, which breeds hatred.

Though he might have been the exception in the Paris Embassy, he felt people from different cultures had more in common than not. "Think about it," he'd often appeal to his subordinates: "We love music; they love music. We like poetry and dance; they like poetry and dance. We all get married, go to funerals, grieve, and celebrate birth.

"There are just so many basic human traits that are universal, that are normal everywhere. We're not so different as you imagine or want to think."

When would people get it? When would we all realize that every one of us is connected? It's not a complicated concept.

His first stop would be the Ambassador's office. They would have to begin to turn the wheels to set in motion the necessary paperwork, approvals, and bureaucracy to allow Dr. Revchenko asylum.

The homeland was now threatened, and for now, he was the only person who could do anything about it.

6

*I*t was five-thirty, and Nathan had less than seventy-two hours to get some solid answers. Overnight, his entire assignment had gone from some simple research to a matter of life and death, not unlike his experience in Libby. Now, however, he had to take care of his family, had to get them to safer ground.

He sat down on the bed and dialed his home, gripping the phone tightly in anticipation of his wife's reaction.

"Stella. It's me. I'm afraid I've got some bad news."

"You're not coming home," she deduced flatly.

"Sweetie, I just need a day more; just one more day. But in the meantime, I need you to do something for me."

There was no response.

"Stella, I want you to take Jennifer to my parent's ranch. Pack up enough stuff for about two weeks. I've already called my mother and told her you'd be coming."

"What are you talking about? What's the matter? What's going on up there?"

"I can't tell you right now, because I'm not sure myself. But I don't want to worry about you. Just do this for me, please. Get in the truck and drive there today. I'll meet you as soon as I can."

"All right, all right. Call me there tomorrow if you can."

"I will, I promise. I love you."

"I love you, too."

Hanging up the phone, he closed his eyes and bowed his head, knowing that he might not be seeing his wife or daughter for a very long time.

*   *   *

Nathan and Stella lived in Helena. His parents' ranch was in Billings about 200 miles southeast of Helena and about 500 from Troy. The prevailing hot summer winds on the plains were from east to northwest, from Libby through to the Canadian border. In the winter, stiff arctic winds blew down from the north, just the opposite.

He knew that she could make the trip in less than a day and that would be the safest place for his family, at least for now. He'd feel better knowing that Stella and Jennifer and his parents were all in one place far away from Troy. Besides, he had no other relatives. Otherwise, he would have sent them further east.

As Nathan locked the door to room 28 behind him, he began mulling over details about every worst-case scenario he could imagine.

By the time he pulled into the clinic parking lot, it was six o'clock. The clinic didn't open until seven, but already there was a crowd growing outside. The unpaved parking lot was nearly full and there was a line of people stretching around to the back of the gray cinder block building. Already the temperature on Nate's dashboard thermometer read 80 degrees.

As his heavy-duty Ford 350 truck skidded to a stop, he noticed the gathering of people outside the clinic. He quickly surveyed the crowd and could see that many of them were holding their stomachs, or had their hands up squeezing their heads, as if to make a bad headache go away. Several women were holding wet cloths over their children's foreheads. All of them looked agitated or scared.

"Are you the doctor from Washington?" one woman asked as the crowd, seeing him, began to push toward the door.

"I'm from Washington, but I'm not a doctor," Nathan answered as he pushed the truck's door open and waded through the throng to get to the office.

"There isn't enough room in here for all of you at once," he said in a loud voice, gesturing the crowd to back up. "Let's take it ten people at a time. You first ten here, come in and sit in the waiting room."

He could sense the panic in their expressions now that he was a breath away—panic mixed with the familiar light-ashen skin tones and the pink-edged eyelids of those who are very ill.

As soon as the first group of people went through the door, the crowd collapsed in to fill the void in the line. No one wanted to be left out, not if there was a treatment.

Not wanting to start a panic, he hadn't yet told the doctors at the clinic what might be happening. But now it was obvious. Something serious was definitely developing, and even if this wasn't meningitis B form of the bacteria, it was bad and getting much, much worse.

He knew he'd be calling Beckman in Washington before the day was out, but for now, all he could think about was his family. He'd give Stella another couple of hours to reach the ranch and then he'd call. The doctors in Troy would have to do whatever they could to provide temporary relief. A thousand scenarios began to race through his head.

July 29, 2010

"There's my girls!" Henry Bannister beamed as he swung open the screen door and gave both Stella and Jennifer a big hug. "Come on in. Make yourself at home."

Henry and his son could easily have been mistaken for brothers. Though Henry was in his seventies, he was still in good physical shape—tall and muscular like Nate, with a full head of thick brown hair.

Stepping into the rambling ranch house, Stella reached down and picked up one of the two suitcases she'd packed.

"Place looks better than ever," she said.

Henry Bannister had built the entire two-story home out of wood cut from the timber on his own land. He'd also done most of the work himself. The interior was lined with knotty pine, and there were huge crossbeams made of cedar running the length of the living room. It looked more like a posh hunting lodge than a house.

Stella had always felt comfortable there, and it seemed Henry always had a fire going in the enormous river rock fireplace—winter or summer—just for her. The smell of fresh smoke and cedar was quite possibly her favorite smell in the world.

"Mom's out back feeding the horses. She'll be in, in a minute. Sit down, I want to hear what's goin' on," Henry said.

"Dad, your guess is as good as mine. I was hoping Nate had told you."

"'Fraid not. But I know him. If it was anything really bad, he'd have shared it with me. And hey, anything that gets you and Jennifer up here to see us can't be all bad. Isn't that right, Jenny girl?"

The three-year-old looked like a miniature version of her mother: with long, soft brown hair and large brown eyes. She stood next to Stella with a small backpack in one hand and a doll clutched in the other.

"Come on over here and see your ol' papa," Henry said, patting his knees as he sat in the large lounger next to the fireplace. Jennifer's face lit up and she charged across the room and hopped up on her grandfather's lap.

Henry clutched her tightly as a huge smile crossed his face.

"I'm so glad to see you, sweetie," he said.

"Me too, papa."

*   *   *

It was close to lunchtime, so Stella fed Jennifer at the picnic-sized dining room table and then put her down for a nap. Joanne Bannister had made a large pot of coffee and she and Stella whiled away the afternoon sitting at the breakfast nook and getting caught up.

Though Henry looked fifteen years younger than he was, Joanne had not aged as well. She had a round, pleasant face, but her nearly white hair and leathered skin revealed the decades she'd spent working in the sun.

Her hard work on the ranch showed, particularly in her hands—they were sinewy, but strong, covered in light brown age spots.

Joanne was trying to change the subject of Nate's research when she took a sip of coffee and asked her daughter-in-law, "So, Stella, tell me what's been goin' on with you. How's school? What're you gonna be teachin' this coming semester?"

"Communications." Stella shrugged to imply that the job really didn't mean that much to her anymore.

"Again? I swear, I don't know why you ever quit that job working with those handicapped children."

"I guess we never did talk about it much, did we? You know, everything just kind of turned into a big administrative mess. It came down to them just plain not knowing what they were doing. Sad, really," Stella answered. "And, by the way, they aren't called handicapped anymore."

"I'm sorry. I stand corrected. So, what's new in the world of communications this year?" Joanne asked, sensing Stella did not want to discuss the past.

"Well, I've been intrigued for a long time with something called Emotion Recognition Software. It's all about how humans communicate so much through expressions, but not the obvious ones like joy or anger that everyone can readily identify. It's more about the science of analyzing people's true motives by recognizing very subtle facial expressions, things your brain sees, but you don't."

"You mean people could know what I'm thinking before I say it?"

"Yes, some people anyway—those that are trained. The whole thing has fascinated me for the last year. I've also been studying how the senses work through the brain. You know, like when you're listening to loud music, how you can't really think too well at the same time?"

"I guess. Is that like when we go into town and Henry plays that corny square dance music so loud on the radio that I can't even think straight?"

"Precisely. And there are other interesting connections as well. Like Nathan can play the piano by ear, but he can't read music. He's just got that gift. It's almost like he hears it in his mind rather than his ears, if that makes any sense.

"Music is a language just like English or mathematics, and Nathan seems to be able to understand it without reading it."

"It does make sense. So, how are you going to put this all together for your students?" Joanne asked. Looking into Stella's soft brown eyes, she drifted off to when they had met, when Nathan brought her out to the ranch that very first time. *Yes, she was pretty, with long brown hair, and a beautiful smile, but her attractiveness really came from within.* Joanne sensed it immediately. *It was the eyes.*

Whenever Stella looked at or listened to you, you sensed that she really cared about what you were saying. She had empathetic eyes, Joanne had decided. *No wonder she was in communications.*

"I'm not sure yet, Mom. But there's a connection through it all. It's really still about communicating effectively. I thought my lesson plan last year was a bit weak when we spent the entire semester talking about advertising. I really want to teach them something worthwhile, something more about people's emotions, and how we all communicate on a level higher than just talking."

Stella took another swallow of her coffee and placed the mug gently back on the table. She smiled at Joanne and said, "God, I wish he'd call. He missed Jennifer's play again."

Joanne immediately sensed her daughter-in-law's concern.

"So do I, dear. So do I."

7

Same day

*H*alfway around the world, Prime Minister Shavkat Mirziy-oyev's Director of Health Services was reading a medical report. To the south in Termez, it appeared that a flu epidemic was starting.

His first thought, because of their proximity to Asia, was that it was the bird flu again; the avian flu that had been so deadly just three years before. This time, though, the symptoms sounded different—more virulent, more diverse—from the familiar nausea to the not-so-usual vertigo and migraine-type headaches. The really worrisome thing was that all 700 of the town's inhabitants were complaining of symptoms.

He decided to send several of Uzbekistan's health officials there immediately to check it out. The avian flu had killed nearly 50,000 people in Afghanistan and another 20,000 in his country. Even in Europe and America, the death toll had been high.

The tab for that epidemic was $1.4 billion, and that was just for Uzbekistan and Afghanistan. Most of that money came from the U.N., which had received the bulk of their funding from the U.S.

He wrote a note on his calendar to alert the Prime Minister as soon as the health inspectors returned or called back. Then, if it was as serious as it sounded, he'd post a notice on the Health Warnings page of the State's Web site to alert countries all over the world.

That would take several days.

8

In the event of a terrorist attack, natural disaster, or other large-scale emergency, the Department of Homeland Security will assume primary responsibility regarding civilian health and well being. As of March 1, DHS (or if Homeland Security Agency, HSA) will ensure that emergency response professionals are prepared for any situation, the Web site copy read.

This will entail providing a coordinated, comprehensive federal response to any large-scale crisis and mounting a swift and effective recovery effort, the paragraph ended.

Yeah sure, swift and effective, Nathan thought as he closed the Web browser on his laptop. *I wonder if that was up on Homeland Security's Web site* before *Katrina? Coordinated? Comprehensive?*

That evening, on the 29th, before Nathan checked out of his motel room, he'd received word from Beckman that time was up. They would have to quarantine at least the city of Troy, maybe a far larger area—perhaps the entire state. He'd also told Nathan to stay put in Troy since he'd been exposed as well.

For now, just the Montana National Guard would be mobilized; not the entire Guard, just E Troop, 163rd Infantry.

Nathan thought, *God, those guys at Homeland. Ever since the debacle during the hurricanes, everything they do is overkill. I guess I can see the point, though. They did take a shellacking after that disaster.*

Since then, things had changed, at least it appeared that way. There hadn't been any real national disasters since 2005, with the possible excep-

tion of the bird flu, but that was more an issue for the CDC, so who really knew? But an assault infantry group? Maybe that's all they had available.

The one thing they did get right was the communications—the frequency problems. It's odd. All the troubles we'd had communicating between various organizations, had ultimately been solved through television.

The FCC had mandated that by 2008, all television sets had to be digital. It had all started years before when HD or high definition cable sets came on the market. The pictures had been so stunning, by 2005, nearly thirty-five percent of the country had them in their homes.

When the government saw how popular they were, they realized if they could force the industry to convert entirely to the digital rather than analogue format, they could free up many of the old analogue frequencies. Not only would America be a "better place" for having crisp television pictures, but they could auction off many of the remaining frequencies and make millions upon millions of dollars—the real motivation.

The real benefit in terms of mankind, however, at least in America, would be that the FBI, CIA, EPA, NSA, Homeland Security, and all the other related agencies would have unfettered access to each other. Walkie-talkies would be compatible; information systems would be nearly seamless; frequencies would work together.

There would be no more "lack of communication," like the mess that occurred in New Orleans.

Right now, though, the two things that worried Nathan were the safety of his family 600 miles away and the similarities to this event that he'd read about on the CDC's Web site. *Apparently, the villagers of a small town half way around the world were suffering from what sounded like identical symptoms. This definitely is not good.*

Contrary to Beckman's orders, Nathan climbed into the cab of his pickup and turned on the ignition. It would be a long drive, but he fully intended to be in Billings by five o'clock tomorrow morning.

To help him stay awake, he tuned his radio to a local country western station and, without giving it much thought, raised the volume so high the knob wouldn't turn anymore.

9

The biotechnology conference at the Amarante Hotel ended the following day, July 30. The lead delegate from Britain, Dr. MacClenden was worried. He'd spoken to Dr. Revchenko prior to the conference, so he knew he was in Paris. *Why hadn't the doctor attended? He was the keynote speaker. His research held the widest interest of those in attendance. Was he sick? Had he been in an accident?* MacClendon wondered.

When MacLendon returned to his room, there were no messages. He dialed room 435 once again; still no answer. He called the front desk to inquire. Next, he tried the two major hospitals. No one had seen the doctor.

It was time to call the Paris police.

*   *   *

"You can't use asylum law to protect everyone from disagreeable things that happen in life. That's not the legitimate purpose of asylum," Director of Immigration Reform Dan Stein told deputy ambassador Baker over the phone from Washington.

"I understand that, Mr. Director. But these are highly unusual circumstances. And regardless of the present situation, the KGB murdered Dr. Revchenko's wife and daughter. It seems to me that *that* would constitute domestic abuse. No, *he* wasn't physically abused, but his family certainly was, and I would think just the horror of losing his family, particularly in the brutal manner that they were killed, would be abuse."

"I sympathize with you and the doctor, Mr. Baker, but the intent and the written laws pertinent that are issued by the INS only consider abuse or persecution based on race, religion, nationality, or membership in a particular social group. It doesn't take into consideration spousal abuse, even by a third party such as the KGB."

"Yes, but, Mr. Stein, it was all political. They threatened the doctor into developing a deadly virus for political purposes—terrorism."

"Mr. Baker, I understand you. However, let me offer you this advice: Despite *our* policy here, a U.S. Embassy can harbor a defector or one seeking asylum indefinitely. The only catch is the individual can't enter the United States. Perhaps this would buy you the time you need."

"Mr. Stein, we really don't have *any* time left, considering there may be thousands or even millions of American lives at stake. Personally, I understand Dr. Revchenko's reasoning. If he gives us the city or cities, then he's got nothing left to bargain with. He won't talk until he's on American soil, at the very least," Baker said.

"I'm sorry, Mr. Baker. My hands are tied. I must go now. Tell Dr. Revchenko that technically he *is* on American soil."

After an abrupt click, the phone went silent.

Baker immediately walked into the planning room upstairs, opting to take the stairs two at a time instead of the elevator. On one wall was an enormous map of the world—ten feet across and five feet tall, each country a different color. He drew a visual line from Termez, Uzbekistan, to the west across the Atlantic Ocean, past New York, Pennsylvania, and into Illinois.

Assuming the Midwest ended with the border between Idaho, Oregon, and Washington, at least on the same latitude as Termez, then he had narrowed his search down to only about 50 million square miles. The line ran along the 44th parallel, intersecting cities like Missoula, Montana; Bismarck, North Dakota; and Duluth, Minnesota—not exactly heavily populated areas—but certainly affecting more than ten million people, at least.

But then, Baker thought, we *don't even know if the doctor is telling us the truth about the location.*

10

July 30, 2010

*D*uring the long drive from Troy, Nathan clung to any alternative explanation for the nausea and slight dizziness he was feeling. *Maybe it was something I ate at that last truck stop. Maybe it's nerves. Maybe I'm just tired.*

Try as he might, however, he could not convince himself of anything other than the truth. He knew that, more likely than not, he had been exposed to the virus. Now, it was just a waiting game to see what symptoms developed and how severely they would affect him.

Cresting a ridge on the lonely dirt road that lead to his parents' ranch, he pulled to the side and stopped the truck as the sprawling home came into view. Still more than a mile away, he shut the engine off and picked up his cell phone.

It was the most difficult phone call he would ever make in his life.

"Nathan?" Stella asked. "Where are you?"

"Not far, sweetie. If you stood on the front porch, you'd see me parked on the side of the road near that giant oak tree we used to swing on."

Something in his voice—a slight flutter—made her nervous. "Why … why are you stopped?"

"Because I'm not coming any closer."

"Oh God," she whispered and released an awful, low moan. "Please don't tell me that you're sick."

A lump formed in Nathan's throat.

"I'm not sure. So far, I've only got a little nausea, but that seems to be how it starts."

"A newscast from about an hour ago said that it could be meningitis!"

"They don't know that yet."

"But even *you* said that they've already called out the National Guard. They wouldn't do that unless it's a real emergency. Oh, Nathan, I'm so scared."

"Listen, honey, they're just being overly cautious. They've got to quarantine Troy just to be on the safe side. So far, there haven't been any other breakouts reported here in the U.S."

"What do you mean by *here in the U.S.?*"

Nathan had never hidden anything from his wife, and he wasn't about to now. "Stella, the CDC just picked up an Internet intercept from Russia, or rather from Uzbekistan. They've had an outbreak there as well—at least the people in a small town are showing pretty much the same symptoms."

"Jesus, Nathan, what is going on in the world?"

"You're guess is as good as mine, sweetheart."

Over the next five minutes, Nathan shared everything he knew so far about the disease.

"First, there's nausea and vertigo. Next comes migraine-like headaches, confusion, and loss of consciousness, muscle aches. Some people report a ringing sensation in their ears."

"Is it lethal?" she asked.

"No one knows. Washington's doing a whole slew of studies right now, but they probably won't know anything certain for at least a couple of days."

The phone went silent, and for a moment he thought the call might have been disconnected. "You still there?" he asked.

"I'm here," she said, her voice quavering. "So what happens now?"

"I don't know, but for the time being I want the four of you to stay put at the ranch. Hopefully, the outbreak won't show up anywhere outside of Troy."

"But, but what are *you* going to do?" She was now sobbing softly.

"I'm not sure, but I'll keep you posted every step of the way. I promise."

He took a deep breath, placing a hand over his closed eyes and settling deeper into the truck's bench seat.

"I'm so sorry, honey. Please tell Mom and Dad and Jennifer that I love them very much."

"Don't! Don't you dare say it like that! Don't talk like you're going away forever."

"All right then. Goodbye, honey. I love you. See you soon, okay?"

11

*O*n July 31, the first contingency of E Troop, 163rd Infantry of the Montana National Guard rolled into the small town of Troy. There were twenty Humvees, all painted in green foliage camouflage, five of them with machine guns mounted on the roof.

At least 100 soldiers walked in lines beside the Humvees, each man with an M-16 automatic rifle, a bayonet affixed, and a HAZMAT gas mask pulled tightly over his face.

To the residents, it looked like a full-scale alien invasion. To Colonel Rybick, it was all just standard procedure. It was a lock-down; a quarantine. He relished the exercise. It reminded him of the good old days, days he had thought would get even better. It took him back to early 2003 when national security was just starting to get to where he was comfortable—when the government acquired the authority to frisk, to question, to delay, and to utterly complicate people's lives—all with impunity and without cause.

But it had only lasted a few years before that sappy President Jordan began pulling the troops out of Iraq, lowering the country's alert levels, and ultimately yanking the carte blanche away from him once again.

The Colonel's own vehicle was parked in the lot at the clinic, while the menacing parade of Humvees slowed to a standstill up and down both sides of the city's main street—Troy Avenue.

A haze of dust kicked up by the lumbering vehicles hung over the area. Downtown residents wore expressions of panic, some clutching each other as they watched the drama unfold.

There had been no emergency radio announcements nor had there been any televised news about the event. The President, along with the governor of Montana, had ordered the Guard to proceed with haste to the town and sequester everyone. No one was to leave. It was a state of National Emergency, but not national notification.

There would be no panic. The citizens of Troy were to go to their homes and remain there. Within hours, a team of Army doctors would fan out and visit each home. Until then, no one was allowed in or out of the town. An Abrams M-1 tank sat at each of the city limit signs to ensure the President's orders were not taken lightly.

Colonel Rybick climbed up on top of his Humvee with an electric bullhorn, placed it in front of the canister on his gas mask, and began to speak in a muffled but loud tone.

"People. People, please don't panic. I am Colonel Jason Rybick with the Montana National Guard. These soldiers here, like myself, are all your neighbors. We're all from Montana, and we're not here to harm anyone."

A crowd began to slowly come closer.

"That's it. That's it," he waved with welcoming arms. "Come in closer. It's okay. We are only here to help you," the Colonel continued.

"Your Governor, Jacob Reynolds, and President Jordan have issued a state of emergency here in Troy. We know most of you have been getting sick over the past week. We are here with medical personnel to see if we can't get to the bottom of this mysterious illness and to ensure that it stops here.

"For those reasons, and for national security, you can all go about your business here, but you must be in your homes by nine o'clock every night. No one is allowed to leave the city. You are officially under a full quarantine."

"You mean arrest!" one man shouted from the crowd.

Rybick rocked his head from side to side and raised his hands.

"I suppose you could call it that, but we're just trying to help," he called back, thinking he'd just as soon climb down and smack the troublemaker upside the head with his bullhorn. Knowing the political leanings of this part of the country, he knew there were plenty more like him.

"Now, please, everyone go home and tell your neighbors to do the same. Stay there until our medical teams have been out to see you. After that, you will be allowed out each morning at seven o'clock, until further notice from me, personally."

As the Colonel lowered the bullhorn and began to climb down, a man in the crowd suddenly fell to the ground and began writhing and twisting in the dust.

The crowd instinctively circled the man, but at a distance. Most of them had seen this before. The man's eyes were rolled back into his head and white foam was frothing from his mouth. His hands were clenched in fists and his legs were drawing up tightly into his gut, as if every muscle in his body was cramping violently.

"Medic!" The Colonel yelled, as he ran to the man and pushed several people to the side.

"Make room. Stand back. There's nothing you can do," he said. "This man's having a seizure."

*   *   *

At the same time the Colonel was issuing his orders, forty-five miles out of town on Highway 90, Manny Parker, a forest ranger from Troy, his wife, and two children were racing toward his brother's home in Utah in their SUV.

Parker would be damned if the government was going to take his freedom away. He had every right to take his family out of harm's way.

"Are you all right?" Parker asked his wife who was holding her stomach, tiny beads of sweat forming on her brow as she watched fence-posts streak by her window. She didn't answer.

"Try to hang in there. I'll stop at the next store I see and get you some Pepto Bismol and aspirin," he said nervously.

Still no reply.

It would be a five-hour ride. Parker took a sip of the coffee in his thermos and kept his eyes intently on the road ahead. His wife stared blankly out the window the entire time.

In the back seat, his daughter was screaming at the top of her lungs because her brother had pinched her hard. Manny and his wife continued to gaze out at the countryside in silence.

They'd be at his brother's house by ten o'clock that night.

Two days later
July 31, 2010

Eighty miles to the northwest Hop Brody was singing along with a country western tune on his radio while he drove toward Troy. Brody was a reporter and syndicated columnist with *The Park Record*, the daily newspaper in Park City, Utah.

It was Brody's annual fly-fishing trek to Troy. He'd made reservations as he always did at Manheim's bed and breakfast, a six-bedroom home in the style of a log cabin located just outside of Troy on the eastern part of town.

He couldn't wait to unload his gear, get a good night's sleep, and rise before dawn to wade out into the river, which offered some of the best trout fishing in the world.

Ahh, this is the life. One full week of nothing but fishing, catching up on all the stories my two buddies will share, and some of that fantastic home cooking of Sheryl's.

Brody's two friends were coming up from Libby to meet him there tomorrow. As Brody's Chevy pickup came around the big loop leading off the highway into Troy, he could scarcely believe what he was seeing. He slammed on the brakes at the sight of the enormous Abrams M-1 tank with the soldier in fatigues pointing a machinegun down on the road.

The massive six-ton vehicle idled at a rumble and poured a continuous stream of pungent diesel fumes into the pristine Montana air.

What the hell?

In front of the tank, a barricade of yellow caution tape was stretched across the narrow road. Another soldier stood behind the taped threshold with an M-16 rifle.

Brody approached slowly. It looked like an invasion or a scene out of a bad sci-fi movie. When he got to the tape, the soldier approached his window dressed in green fatigues, flack jacket, steel helmet, and a full gas mask.

"I'm sorry, sir. No one is allowed into Troy. You'll have to turn around."

"What in the hell are you talking about? No one is allowed in the city?"

"That's right, sir. Please turn around."

"This is bullshit. I've got hotel reservations. This is my annual fishing vacation. I've just driven three hundred and fifty miles to get here. No one said anything about military checkpoints. And how can you just close down a town?"

"I can't tell you that, sir. All I can tell you is that you have to turn around and leave. No one comes in or goes out of Troy."

"Are you with the Army?" Brody asked with a look of total bewilderment.

"National Guard, sir. 163rd Infantry."

"Has something happened to the people there?"

"Sir, I can't tell you that. I can't tell you anything except to turn around. If you don't leave, we'll be forced to arrest you."

Brody could not begin to make sense out of what was happening.

"So is the road blocked on the eastern side as well?"

"All I can tell you, sir...."

"I know. I know—I've got to turn around."

Brody backed the car off the shoulder of the road, and turned back down the same way he'd just arrived. He was angry that his vacation had been interrupted, but the reporter in him was intrigued beyond measure. He knew that he would have been one of the very first people to hear about any kind of military lock-down, so he immediately sensed that a major problem was brewing. And major problems always ended up being major news stories.

If the National Guard was keeping people out of Troy, a city where nothing ever happened, he assumed that they had arrived within the last twenty-four hours.

As he headed northwest again, he got on his Blackberry to call his two buddies. They didn't answer. Then he called his editor at *The Record*.

"Tom, it's Hop. You're not going to believe what just happened to me. Can you hear me?"

"Hey, Hop. Yep, I can hear you, but just barely. You still using that crappy old cell phone of yours?"

"It's not a cell phone. It's a Blackberry, and it wasn't cheap."

"Well, then, let me be the first to welcome you to the twenty-first century."

"Yeah, yeah. Very funny."

"And what are you doing calling here anyway? I thought you went completely underground on your vacations."

"Usually I do but … Oh, shit!"

"What's the matter, Hop?" Tom asked.

"There's a cop behind me with his lights on. No, wait, it's not a cop. It's an M.P. Jesus, what the hell is going on around here? I'll call you right back, Tom."

Hop Brody pulled over to the side of the road. He'd only traveled about a mile and a half when he saw the lights. It was a green military vehicle, a Ford Crown Victoria with rotating yellow and red lights on top.

Hop stayed in the car and kept his eyes in the rearview mirror, watching as another soldier in a gas mask cautiously approached on the driver's side. Hop could see that he was carrying a side arm and wore the insignias of an officer.

"Good morning, sir. Can I see your ID?" the Colonel asked politely.

"Who are you? You don't have the right to pull me over."

"Sorry for the inconvenience, sir. And, yes, I do have the right. Now, can I see your driver's license?" The Colonel asked, making a not-so-subtle gesture of unsnapping the safety strap on his gun's holster.

Though growing more agitated and confused by the minute, Hop pulled his wallet out of his fishing jacket and removed his driver's license from its plastic sheath.

"You're from Utah, huh? What brings you to Montana?"

"I don't have to tell you what I'm doing here. Now, do you mind telling me what the hell is going on? Obviously, you're with the National Guard unit back there in Troy."

Without acknowledging Hop's observation, the Colonel said, "Uh, Mr. Brody, can I see that other ID in your wallet, the one that says Press?"

Hop gave a sigh of frustration and pulled out his Press pass.

"You're a journalist, is that right?"

"That's what it says."

"Where do you work?"

"*The Record.*"

"I read that newspaper."

"Yes. We've got lots of readers throughout the West and Midwest."

"That's what I was afraid of. Mr. Brody, I'm going to have to ask you to step out of the car."

"Wait a goddamned minute. You can't search me."

"I'm not going to search you, sir. I'm arresting you."

"What! What in the hell for?"

"For national security, sir. I'm afraid I can't tell you more than that. Will you just step over here and have a seat in my car?"

Hop was boiling over, but he knew he didn't have a choice. As the Colonel turned, Hop grabbed his Blackberry, switched it to vibrate, and slid it into his jeans pocket.

"Where are you taking me? I have a right to know."

"Where you'll be safe, sir. Now watch your head."

*   *   *

Tom Hawthorne, Hop's editor, sat in his office stroking his chin in thought. *What did he mean by an M.P.? Military Police? But why would the military be in Troy?*

He waited five minutes more and then dialed Hop's phone.

"Hello. You've reached Hop Brody. I can't come to the phone right now, but leave a message and I'll return your call as soon as I can. If this is an emergency, call my editor, Tom Hawthorne at *The Record*," came the familiar voice-mail.

"Hop. What's going on? Give me a call as soon as you can."

As the green sedan kicked up plumes of dust into the pine trees that lined the two-lane road, the radio crackled with cross conversations, lots of military jargon. The Colonel quickly reached over and turned down the volume, then kept his eyes straight ahead and did not utter a word.

Hop sat staring through the steel mesh that separated the driver from whatever passengers were unfortunate enough to be riding in the back. He glanced over to the left side door—no handle, no lock; same on his side.

It was a short ride, heading back to the cutoff where the Abrams tank sat and then beyond it a half mile or so. After a few minutes, the Colonel pulled off on a small road, more like a dirt driveway and drove back into the woods.

This is just getting too weird, Hop thought. *Had martial law been instated and he hadn't heard about it. That was impossible.* Hop Brody was an award-winning political columnist. He'd have known if there was anything that scale going on.

Hop judged that they were nearly a mile off the main road now and as the car made a slight left turn, he could see a large, beige, doublewide trailer. It had a satellite dish mounted on top and there was a soldier standing outside with an M-16 slung around his shoulder.

The car stopped abruptly near the front door. The Colonel got out and came around to let Hop out.

"Mr. Brody, I'm going to have to ask you to, um, *lodge* with us here for awhile. No harm will come to you."

"What! You can't lock me up. This is kidnapping. And when I get out of here, you better believe the shit is going to fly—the whole world's going to know about this."

"No. No sir, they won't. Now, if you'll just follow this soldier here, he'll make you comfortable inside."

Hop was hissing through his teeth and his hands were rolled up into fists, but he knew enough not to do anything stupid. This was too much like the wayward weekend he'd spent in New Orleans on his furlough back in the states from Vietnam. Sure, he'd been a little loud, maybe caused a little bit of trouble, but hell, he was only nineteen and just blowing off a lot of pent-up steam.

But the two policemen summoned that night by the bouncer didn't see it that way, and they cuffed him and beat him pretty badly with two long plastic batons. That was how he'd gotten his moniker. His real name was Benjamin Brody, but after the cartilage in his knee was snapped at the force of one of those baton blows, it never grew back right. From that point on, his friends called him Hop, short for Hopalong.

The soldier motioned to him to climb the short portable stairway to the door. When he reached the top, he opened the door and stepped in. His escort was less than three inches behind him.

Inside, another soldier was sitting at a desk and typing on a rugged notebook computer. Hop looked to the opposite side of the trailer. *Holy shit*, he thought. *This is a friggin' jail cell.*

The trailer was similar to any large mobile home in a typical residential park, but it still had its wheels and, with nothing more than four cots situated behind a sliding cell door, was far less inviting. When servicemen on leave got drunk or rowdy, they would be delivered to the mobile unit and kept there until an M.P. showed up to take them back to the base.

Hop noticed the steel bars covering every window—bars that were screwed into the sides and the floor of the trailer. Not exactly maximum security, but he certainly wasn't going to be breaking out.

The soldier guided Hop through the cell door, closed it, and turned the key. Then he went back outside, leaving the prisoner with the clerk who was still typing.

Hop looked around. There was another door on the other side of the clerk that was closed. He guessed it was either another office or a bathroom.

"Ahem, excuse me, soldier. But is there any water in here?"

"Sure. Want some?"

"Yes, thank you."

The young soldier stood up and opened the door next to him and disappeared for a moment.

Hop reached into his pocket and pulled out his Blackberry. He saw that he did not have much battery life left—maybe enough to make three or four calls. Not wanting to alert the soldier by talking, he quickly used his thumbs to peck out a text message to Tom.

"In deep sht but ok. Hot stry. Don't call. Will call u soon."

August 1, 2010

Manny Parker and his family arrived at his brother's house in Utah the following day, bringing the virus with them. It never occurred to him that there was a good reason for quarantine, that the National Guard locking down his town might have had grounds to contain the citizens.

Manny was still a hippie. He'd lost a lot of good friends in Vietnam and had become disillusioned with the war, so when he returned home in 1969, he joined the protestors, marched on Washington, and generally became extremely distrustful of just about anything the government did.

No Gestapo National Guard Colonel is going to tell me when to go to bed or if he could come and go. He'd go any damned place he wanted, and he'd go any time he wanted. *For God's sake, this is America.*

Besides, he'd watched as his neighbors became sick and he wasn't going to risk his family. He was just too stubborn to realize it was far too late.

12

As Colonel Rybick sat looking out the window of his temporary operations facility at the post office, a white van with large yellow letters spelling out *HAZMAT* cruised slowly down Troy Avenue.

Under the large *HAZMAT* lettering, the words *Official Test Vehicle—Environmental Protection Agency* were printed in black. Next to that, a warning was printed that read: *Hazardous Materials Inside. Keep Clear. Dangerous!*

Inside the van, the driver was steering with one hand while punching information into a laptop computer that was affixed to the dashboard. On top of the vehicle were several satellite dishes and an odd looking piece of equipment roughly the size of a laptop computer. It was two inches thick and twenty inches square, and it sat on the top of a steel tube, which was attached to the roof of the van.

The leading surface of the apparatus had the appearance of a giant gray waffle. It was a collector specifically used to trap minute particles in the air.

When the van moved forward, microscopic particles were trapped in the waffle's folds of "aero gel," a porous substance originally developed for NASA to use in space to obtain comet dust samples.

The EPA had already confirmed the presence of the bacteria that caused meningitis in the blood samples of the people of Troy. Now they were trying to determine how it was spreading, for if the bacteria was airborne, a wide-scale epidemic was virtually eminent.

Closing the borders of Troy would be as effective as closing the screen door on a submarine.

After navigating the town's main streets, the driver got out and climbed to the top of an aluminum ladder mounted to the back of the van. He then unfastened the waffle, put it into a special cellophane bag, and stored it in a freezer unit inside the van. Once frozen, it would be packaged in a special box and sent via Fed Ex to the EPA in Washington. The test results would take two days.

Nathan's boss in Washington, Avery Beckman, would take the waffle and submerse it in a special solution of chemicals to draw out any particles trapped in the aero gel. He knew that if there were more than 500 parts per million of the bacteria, they would be in trouble. In that case, he would use a model that had been developed in 2005 to track the movement of the disease.

The model had originally been developed by a German company that used data from a cash-tracking Web site to trace more than $450,000 worth of one-dollar bills through the continental United States. This data allowed scientists to develop a model of human dispersal that later on proved crucial in fighting flu and other contagious diseases.

The aim of the original study was to attach a number to human traveling behavior. Scientists knew that in order to understand how epidemics spread, they needed to make some assumptions about how humans move about.

Originally, the researchers used data from a Web site as a proxy for how people move around. It had all been fascinating to Avery, the fact that tracing money could actually lead to tracking a virus.

He found that the Web site allowed users to specify where they found any particular marked bill. Each set of entries yielded a unique travel diary of that bill. For example, one bill passed through eights states, assorted restaurants, a racetrack, and a strip club on its journey of at least 4,191 miles.

The study had scrutinized the first and second recorded locations of 464,670 one-dollar bills—most reappeared within six miles of their origins. However, a smaller but significant number turned up over 500 miles away. All of the data eventually allowed the scientists to create a mathematical model of the movement of people.

Avery knew that in a sparsely populated state like Montana, the travel of individuals would not be as fast or as far. Nevertheless, he hadn't yet figured out if the virus was an airborne version, or would be relatively contained through actual physical contact with an infected person.

*   *   *

Manny Parker could not shut off the screaming inside his head.

God, I shouldn't have come here. But what else could I do? I had to get out of Troy. I had to protect my family. I thought we'd been spared.

"Alan? Alan. Come upstairs. I need to talk to you," Manny called out as loud as he could manage, then rolled onto his side and clutched his stomach again. With sweat pouring down his neck, he reached over the side of the bed and pulled the wastebasket closer.

That evening, 425 miles away from Troy, in northern Utah, Manny, his wife, and two children were suffering through the worst of the symptoms. Manny's brother and sister-in-law said it looked like the flu—vomiting, high temperatures, dizziness, and crushing headaches. They called the doctor, but Manny knew there would be nothing a physician could do to ease their pain.

Now, in addition to feeling like death was at his door, he was also wracked with guilt for not having told his brother the truth. Within days, his family would be going through the same debilitating symptoms. And it wouldn't be just them. Recalling their trip from Troy, he thought about all the people they had come into contact with along the way; the gas station attendant and the bank teller. The customers and workers at the grocery store near his brother's house.

August 2, 2010

"Your IDs, please," the uniformed guard said to the two men inside the late-model Mercedes sedan.

The border guard took the two driver's licenses into the guard-house and scrutinized the pictures.

The pictures matched but, from experience, he knew that didn't mean anything. The men were olive-skinned. Both had oily black hair and identical, three-day-old stubble on their faces. Their teeth were the color of cornhusks, and the inside of the car was pungent with the smell of body odor and cherry-scented air freshener.

As a private citizen, he'd been taught not to judge people by their appearances; but as a border guard, everyone was a suspect, particularly those who looked Arabic. He wished that passports were still required. He felt, as did most of the guards, that it had been a stupid idea to roll back the passport requirements. All these two had were New York driver's licenses.

In fact, there were a lot of stupid rules that governed Canadian Border Guards. For one thing, they were unarmed, with the exception of a small can of pepper spray. In fact, some of them routinely walked off the job because they had no way to protect themselves from dangerous armed men coming up from the U.S.

Those in the government and tourism industries felt it inhospitable and rude that armed guards would greet people coming into their country—their first impression of Canada. Don't depend on the border guards, let the Royal Canadian Mounted Police deal with it later, was the philosophy.

Many members of the border patrol worked in places like this one: extremely remote outposts and often staffed with only one or two guards.

When he was done looking at the IDs, the guard came back to the car and handed them to the driver.

"What is your purpose in Canada?" he asked.

"Vacation," the driver responded.

"How long will you be here?" the guard continued.

"Less than a week. Then we return to France," the driver answered.

"Are you bringing any equipment or food into the country?"

The guard leaned down and glanced in at the passenger who was staring straight ahead.

"No, sir. No equipment or food."

"Will you open your trunk for me, please?"

"Certainly," came the reply.

The driver pulled the keys from the ignition, got out, and went around to the back of the car and opened the trunk. The guard rummaged through the luggage in the trunk, and the driver went back to his seat and began talking with his partner.

"Arnot, what are we going to do?"

"Nothing. We have no reason to worry. We have no evidence with us. He will find nothing and then we will be gone. I've told you this is part of our plan, so do not panic now.

"The canisters we opened contained *all* the virus. By now, I guarantee you it will have spread through at least three states, maybe more, though they won't know that immediately.

"Remember, this was our plan all along, to get out of the country before they knew it was an epidemic, before too many people got sick. It's only been ten days, and it takes that long before the symptoms to start to show up. Remember Termez?"

Arnot's traveling companion's real name was Anbar Abazaid. He was young and new to terrorism, having been recruited after the showdown between the U.S. and his homeland over the development of nuclear fuel—a shot heard 'round the world. Both men were French citizens now, living in the Muslim area of Paris.

His country had lost the confrontation with the U.S. and though the enriched uranium they had managed to develop was never found, he knew it wouldn't be long before they would be able to develop at least one weapon in the secret lab in Uzbekistan, far from his borders.

Losing the war of wills to the U.S. had been humiliating to his country. The ensuing embargo had made life very difficult, not at all like the relative comfort he'd enjoyed growing up. He couldn't wait for the infidels to suffer.

"The stupid Americans will not know what hit them and we will be safely back in Iran. They are all focused on our so-called nuclear weapons program. If only they knew. We do not need nuclear weapons. The fools," Arnot said. "We will turn Americans against themselves. There will be total chaos. The rest will take care of itself."

"The Canadians are even more stupid, they don't even allow these border guards any guns. They are helpless. Hah!"

The driver could feel the trunk lid slamming shut and out of the corner of his eye, he saw the guard approaching.

The passenger turned his head to look straight out the windshield, trying to avoid any eye contact. He was still worried, and he knew his facial expression could make him appear suspicious.

The Canadian and American Immigration authorities had long been working with ERS, or Emotion Recognition Software. The Americans introduced it to the Canadians first. The INS and other law enforcement officers had been undergoing training for years to recognize the signs of fear or to tell when someone was lying. Often, it was simply a few facial expressions. Other times, it involved how people moved, what gestures they used, the words they chose. It was all quite sophisticated and quite effective.

It had been particularly effective at the borders with California, Arizona, and Mexico.

The driver had also been trained, but in a different way. Arnot could pass a lie detector test with ease. He would have been a master at poker, if he'd chosen another field.

His passenger, on the other hand, was a novice at hiding his emotions.

The guard leaned down to the driver and said, "Okay. You can go. Drive safely, sir."

The dark blue compact pulled away slowly and within a few seconds was back safely on the highway and far beyond the sight of the border guards.

"Sergeant, look at this," the officer said, sitting in front of a bank of computer monitors and pecking at the keys. With the touch of the mouse, the picture on the largest monitor zoomed in on one of the men's faces—the passenger that had just gone through the crossing.

"He's scared. See that?" The guard asked, pointing at the screen.

"Yeah. You're right. Look at his eyes and mouth. I'd say he was more than scared."

"Yeah. I'd say he looks guilty as hell, but of what?"

"Let's find out," the Sergeant replied. "Call headquarters and tell them to pick this team up coming out of Glacier National Park at Ft. McCleod. Tell them not to stop them, just to follow them. Tell them they're probably headed toward Calgary."

13

By ten o'clock that night, Hop was bored enough to begin to doze off on the narrow canvas cot in his cell. He'd tried to make conversation with the clerk but gave up after the first few tries.

He wished that the soldier had been a smoker. That way, he could have asked him to step outside, giving him enough time to call his editor. As it was, the clerk only left the room once to use the bathroom and even then, only for a few seconds.

Hop closed his eyes, wondering how long he would be a prisoner, then the phone on the clerk's desk rang.

"Hello. Corporal Davis," he said. Hop peaked out of one eye. The soldier had turned his chair toward the bathroom door, away from the cell.

"Yeah, we're going to be here awhile, I'm afraid."

The soldier was silent as whoever was calling kept talking.

"Well, they haven't told us yet. Don't know that they will. I do know they're keeping all the ranks on the perimeter of the city now. Everyone in the whole damned town is sick and they don't want any of us getting whatever it is. All of the unit downtown is in full riot gear and masks."

Suddenly, the clerk realized that Hop might be listening. He quickly jerked his head around to see the prisoner sound asleep.

The soldier lowered his voice to nearly a whisper, "Dan, I've gotta go. They're coming to relieve me in a minute. I can tell you this, though—I'm not happy about being here. I was in a unit five years ago in Iraq and we pulled the same duty in a little shit hole over there. Turned out it was a smallpox scare."

Hop's ear twitched at the soldier's revelation. *Oh my God. I've got to get out of here. Somehow, I've gotta get out of here.*

Hop never did fall asleep. He could think of only two things: his daughter Amanda and his son Casey, who were staying with his ex-wife. The two had joint custody, and Hop had planned his vacation to coincide with her having the children. He felt relieved with at least that knowledge, though he did tell his ex that he'd call them everyday. At the moment, however, it was far more important to get a call through to his editor.

Hop was filled with competing emotions: dread, anger, and helplessness. He had to think of a way to get out of the cell.

It all made perfect sense now, the town was under quarantine. This was going to be one of the biggest stories he'd ever reported, not so much because of the quarantine, but because it was all being kept so secret. The public had a right to know.

August 4, 2010

"Jesus Christ, Bannister. You've really done it now. You know these guys here in Washington already had it in for you. And now you've gone and defied official orders to stay in quarantine?"

Nathan was curled up in a fetal position in the bed of his truck, protected against the evening wind by a camper shell. Still, he shivered as if he were freezing.

"Listen, I witnessed first-hand how the government handled the Libby situation. Do you really think I would just sit around and let them do the same thing to my family? And don't worry, I got us all out of the area before any of us presented any symptoms."

"And you're all okay?"

"We're all fine," Nathan lied.

"Where are you?"

"I'm not going to tell you that."

"I see. So, do you want to hear what I've found out?"

"Why do you think I called you?"

Avery quickly pulled the phone away from his hear to see if there was any caller ID. He figured Bannister was using his cell phone, but there was always a chance. The ID showed "Incoming Call" but no number.

"Okay, it's bad, real bad. It *is* the bacteria—the type B meningitis. Highly contagious and very ugly."

"I see."

"And it gets worse. I found an aerosol molecule mixed into the virus."

"What does that mean?"

"It means someone released it on purpose, probably using some kind of liquid propellant to get it to spray into the air. As much as I hate to say it, I definitely believe we've got a terrorist situation on our hands."

"So it *is* airborne," Nathan said.

"'Fraid so. What's more, it seems to be able to survive for days in the atmosphere."

Nathan rolled onto his back, feeling like the air had just been punched out of him. "Jesus Christ, Avery. You do know that this could be the biggest disaster in American history."

"I'm aware of that. We're doing what we can."

"What can I do to help?"

"You can start by telling me where you are."

Before Beckman could build a convincing case as to why he should go back to Troy, Nathan pulled the phone away from his ear and folded it closed.

14

August 6, 2010

*N*athan's symptoms had somewhat stabilized. He was vomiting less and the bouts of vertigo were not as intense. There was the occasional ringing in his ears, but it was not nearly as bad as some people had described it.

Parked under a massive oak tree, he basked in the warmth of the sun rising over the vast Montana horizon. It was almost seven o'clock local time, two hours earlier than Washington. He flipped open his phone and hit the speed dial button connecting him directly to Avery's office.

Avery recognized the number immediately. "Glad you're still with us," was how he answered the phone.

"Not as glad as I am," Nathan joked back. "Any new developments to report?"

"Well, the Center for Disease Control has taken over for the EPA. Their position is that this situation doesn't have anything to do with pollution, or water contamination."

"Like hell it doesn't. I'd say this is just about the worst type of pollution we're ever going to see."

"The President's cabinet isn't seeing it that way. The CDC is taking over and there's not a thing we can do about it."

Nathan huffed a sarcastic laugh.

"Great. Now we've got the fox guarding the henhouse. I just hope they don't find this virus to be as harmless as they did those trailing piles in Libby."

"Oh jeez, not that old story again."

"Yep—that old story. Never gets old to me. And I don't care if the CDC's taking over or not. I'm still on this thing."

"Well, I won't preach to you about what you're up against, because I know you're a smart man. Just watch your backside, and do everything in your power not to catch this thing."

"I will. And thanks, Avery. I'm sure you could have put out an APB on me and had me dragged back into quarantine."

"Still could, so don't do anything stupid. Oh, and one more thing."

"What's that?"

"There's a worldwide health alert out on the Internet. Seems something very similar has been going on in Uzbekistan. The Health Ministry published it a week ago. At first, they thought it was a recurrence of the avian flu."

"So, what's being done about it?"

"The government has asked the U.N. for help. Of course, they sent a team from the CDC."

"Of course. What have you heard so far?"

"It's strange. It looks like its been contained to the town of Termez, probably because it's surrounded by mountains. By coincidence, the city is about the same size as Troy."

"That's a disturbing coincidence. And when was the first case reported?"

"About two weeks ago."

Nathan needed to ask the question, but he knew he might not be prepared to hear the answer. "Anyone dying from it?"

"So far, there've been no fatalities. Guess if you look hard enough you can always find a silver lining, eh?"

"I guess so. Who's doing the research?"

"Funny you should ask. They have a Russian scientist there studying it. He's quite well known—a biochemist named Revchenko. He's there with the head guy of CDC."

"That's not really so odd," Nathan deduced. "It wasn't that long ago that Uzbekistan was part of Russia, or rather the Soviet Union."

"I know. But two weeks ago, this guy was in our embassy in Paris asking for asylum to the U.S."

"And how would you happen to know all this?"

"I've got my sources. They gave him asylum but then immediately sent him to Termez. My source tells me he's also got a couple of heavyweights with him. Spooks, if you know what I mean.

"He never put a foot on U.S. soil. I'm guessing he might be a little scared. You don't ask for asylum unless you've got a good reason, but now he's right back in the thick of things. There are plenty of people in Uzbekistan that didn't really want to secede from the U.S.S.R."

15

G ot to figure a way out of here, was all Hop could think, though as long as he was locked behind bars and that corporal was sitting in the room, he didn't have a clue how that was going to happen.

Then he reached in his pocket and wrapped his fingers around something he forgot he had.

Hop asked the soldier, who was still typing, to let him out to go to the bathroom. He knew there was probably a window in there for ventilation and perhaps he'd be able to see if any other men were stationed out front.

"I'll have to cuff your hands behind your back, sir," the young soldier said.

"Then how in the hell am I going to take a piss? Are *you* going to hold it for me?"

The soldier threw his head back and grimaced.

"Not in a million years. Guess I'm just gonna have to trust you," he said as he walked over and unlocked the cell door.

With that, Hop went into the bathroom and closed the metal door behind him. Using the toilet seat, he stepped up and peered out a tiny window to the front of the trailer. No guards. He looked to both sides—no one else around, only an old military jeep sitting about fifty feet away between two trees.

Stepping back down, he flushed the toilet and began calculating what his next move should be.

"Hey, you done in there?" the corporal asked.

The door swung open, and Hop ambled out tugging on the zipper of his already zipped pants. In his right pocket was his nearly dead Blackberry; in his left, a book of matches.

The soldier motioned toward the cot without saying anything and Hop dutifully crossed the linoleum floor into the cell. Sitting down on the cot, he watched the soldier pull the self-locking door behind him, then amble over and put the cell's keys in the top desk drawer before going back to work on the computer.

The plan was so easy; it practically figured itself out on its own.

"I think I'm going to lie down for a bit," Hop said with a yawn, then stretched out on the cot with his back facing the soldier.

"Sure. Whatever," the officer said without looking up.

Within a minute, the clerk was typing again, intent on the monitor in front of him.

Hop took one last peek over his shoulder, and then lit a match as he coughed to muzzle the sound.

Holding the match against the edge of the government-issue bed sheet, he knew it was not going to burst into flames. It would just smolder, creating a dark gray trail of smoke.

Hop lay perfectly still on the cot as the match began to melt the edge of the fabric.

"What in the hell is that smell?" the clerk said as he waved his hand back and forth in front of his face. "Jesus. Smells like burnt hair or...."

"Oh my God!" Hop screamed, jumping out of bed and frantically patting his shirt as if putting out flames. "Get me out of here, the bed's on fire! Get me the hell out of here!" He pushed his back into the corner of the cell as a billow of smoke rose off the mattress.

"Stay back. I'm gonna open the door," the soldier yelped as he sprang into action. He jammed the key into the lock, opened the door, then took off his shirt and started slapping it across the smoking bed sheet.

With unexpected agility, Hop lunged behind the officer, bounded out of the cell, and yanked the self-locking door behind him.

"Hey! What the fuck do you think you're doing?"

"I'm getting out of here, that's what I'm doing," he said as he pulled the cell door keys out of the lock and tossed them across the room. "Now, where are the keys to that Jeep outside?"

With a sly grin, the soldier reached into his pants pocket and pulled the keys out, dangling them in front of Hop. "Right here, old man. Why don't you come in here and get them?"

Hop's mind had always reacted well under pressure. Recalling the Jeep parked outside, he knew it to be of '60s vintage. More likely than not, it was a mechanical clone to the Jeeps he'd hot-wired dozens of times during his tour of duty in Vietnam.

"You hold on to 'um, son. Tell your superior you put up a hell of a fight to keep them away from me. I'll back up your story if anyone ever asks."

"Fuck you," the young man sneered as he watched Hop slink out the trailer's front door.

Hop peeked carefully around the corners of the trailer. Not seeing anyone, he made a hobbling dash for the Jeep, but stumbled and slid into the dirt, his limp forsaking him. As he began to push himself up, he heard the sound of two, maybe three men approaching. It wouldn't be long before they noticed the smoke coming from the trailer.

As expected, the men bolted into action with a flurry of cussing and yelling, one of them obviously shouting their predicament into a radio. If Hop timed it just right, he could slide into the jeep just as they climbed the stairway to the trailer. He knew he would only have a few seconds to get it started.

Here goes nothin', he said under his breath as he clambered up into the vehicle.

Keeping his eyes on the trailer, Hop reached under the dash and laid his Chevy key lengthways across the backside of the Jeep's ignition switch, which created an electrical arc across the car's starter solenoid terminals. The trusty Jeep fired immediately.

"Holy shit!" he heard one of the M.P.s yell as the soldier bolted out onto the front steps. As the two men ran towards him, Hop jammed the gearshift into first and floored the gas, spewing out a huge cloud of exhaust into the faces of the two pursuing men.

As Hop careened down the dirt road towards the highway, he heard a rifle shot. He ducked his head instinctively and kept the accelerator to the floor. The gamble now was if he should stay in the Jeep or try to make it back to his own truck. It was probably still sitting on the side of the road, but who knew if the keys would be in it. Either way, he'd have to head down this road for at least another couple of miles before he could get out onto the highway.

Reaching into his pocket, Hop pulled out the Blackberry, pushed the power button, and waited to see how much battery time he had left. He estimated that there was maybe enough for one conversation, and quickly decided that that one conversation would have to be with Tom. He pushed the speed-dial button.

"Hey, Hop. Are you all right? I've been trying to reach you all day."

"Tom, it's a long story and I only have a minute of battery left. Someone—I'm assuming the Governor—has quarantined Troy. The National Guard is all over the place. They even have an Abrams M-1 parked at each of the city limit signs."

"What? Are you sure? Why haven't I heard anything about this?"

"I don't know. But when I was calling you earlier, some colonel caught up to me and threw me in a temporary holding facility parked in the woods.

"Fortunately, he was too stupid to take my Blackberry. I escaped about ten minutes ago, and I'm thinking that the best thing for me to do now is to go into the next town and get a rental car. They're going to be looking for the Jeep I stole."

"You stole a Jeep?"

"Yep. Army issue."

"Oh Jesus, Hop. You realize all of this is felony territory, don't you? When the Army takes over during quarantine, it's just about the same as martial law. They can put you in prison and they don't have to tell anyone where you are."

"Yeah, I know. Listen, I'm about out of juice. I'm going to find a rental car and get this damned thing charged up somewhere. I'll call you back as soon as I can."

"But where are you gonna' go? They'll have someone on every road waitin' for you."

"Not every road. And I know this may sound stupid, but I think I'm going back to Troy."

Hop turned off the Blackberry before his editor could talk him out of his plan.

1 6

By the following day, Avery Beckman had been able to track most of the virus using the same principles as the cash-tracking system that he'd learned, along with several algorithms.

It was six-thirty in the morning and Avery sat analyzing the data on his monitor, sipping coffee from a large Styrofoam cup, when his private line rang. The caller ID displayed Nathan's cell number.

"Good morning, Nathan."

"Morning Avery."

Though Beckman recognized Nathan's voice, there was something different about the way it sounded. He couldn't put his finger on it exactly, but he pictured in his mind that Nathan's neck and throat were swollen. "How's everything going?" he asked.

Through the earpiece of his phone, Beckman could hear the sound of Nathan's breathing. He could even hear birds chirping in the background.

"I said, how's everything going?" he repeated louder than before.

"Huh? Oh fine, fine." Nathan answered. "Just trying to keep up with everything. Any news?"

Beckman stood up and paced the confines of his office. "Oh, there's news all right—just about all of it bad."

Nathan looked down at his Palm Treo 1150 phone, making sure the volume was turned all the way up. "Yeah? Care to enlighten me?"

"Well, the CDC sent me an email this morning, and together, we've been able to track outbreaks of this thing all the way to Pennsylvania, down to Atlanta, and out to Denver."

Nathan could feel his chest tightening as he listened to Beckman's update. "Jesus, Avery. How could it spread so fast in less than two weeks?"

"We're not sure, but it is a resilient strain of bacteria that doesn't seem to mind floating around in the atmosphere for a while."

Nathan did not reply.

"Which reminds me, how are you doing? Any signs of nausea or vertigo?"

"No. Guess I must have got out of Troy just in time."

"I see," Beckman pursed his lips and nodded—a look that would have conveyed his suspicion had Nathan been there in the room with him.

Nathan walked over and sat down beneath the tree he'd been camping beside for the last couple of days. "I assume Montana's seen the worst of it," he said, preparing himself to hear the worst concerning his family holed up in Billings.

"Actually, the bacteria appears to be kind of leap-frogging its way south and east. There'll be a reported case two towns past the last outbreak. We're still trying to figure it out."

"Any way to slow it down?"

"We don't have an antidote, if that's what you're asking. Hell, we don't even have a realistic treatment to alleviate the symptoms or quell the pain. What's worse, at the rate it's moving, this whole country could be infected within weeks. I'd say we're just about to jump into Shit Creek with both feet and no paddles."

"You seem a little cavalier about it all Dr. Beckman."

"I'm not being cavalier. I just don't have any answers, and neither does the CDC. Besides, like you, I'm a scientist. I have to take a calm approach to this thing or I won't be any good to anyone."

"You're right. Now, back up a bit. You said that *almost* all the news was bad. Does that mean there's some good news?"

Beckman sat down at his desk and opened a file that had been emailed to him just yesterday.

"Remember my source I talked to you about the other day? The one who gave me information on that Revchenko guy, the scientist in Termez?"

"Yes."

"Well, apparently, the virus there *has* been contained within the borders of that city, thanks to Revchenko. The people are getting over the vertigo and nausea, and no one is having the seizures. The only residual effect seems to be varying degrees of hearing loss, but other than that, they appear to have contained it."

"How?"

"I knew you'd ask that. You on your Treo?"

"Of course. I'd be dead without this thing."

"Good. Here, I'm emailing you a report I got yesterday. Let me know when you've opened it."

Nathan flipped up the phone's screen, accessed his email account and opened the file. "Got it."

"Good, now scroll down a bit until you see the photos they took with a microscope."

"Okay, I'm there. What am I looking at?"

"That's the million-dollar question. Meningitis B is a bacteria, only this acts like both a virus and a bacteria. It appears to have mutated into something else, which, of course, makes it even more difficult to deal with."

"Is it synthetic?"

"Ah, yes. And that's where dear Dr. Revchenko comes into the picture. Apparently, he was forced by the KGB to create a biological weapon of mass destruction. But as it happened, he ended up stealing the entire batch of it after they murdered his family. That batch has been floating around in storage for the last twenty-five years, which may explain the odd mutation."

"Wow!"

"Wait, the story gets a lot more involved. Apparently, a faction of Iranian terrorists recently stole the virus from *him*, and that's who we believe released it in both cities.

"The good news, though, is that Revchenko also manufactured an antidote, one that he had concocted, unbeknownst to the KGB."

"Okay. So that's what he's been using in Termez?"

"Precisely. Only now, he doesn't have anymore and he needs a lab to develop another batch, or, should I say, many batches."

Nathan stood up and leaned his back against the tree. Part of his mind was drifting off to Stella and his family, while the other part was slipping into investigative mode.

"Well, for Christ's sake—why don't they give him a lab?"

"They're working on it."

"Well, they better speed it up. We've all got family out there who could come down with this at practically any minute."

"You're preaching to the choir, Nathan. I'm doing everything I can to help. And I'll keep sending you whatever information I get."

"Thanks. And tell me. Your guy must be embedded pretty close to the source to know all this."

"About as close as you can get."

"Yeah? Like who?"

"Revchenko himself."

"Huh?"

"My contact's one of the spooks guarding him. Special ops guy who was in Afghanistan. Also happens to be my brother-in-law."

"Boy, doc. You're something else. I had you pegged entirely different," Nathan said as he walked over to the cab of his truck and grabbed a pad of paper and a pen.

"What do we do now?" he asked and starting writing some notes to himself about the virus.

"We? Are you sure you don't want to get back to your family first?"

"Hell yes I want to go back to them. But right now, I … I can't."

"That's what I thought," Beckman sighed compassionately.

17

$\mathcal{N}$ ight was falling, though Hop could still see the heat waves rippling off the concrete highway. He pulled the Ford pickup off the road about three miles from Troy, turned off the lights, and unplugged the Blackberry from the cigarette lighter attachment.

Thank God for Blackberry, he thought.

It wasn't just his phone and email tether—he used it like a tiny laptop to access Internet sites and to do research on the road. That day, after he'd picked up the rental truck, he went into a roadside diner and spent the better part of two hours Googling words like: *virus, quarantine*, and even *martial law*.

Hop was intent on getting his story right from the source—someone in the town.

No sooner had he gotten online than the unit's vibrator began to signal him of incoming calls and emails. The incoming profile indicated that Tom had tried to reach him six times. He chose not to answer him—not yet. Two missed calls were from his daughter and one was from his son.

Hop took a deep breath after seeing those two IDs, but he knew his children were in good hands. Besides, there was absolutely nothing he could do at the moment.

Hop had been coming to Troy for eight years to fish and to enjoy his two weeks off in the summer. He knew the area better than probably half of the people who lived there. He'd hiked mile upon mile into the forests and followed uncountable streams, always in search of more or bigger trout.

There was an abandoned mineshaft just outside of town about a half mile away, right near the edge of the woods. He and his fishing buddies had discovered it years ago, and though they knew it was boarded up and probably dangerous, a night of drinking whiskey convinced them it would be fun to explore.

Once inside, they'd walked and crawled around under the supporting timbers using a camping flashlight until they'd gone about as far as they dared. Their trek had taken them to within about fifty yards of light—another entrance. But, when the dust and rock started to crumble overhead, and the supports began to creak, they sobered up quickly and made their way back to their campsite, never giving it much thought after that other than to embellish upon the mini-adventure.

Each of the men repeated the story for years until it had grown into a vivid tale about them finding some strange prehistoric, bear-like animal, perhaps even a Sasquatch inside and how they had just barely escaped with their lives. Whenever asked, each man would not only back up the ridiculous story, but more often than not over the years, add something to it.

He would use the tunnel to steal into town and then make his way to his friend's bed and breakfast. Hopefully, she hadn't been stricken yet and she would be able to tell him what was happening.

By ten o'clock, Hop emerged from the other entrance only a hundred yards across a field from downtown Troy. There was no moon out and very few lights glowing from the homes. He couldn't see any soldiers, but he did hear the rumble of a large truck and someone making announcements through an electric bullhorn.

"Attention, Troy residents. The nine o'clock curfew is in effect. No one is to leave his home. Keep all doors locked. Do not come outside until seven in the morning. Anyone caught outside is subject to immediate arrest."

The same message was repeated a few minutes later as the truck made its rounds through the town.

By that morning, Hop had heard all he needed and was only waiting for nightfall to make his way back out the tunnel to the rental truck. He'd gone to Sheryl's place, the bed and breakfast he always stayed at. He knew her better than anyone else in town, except for Mike, the guy who owned the bait and tackle shop.

They'd spent the better part of the night talking in the basement. Turned out she was sick, too, but he had to take his chances. She'd told him about the EPA man, how just about every person in town was sick as dogs, and then what the Army Colonel had said.

Hop knew, from his research, the power the Colonel and the government had. Quarantine was essentially no different than temporary martial law. The Colonel *was* the law. Forget about constitutional rights. All the phone lines had been shut down and anyone who had a short wave radio had it confiscated. "Of course," Sheryl had said, "they couldn't shut down the Internet, but not too many people out here use it anyway."

The people were allowed to keep their televisions and regular radios, at least for the time being. An enormous Army hospital tent had been set up next to the clinic, and there had been several quarter-ton trucks with red crosses painted on the side that unloaded a slew of guys in white coats. But, according to Sheryl, they hadn't accomplished much and everyone was still getting sick. In fact, she only knew of four that were still okay.

"Hop, you be careful. Some of these soldiers might look like punky young eighteen-year-olds, but now they've got their first taste of real power, probably for the first time in their lives, and some of them are meaner than they look," Sheryl told Hop as he climbed out the back window.

The black Ford pickup was on the main highway within an hour and by two o'clock that afternoon, he'd pulled into the parking lot of a Starbucks.

He knew he could use the wireless hot spot there to write his story.

That story, finished in less than an hour, was a powder keg ready to explode. He felt like Bob Woodward breaking Watergate. Before nightfall, it would be on all the wire services, on the Internet, and at every television and radio station he could imagine. After reading through it one last time, he emailed it to Tom at the office, along with a note to call him on his Blackberry.

The world was about to find out about Troy, the government cover-up of the quarantine, and the lethal threat facing every citizen. Hop had to catch his breath before leaving the quiet coffee shop.

*   *   *

The thought never entered his mind that shouting his story from the rooftops might not have been the best plan of action.

That night, the headline hit the Internet, but it was late and most people were asleep:

Deadly Virus Quarantine
A Government Cover-up

The following afternoon, the same headline or a version of it followed in every major newspaper in the country. Unfortunately, Hop's story caused sporadic panic—the very thing that President Jordan had been discussing the night before with this cabinet in the White House in preparation for his State of the Union Address.

PART

II

18

Two weeks after the initial outbreak in Troy
August 9, 2010

Robert Jordan, a handsome man that reminded people, at least in appearance, of Robert Kennedy, had won the presidency with nearly sixty percent of the vote. The first Independent candidate ever to win the office, he was also the first president to have a female vice president. Her name was Madlyn Kramer. Candid, dynamic, and fashionable to a fault, Kramer was widely acknowledged as the driving force behind Jordan's victory.

The country had finally grown up. It was time for a dramatic change. Jordan and Kramer represented the first truly fresh air to blow through Washington in nearly forty years.

Now, not even two years into his term, Jordan was faced with what he knew would be the defining challenge of his presidency—an epidemic of catastrophic proportions.

The Uzbeks had managed to isolate the virus and also provide a sort of living laboratory where health officials from all over the world were studying the effects. Fortunately, no one in the town had died, but nearly all of them contracted the disease.

Jordan's main concern was that the bacteria had already spread too rapidly and too far to contain as easily as it had been in Termez. In fact, it was already reported in eight states and showed no signs of abating.

So far, the worst long-term effects of the meningitis were related to damage to the inner ear, in particular the cochlea and the nerve pathways to the brain that help interpret sound.

Jordan had pored over all the research he'd been given by the CDC and the medical experts. Apparently, the age of Dr. Revchenko's virus had caused it to mutate. The good news was that the disease did not appear to be fatal. The bad news was that, after being violently ill for weeks, people were beginning to experience sensorineural hearing loss.

Sensorineural hearing loss, Jordan was told, meant that sound reaches the inner ear, but there's damage in that part of the ear or to the nerve pathways from the inner ear to the brain.

Traditionally, this follows the use of certain drugs, exposure to loud noises for prolonged periods of time, or from an infection, heredity, a birth defect, or meningitis.

No one could predict if the hearing loss would be permanent, but everyone could envision the myriad consequences to the nation's health, the economy, and the country's security if enough people were affected.

Upon hearing the worst of it, Eric Jennings, head of the Department of Health Services, had related to the President that he felt the bacteria would be manageable. After all, no one was dying; most recovered from the physical effects, with the one exception of the hearing loss. What's more, there seemed to be a good chance that Dr. Revchenko would be able to duplicate a vaccine that had worked on the people of Termez.

To him, the problem was more about the immediate isolation of the President, his cabinet, certain military leaders, people in the financial industry and law enforcement; NSA, CIA, and FBI operatives; and others, including himself, that would be needed to run the country—the people who would have to continue to communicate in a "normal manner," meaning they could speak—and hear.

President Jordan sat at his desk in the Oval Office. Seated around him were the Vice President; Eric Jennings; Halley Weber, the Secretary of Education; and several others. Once this inner circle made some decisions, the Joint Chiefs of Staff, members of Congress, and others would be included.

"Mr. President," Vice President Kramer said, "I disagree with Mr. Jenning's rather callus assessment of the situation.

"My God, think about this. Are you grasping the scope of the disaster this country is facing if hundreds of thousands, perhaps *millions* of people suddenly go deaf? How will Air Traffic Controllers talk to pilots? Our entire air transportation system would shut down overnight. With all due respect, Mr. President, Mr. Jennings hasn't thought this through very well.

"Here's another thought: The financial markets would have to close. How are the traders on the floor of the stock exchange going to get their buy and sell orders handled?

"I can think of hundreds of other examples. In short, we would experience a complete and catastrophic economic collapse. Phones will be useless, radios will be obsolete; and how are the law enforcement agencies going to talk to each other?

"Can you imagine a patrolman in a cruiser with no radio communications? No one will be able to call nine-one-one. The list of disasters is practically endless when you think about how much of our lives depend upon our hearing."

Vice President Kramer paced back and forth in front of the President's desk.

"With all due respect, Madame Vice President," Jennings broke in, "don't you think you're letting your emotions get in the way of reason? After all, we have no idea how many people will be afflicted. For all we know, this may be contained to just eight states. And even if it *does* spread a little further, there are always people who can step in as back-ups for all these jobs."

The Vice President listened, took a deep breath, and calmly responded to Jennings.

"Mr. Jennings, right now we need to be thinking about *worst-case* scenarios.

"Are you forgetting the impact nine-eleven had on the global economy? And not to diminish the tragedy, but that was just *two buildings and three thousand people*!

"Have you thought about the effect this situation would have on the financial market? The sheer panic of how this country would adapt, would send the stock market into a tailspin."

The President had heard enough for the moment. "I agree," he said as he joined the heated conversation. "This is a potentially the worst disaster to ever hit this country. But before we get into the logistics of crisis management, a more immediate issue is how we're going to bring the American people up to speed on what's going on. If we don't give them some honest answers soon, we'll have a revolt *and* an epidemic on our hands.

"When the people become skeptical, as they were a few years ago after Katrina, fear becomes as epidemic as the bacteria. That leads to confusion and anger. And we all know what that kind of anger leads to. Just look at the looting in New Orleans—the armed riots—only now we're talking about a nation full of scared and angry people, not just one part of one city. And if you add the fact that no one will be able to talk to anyone else ... well ...

"One of the most difficult challenges we have is to prepare the country for a public health crisis, the likes of which the United States hasn't seen in more than one hundred years."

Jordan had done his research. In the many folders given him by the CDC, there were files on an epidemic most people had not been aware of, partly because it happened in 1894—the smallpox outbreak in Milwaukee. It was a vivid illustration to him just how important trust was if a deadly virus swept the country or the world.

When smallpox struck Milwaukee, "Health officials permitted middle—and upper-class residents to be quarantined at home, but ordered residents in the city's crowded immigrant sections to an isolation hospital known as the "pest house," the *Los Angeles Times* article read.

The article went on, "Angry at the injustice, immigrant groups hid smallpox victims from authorities. The health commissioner told a newspaper reporter: 'I am here to enforce the laws, and I shall enforce them, if I have to break heads to do it.'

"Riots broke out and smallpox raced through the city. By the end of the outbreak, 1,079 Milwaukeeans were infected and 244 died."

"However, when the epidemic reached New York, they handled it differently," Jordan said. "They alerted everyone in the city and they had vaccines ready. They told the people exactly what they were faced with and as a result thousands upon thousands of people were inoculated within days and the epidemic never took hold."

In Jordan's mind, those Milwaukee and New York numbers were far smaller compared to what the country was faced with now. Yes, no one had died, but that didn't mean they wouldn't. Millions upon millions would be affected and panic would most certainly follow.

Jordan's Oval Office meeting was an open forum and he encouraged each member to speak his or her mind.

Press Secretary Gordon Boggs spoke up first.

"Mr. President, at this moment, communication with the people is what matters most, and the core of crisis communication is demonstrating competency, transparency, and compassion.

"With that in mind, if this turns into an epidemic, and it looks like it will, we have to make sure that words from the White House won't fall on deaf ears—no pun intended. So far, the country has your trust. We can't squander that. We can't screw up like they did before.

"Under the last administration, DHS and FEMA were late and inept. The color-coded terror-alerts were a joke. The still-unsolved anthrax scare without a solution was a debacle. We still have troops in Iraq after seven long years. We all know how all of those things were treated. It was all as opaque and dishonest as it gets.

"First, the Patriot Act slipped through Congress because everyone was so scared. Then the illegal phone taps started and then the tracing of millions of emails got out of hand—all of which had been very secretive and still would have been when you were elected, had it not been for the press. Everything could be justified under those magic words, 'In the interest of national security'—everything.

"Mr. President, communications coming from this office need to be frank. People have to know they are going to get sick, that they may lose their hearing; that they might even die.

"Great communicators help citizens steal themselves for suffering, while also protecting them. That means you have to admit that something tragic is happening."

In the far corner of the room sat an attractive woman in her early forties. Though she had a youthful face, she wore heavy, narrow black glasses that made her look bookish and very conservative.

She hadn't yet participated in the dialogue but her mind was racing ahead of the immediate consequences. Her name was Halley Weber. She was the Secretary of Education. Her first thought was, *Why have I been invited to this meeting? The Joint Chiefs should be here.* Then it became apparent once the meeting began.

Ms. Weber was a single mother of a nine-year-old daughter. Oddly, she had been the first person to hold the post that was also a parent.

According to Ms. Weber, her experience as a mother of a child in a public school, struggling with English classes, gave her a better understanding of what parents want in a public school.

The additional fact that her only daughter was hard-of-hearing since birth, gave President Jordan a very good reason to include her.

Just then, one of the President's aides came into the Oval Office.

"Mr. President, I'm sorry to interrupt, but I've got some vital news—not good I'm afraid."

The room went silent as all eighteen pairs of eyes focused on the young man.

"What is it, Daniel?" the President asked.

"In a word, Chicago. I'm also getting reports of symptoms as far east as Pennsylvania and as far west as Denver."

Jordan swiveled his chair to the left, stood up, and walked to the window without speaking. He stood there, silent for more than a minute, when Vice President Kramer spoke.

"Mr. President. Are you okay?"

Jordan turned slowly, as serious as anyone in the room had ever seen him. His face was drawn—most of the color gone.

"Get the Joint Chiefs in here. I also want you to alert the National Guard commanders in Maryland and Virginia," he said to his Chief of Staff.

"We've got a lot to do and not much time to do it. Go to code red immediately, but do not, and I repeat, do not, talk to the press."

"But, sir, how can we go to code red without telling the press?"

"Quietly for now, very quietly. Only those in the Pentagon and the security agencies should know. And I don't want it put out to the states yet, either. I've got to have some time to think. And find out how many troops we've still got here in the States in the Guard and how many in each state. I want that information by the end of the day."

"Sir, at the risk of speaking too soon, what do you think you're going to propose to do about all this?" Jennings asked.

"Martial law, Mr. Jennings, or at the very least, a prioritized martial law."

"Oh Jesus. What do you mean *prioritized*?"

"I mean we'll institute martial law on a *need* basis, wherever we've got a crisis."

Madyln Kramer spoke up. "Mr. President. If I may offer a different opinion, I'm not so sure that martial law, even a limited action, is such a good idea. I didn't agree with the quarantines and I don't think this is ultimately the right decision."

The room came to a hush. Everyone looked at Jordan.

"That's all right, Ms. Kramer. We're all free to speak openly. Go on."

"Sir, quarantines and martial law only serve to make people feel like they're caged animals. They'll begin to feel that they're cut off from the rest of humanity. Besides, at some point soon, it won't matter. The disease will run its course, no matter how many people you lock up."

"Well, Ms. Kramer, we obviously have a difference of opinion. For now, though, we're going with mine."

"What about Tennessee?" A cabinet member asked from across the room.

"What about Tennessee?" Jordan retorted with a touch of anger in his voice.

"They don't recognize martial law. In fact, it's outlawed in the state."

"Pardon my French, but fuck Tennessee. I'm the law now—in all fifty states! We've got to get control of this thing, and we won't do it if everyone is able to run around in a panic."

Three weeks after the initial outbreak in Troy

Hop Brody was already extrapolating out the government powers to quarantine, which was just one step behind full martial law. He sat at his computer using Google to search for the term: martial law. What he found astounded even him—something he'd never heard of.

According to an article written seven years before by Ritt Goldstein, (July 27, 2002) entitled, *Foundations Are in Place for Martial Law in the U.S.*, Ritt said, "Recent pronouncements from the Bush Administration and national security initiatives put in place in the Reagan era could see internment camps and martial law in the United States."

Jesus, Hop thought, *internment camps?* The article went on: "When President Ronald Reagan was considering invading Nicaragua, he issued a series of executive orders that provided the Federal Emergency Management Agency (FEMA) with broad powers in the event of a 'crisis' such as 'violent' and widespread internal dissent or national opposition against a U.S. military invasion abroad.'

Holy shit! Why didn't anyone know about this back in Reagan's time? Certainly, both Bushes knew and almost just as surely, President Jordan knew about it, Hop thought as he continued to read.

"The powers were never used. But, with the looming possibility of a U.S. invasion on Iraq, recent pronouncements by President George Bush's domestic security chief, Tom Ridge, and an official with the U.S. Civil Rights Commission, should fire concerns that these powers could be employed, or a de facto drift into the deployment could occur.

"On July 20, 2005, the *Detroit Free Press* ran a story entitled, *Arabs in U.S. Could Be Held, Official Warns.* The story referred to a member of the U.S. Civil Rights Commission who foresaw the possibility of internment camps for Arab Americans. FEMA has practiced for just such an occasion."

Hop could hardly believe what he was reading. With his eyes glued to the monitor, he continued: "FEMA, whose main role is disaster response, is also responsible for handling UW domestic unrest.

"From 1982-84, Colonel Oliver North assisted FEMA in drafting its civil defense preparations. Details of these plans emerged during the 1987 Iran-Contra scandal.

"They included executive orders providing for suspension of the constitution, the imposition of martial law, internment camps, and the turning over of government to the president of FEMA."

Internment camps!

"A *Miami Herald* article on July 5, 1987, reported that the former FEMA director Louis Guiffrida's deputy, John Brinkerhoff, handled the martial law portion of the planning. The plan was said to be similar to one Mr. Guiffrida had developed earlier to combat 'a national uprising by black militants.' It provided for the detention 'of at least 21 million American Negroes' in assemble centers or relocation camps.

"Today, Mr. Brinkerhoff is with the highly influential Anser Institute for Homeland Security. Following a request by the Pentagon in January that the U.S. military be allowed the option of deploying troops on American streets. The Institute, in February, published a paper by Mr. Brinkerhoff arguing the legality of this—all of which had been approved by Reagan."

The article continued on for several more paragraphs, but Hop had read enough. He realized that what he'd feared as a journalist was coming true. The country had come to a dangerous intersection where civil rights, national security, and technology were about to converge in what might be a very violent collision.

19

August 15, 2010

*H*enry Bannister sat in a large recliner chair facing the fireplace while the girls prepared dessert in the kitchen. On the fireplace mantle, commemorative plaques and display cases full of medals bore the testimony of his years of service in the Korean War.

He'd been a rancher from the day he left the military, forging a simple and rugged existence in places like Billings—places where cows and horses outnumbered people—for himself and his family. Not once had he ever wished to live any other way.

Henry read the day's newspaper while keeping an observant ear on his portable ham radio sitting next to him on an end table. He was a hobbyist that enjoyed listening to broadcasts late at night from all around the world. With the thirty-foot-high antennae he'd erected out by his barn, he could pick up Moscow on a good night.

Because he was an avid listener, Henry had many hobbyist friends all over the world—people he'd never met, but shared common interests with nevertheless.

On this night, as he fiddled with the myriad dials and switches on the radio, he picked up a transmission from a man in Toronto, Canada.

The man was not a regular member of Henry's network of ham operators.

"CQ, CQ, CQ. Anyone receiving this transmission?"

The voice crackling through the radio's speaker seemed agitated, or nervous, or both.

Henry picked up his microphone and hit the transmit button. "Go ahead, CQ. This is Alpha Bravo Tango, one-three-niner in Billings, Montana. Over."

"Greetings, Montana. My name is Walter Cromwell, and I'm transmitting from Toronto. I don't have much time. This is extremely important. Although I live in Canada, I am an American citizen," came the gravely voice.

Henry tweaked the dial just a bit to get rid of the static. *This sounded interesting.*

"Hello, Walter Cromwell. You've got Henry Bannister here. How the heck are ya? Over."

"Listen, Mr. Bannister. There's no time for small talk. You folks down there, especially in Montana, are in grave danger. I don't know what to tell you other than the truth. No time to tell you how I found out, either. Just listen up, okay? Over."

"Roger that Mr. Cromwell. Go ahead. Over."

"There is a terrible virus spreading throughout the United States...."

The statement sent a chill up Henry's spine. *I thought Nate told us this thing had been confined to the Troy area. How could a guy in Canada know about it?*

"Mr. Cromwell, my son works for the EPA and he assured me just a few days ago that the virus had been contained in a small area up north. And how did you find out about it? Over."

"I can't tell you that, and I don't know what your son knows. All I *do* know is that it's beginning to spread throughout several of the lower forty-eight. And, believe it not, that's not even the worst of it."

Henry turned the volume down as the fire crackled in front of him. He didn't want the women to hear what this man might have to say.

"Look it, Mr. Bannister, you may not believe this, but later tonight, President Jordan is going to declare martial law. Do you know what that means? Over."

"I sure as hell do. Over."

"Better get prepared. Turn on your TV tonight."

"We don't have a television."

"Then listen to the radio. I'm sure it'll be everywhere.

"I don't know how old you are, but I was down there when Executive Order 10995 was issued," the man said. "Virtually overnight, the government shut down all communications media, including radio, TV, newspapers, CB, ham, and telephones. I don't care how old I get; I'll never forget that. Got to go. Good luck, Henry Bannister. Out."

Henry knew exactly what Cromwell was referring to. He even remembered his older brother telling him how Hitler shaped Germany into a Nazi dictatorship through a similar executive order. That's how it all began. *When you don't have the ability to communicate, you're in deep shit,* he thought. *Ultimately, the only thing that ensures freedom is unhindered communication.* At that moment, he knew he had to do everything he could to keep all possible channels of communication open. *Someone has to keep an eye on the government, and someone has to tell the truth.*

Stella's voice lilted out from the kitchen. "Henry, do you want some dessert? Mom's made a delicious apple pie, and we have some vanilla ice cream to go with it."

"No thanks, darlin'. I'll pass. I've got a guy here on the radio that I need to talk to. I'll be with you gals in a minute."

Henry's mind started running off in four different directions at once. *Is Nate okay? Should I pack up the family and head out of Billings? And if we do leave, where should we go?*

Henry remembered what Cromwell had said. His own father had related the same kind of information to him years ago. *Be prepared. The more self-reliant you are, the better. Be prepared to stay one step ahead of the bureaucracy.*

The good thing is that we live outside any major population center he thought. *At least there won't be the chaos that people in big cities are going to experience.*

He also remembered the cardinal rules his father related to him:

Become as transparent as possible. Do not draw attention to yourself or your family. Form alliances with like-minded neighbors and friends. Stay away from populated areas and, above all—remain calm.

Henry stared into the fireplace, stroking his chin, deep in thought. *A declaration of martial law means our rights are suspended. Our constitutional rights no longer apply. People can be arrested and imprisoned indefinitely without charges. No freedom of speech, freedom of assembly or press. Gun ownership will come under attack, and search and seizures without notice or warrants will become commonplace.*

Nothing worse than the loss of liberty.

Henry stood up, turned off the radio, and went to the basement door. Opening the door, he yelled out, "Ladies, I'm going down into the cellar. I'm not to be disturbed."

Stella turned to Joanne with a look of surprise and said, "Now what in the world is he up to?"

"Oh, don't pay him any attention," Joanne said, swatting at the air with her open hand. "He likes to mess around with his radios down there. Well, his radios and his guns, that is."

2 0

August 16, 2010

The unmarked plane touched down at the Quantico Marine base in Virginia at midnight. On board were two CIA agents, two pilots, and a frail, gray-haired man in a camel's hair coat sitting bolt upright with a black briefcase on his lap.

When the jet way came up to the plane and the old man stepped out onto the first stair, he could see five different black sedans arranged in a semicircle at the bottom of the stairway.

Outside one of the cars, standing near the front grill, were two Marines, each with a sidearm in a holster and an M-16 in their arms. The two CIA agents followed the old man down the stairs, and when he'd touched the tarmac, they escorted him to the car with the two Marines, advising him to watch his head as they guided him into the backseat.

Dr. Revchenko, though he may have appeared feeble to the agents, was afraid of nothing. He'd seen everything in his eight decades and had met more than his fair share of spies, dictators, and assassins.

In the black case he carried were two vials of liquid. Each one was four inches tall and the width of a ballpoint pen, and fastened tightly to the bottom of the case with a Velcro strap, then covered with a piece of two-inch thick foam.

Within minutes, he'd find himself within the confines of a holding room deep inside the Marine base in a nondescript, two-story building. The only way into the city of Quantico is through the base, or via the river that flows through the city.

Within minutes, one of the agents from the plane was in an office talking to Avery Beckman.

"Well, dear brother-in-law, how does it feel to be back in the U.S.?" Avery asked.

"Avery, I've gotta tell you: With everything that's going on around here, I kinda' miss Afghanistan," he said only half-jokingly.

The two men sat down on a large leather couch, and the agent removed his coat.

"You're going to miss it even more when you hear how bad it's gotten in the last twenty-four hours," Avery said. "Want some coffee?"

"Naw. But I could use a stiff belt of scotch. So what are we talkin' here—a full-blown epidemic?"

Before he answered, Avery walked over to a credenza filled with books. In the center of the credenza was a hidden storage cabinet filled with scotch, vodka, rum, and schnapps.

"Boy, you know your way around here pretty well, brother."

"This is a friend's office. I asked him if we could borrow it when you got in."

Avery poured a glass half full with a golden brown liquid and brought it over to his brother-in-law.

"Getting back to our conversation."

"Well, Major Reynolds, right now the whole country's gearing up for the President's State of the Union Address. It's no secret that there are a lot of sick people here. If that nosey newspaper reporter in Utah hadn't broken the story, we wouldn't be seeing the beginnings of a massive panic, at least not yet."

"How far has it spread?"

"From Denver to New Orleans and from Pennsylvania to North Carolina. Ten states have reported. Fortunately, this Brody guy only knew about the quarantine in Montana. There are plenty of sick people, but they really haven't put two and two together yet. His beef is that the government covered up the quarantine in Troy—kept it a secret.

"These damned do-gooder liberal journalists just don't get it. There are times when the public *doesn't* need to know.

"You brought the keys to the kingdom in with you from Uzbekistan. He's our only hope."

"Yeah. We've been talking ever since we touched down in that country a couple of weeks ago. I've never seen anything like it. We went around with him almost house to house in Termez. He mostly just talked to people, but they were all very sick."

"Vertigo, nausea, seizures?"

"Yep. Looked like the whole village had the plague. They all looked like they were going to die any minute and then bingo, one by one, after the doctor inoculated them, they started coming back within a few days."

"Anything else you can share with me?"

Major Reynolds stood up. "Well, of course, there's the whole loss-of-hearing thing related to this virus."

"That's to be expected if we're dealing with spinal meningitis. Frankly, I'm more worried about people dying. If I lost my hearing, but lived to tell about it, I think I'd consider myself lucky."

The Major took another swallow of his scotch and drained the glass, then walked over to the hidden bar and poured another.

"There was *one* thing, though—about the hearing. The first home we visited when we got there … actually, it was no more than a stone, one-room box. There was a small family, a mother, father, and a little baby.

"The first thing I noticed when we came in was that the baby had a huge black and blue mark on her jaw—like she'd been clobbered. I was immediately suspicious. Child abuse isn't just relegated to the United States."

"Yeah. So?"

The Major took another healthy slug of his drink and came back to sit beside Avery, almost as if sharing a secret quietly.

"Well, the parents didn't seem to get it. I mean it was almost like they didn't know they couldn't hear. The woman kept picking up this old phone they had and kept pointing to it, as if the line were dead. They were sick as hell, too.

"I felt like saying, Ma'am, it ain't the phone, it's your ears. I don't know; it was weird. Then she got a little frantic and ran around looking for something. Eventually, she found it—a pencil and paper. She came over to me and scribbled something on it, but hell, I couldn't read it. I don't speak Russian or Arabic. They were Muslims, just like most of the country."

21

"What in the world are you doing down there, Henry?" Joanne Bannister called down the stairwell into the concrete cellar. "My Lord, it's been over an hour."

"I'm getting ready, Joanne. And I asked not to be disturbed."

"Henry Bannister, don't you dismiss me. I want to know what you're up to. Getting ready for what?"

Henry didn't answer. He knew his wife probably wouldn't come down into the cellar. It always bothered her that he kept so many rifles and guns down there, but over the years managed to live with his passion. Henry had been a hunter since he was a child. She came from a wealthy New York family that thought hunting was an unnecessary, barbaric activity.

The basement was also a dank and foul-smelling room. Years ago, she'd had Henry install plumbing in the garage to hook up the washer and dryer, rather than trudging down to the cellar to do it. After that, the room was pretty much Henry's.

Henry sat on the large tattered sofa he'd brought down there, inspecting one of his three shotguns. He also owned a high-powered 30/06 rifle, an old M-16, and several Smith and Wesson .357 caliber revolvers.

A single fluorescent light hung from the ceiling; a long workbench stretched the length of one wall underneath it. In that workbench was a locked cabinet that contained all his ammo—enough to kill every living thing within ten miles, or to stage a small war.

One by one, he cleaned each weapon thoroughly, inspecting firing pins and oiling them well.

Henry began to think about the cabin. He was sure no one besides his son knew about the getaway they'd both built twenty years ago; not even his wife knew about it. It was their secret father-and-son-bonding place, which they used on many hunting and fishing trips. It was deep in the forest, off any normal paths, even the areas that other hunters walked. The cabin had three rooms: a living and kitchen space with a large fireplace and one bedroom with a bathroom. It was nearly ten miles' walking distance from the house to the north.

Henry always kept it well stocked with canned goods, freeze-dried camping and military meals, distilled water and, of course, another ham radio and lots of batteries. It was the perfect sanctuary. The cabin sat on a small rise backed up to a steep hill. He could see out the five windows in all directions.

Henry never liked to think of himself as paranoid, but his father had taught him long ago to be prepared for just about any contingency. Hell, there had been the cold war, the '62 missile crisis, the threat of nuclear war, and God knows what else. Not that the cabin would have prepared him for a nuclear bomb, but he could withstand just about anything else, including his own government, if push came to shove.

He'd be ready for the President's State of the Union Address. He had a feeling he knew what was coming.

22

$\mathcal{E}$very news media outlet in the country was present. Cameras were trained on the dais from every conceivable angle in the room—the hallowed halls of the U.S. House of Representatives. Not a single congressman or senator was missing from his or her seat, and the gallery was packed to standing room only.

It was prime time—6:00 p.m., August 16, 2010. Nearly every television and radio in America was tuned in to see or listen to President Jordan's State of the Union Address. It had been leaked deliberately to the media that this would not be the standard "pep rally" political address.

"This will not be a litany of my administration's accomplishments," the President was reported to have said. "Instead, this will be an honest and extremely candid message that will affect every single man, woman, and child in this country."

Needless to say, Jordan had a rapt audience when the Sergeant at Arms announced his arrival through the doors of the House: "Mr. Speaker, the President of the United States."

Jordan was tall, an imposing figure. He was only forty-nine, but his gray hair made him look older. His politics were straight down the middle of the Independent Party. He was known as fair, honest, and a champion of civil liberties. Oddly, when it came to government involvement in the daily lives of the American citizens, he was more closely aligned with the Republican Party—the less intrusion in people's lives by government, the better.

Tonight, however, all of his political philosophies would be put on hold. He knew this would be the defining moment of his presidency, probably the defining moment of any presidency since Lincoln. For the second time in less than a decade, the country would be faced with life-changing, society-altering, and politically-amending circumstances.

Jordan strode down the aisle toward the center of the room, his face tightened in a serious expression. He chose not to smile, or to shake hands with the many congressmen and senators that were seated nearest the aisle—the custom for nearly two hundred years.

The room was uncharacteristically quiet, nearly silent as he climbed the four steps to the podium.

As is traditional, Vice President Kramer and the Speaker of the House sat just behind the podium and several feet higher than the President. As the President arrived, the Speaker pounded his gavel loudly and said, "Members of Congress, I have the high privilege and distinct honor of presenting to you the President of the United States."

Jordan did not bring notes. He did not even use the dual transparent Teleprompters placed to either side of him. Instead, he began abruptly, "Mr. Speaker, Vice President Kramer, members of Congress, distinguished and fellow citizens.

"Tonight, I speak to this august chamber with a heavy heart and deeply troubled mind. As you are aware from the various media reports of the last few days, we are quite probably experiencing an epidemic in this country."

The President's delivery was blunt and forceful.

"As far as the CDC and DHS have been able to determine, more than one million people have already been affected.

"In past years, our most serious threats have been from abroad in the form of terrorists bent on destroying our way of life. Tonight, I am here to tell you that we face a threat far more serious than that—we face an insidious disease that has the potential to maim without discretion.

"It appears that it started in the Midwest and has now spread to at least fifteen states."

The entire audience let out a collective gasp as they sat on the edges of their seats.

The President cleared his throat and looked up to his wife and child who were seated in the gallery.

"You should know, however, that at this very moment we are working on an antidote to combat this disease, which appears to be a bacterial form of spinal meningitis. The same disease has afflicted a city in the formerly Russian territory of Uzbekistan, and they have been able to contain it within their borders, thanks to this antidote. So there is hope.

"Our renowned doctors and scientists feel certain that most of the symptoms will disappear within weeks. But there is one profound symptom—severe loss of hearing—which may become complete and irreversible."

The President paused to sip water and to gauge the response in the room. Most people sat with their hands over their mouths, breathing deeply.

"Ladies and gentlemen, every aspect of our way of life is threatened—our economy, our healthcare system, and our very constitution. Without the ability to hear, phones, emergency audio transmissions, air traffic control, and most other forms of communication will be useless.

"I am being direct because we all need to recognize the severity of this challenge. This is not a time for any form of partisanship, other than your citizenship, your status as an American.

"For these reasons, I, with the power bestowed upon me as President of the United States, am tonight doing something I am loathe to do, something that has only been needed on a national level one other time in history—I am instituting a limited form of martial law."

There was a collective enormous sucking of air in the room. Many of the journalists jumped up and ran for the door in an attempt to be the first to break the news; uniformed Marines standing at each door stopped them all.

"Please, ladies and gentlemen, we must remain calm. You must understand that it is incumbent upon me to be forthright with this nation. Given these events, it is my duty to maintain order. It is my responsibility to inform you honestly so that, as a nation, we may defeat this disease and maintain civil order.

"Together, rationally and calmly, we will defeat this menace. You need to know that under this temporary—and I emphasize the word *temporary*—order of martial law, the government will take over control of some of the media as needed. In some cases, there will be quarantines, as we've had to implement in Montana. At any rate, marital law and quarantines, and any other measures needed, will be monitored carefully and will only be instituted where no other choice is available.

"There will be daily notifications on the emergency broadcasting system that will inform and alert you as to our course of action. These will also be broadcast in text form on the television, or open captioning.

"The DHS has already implemented some initial measures to deal with this problem—these involve talks with my Secretary of Education; various organizations that teach some signs, speech and lip reading; and medical hearing specialists to assist those whose hearing has become impaired in any way possible.

"Obviously, the free-flow of communication between us must continue. We will have to change our way of life, at least for the foreseeable future, to adapt to the challenges that lie ahead.

"It is also important for the American people to know that we will not shut down the Internet. Citizens will be actively encouraged to use this medium to contact the various Web sites that will be published, beginning tonight at midnight. These three sites will be the only sanctioned and official sites for honest, up-to-date, and accurate information.

"We also ask people to keep their radios tuned to the emergency broadcast frequencies as long as they are still able to hear.

"And finally, for those who would question my executive power, let me make it abundantly clear that I do indeed have the authority to establish martial law under our constitution. In an emergency that seriously degrades or threatens the national security, emergency preparedness shall be established by the President," he repeated the law for the benefit of both Republicans and Democrats.

"This order includes the federal takeover of all local law enforcement agencies, and controls travel into and out of the country as long as that is possible, in addition to many other broad powers that I may or may not deem necessary to your safety and well-being."

When the President finished speaking, the clamor, furor, and conjecture began all at once. The stampede to the doors was a human wave of panic that the Marines could not contain. And so, it burst forth into the halls and eventually out into the parking lots.

Nearly everyone was on a cell phone and many of the journalists camped out on the steps used their wireless laptops to recap the President's most astounding announcement.

Within hours, contingents of the National Guard who weren't already deployed overseas, would take control of several major cities in America. From this moment on, these cities would be under federal, not state, control.

The House of Representatives was completely empty within five minutes, though the President was cautioned by his Secret Service contingent to remain in the secret office in the back of the building—a *very* secret office that not even many of the congressmen were aware of.

He was told it would be better to wait out the confusion and initial "anxiety" of the attendees, until it would be safe to return to the White House.

Jordan was seated on a leather couch facing a desk and two chairs, his long, lanky legs stretched out before him. There were no windows in the room. Light came from two low-watt, fluorescent lamps recessed into the ceiling. On one wall was a large embroidery of the Presidential Seal.

He sat quietly alone; two Secret Service agents stood outside the closed door. He took a deep breath as he tried to assess the response to what he'd just said—to what he'd just done. Martial law was not something he had wanted to resort to; yet, he was certain that it was in the best interests of the nation to impose it.

23

*I*n a laboratory in San Diego's biotech area, two men stood arguing near several microscopes. One wore a long white lab coat, the other an expensive Armani suit—one a chemist, the other the CEO of the prominent firm, BioGem, short for Biological Genetic Medicine.

In the background, one entire wall was dedicated to five mainframe IBM computers, each whirring with the sounds of their cooling fans.

BioGem had been one of the darlings of the investment world. The company's work in nano-technology, particularly in the area of personalized medicine, had been the most promising story of the 2007 stock market boom.

The company had partnered with IBM in a joint venture to work on infectious diseases. IBM wanted to develop its own life sciences division, so the venture was a natural and IBM's name had lent a great deal of validity to BioGem's claims, promises they had made during their drive to develop an IPO.

In that initial public offering, BioGem had raised $250 million and made several of the founders very, very rich. One of them, Daniel Segar, was now the CEO, and his short-lived empire was about to come crashing down.

The company's first product, a supposed nano-tech cure for obesity, had sent the stock price soaring past $125 a share. The only problem was that the drug, although the Food and Drug Administration had deemed it safe to consume, didn't actually do anything. Daniel Segar had known of the product's ineffectiveness, but continued to tout the miracle compound during the IPO—a class-one felony, among other things.

So far, he'd managed to keep a lid on things with the help of his chief chemist, but that wasn't going to last long. The SEC might never find out he'd cheated on the tests, but the marketplace would destroy them when it was determined the drug was essentially worthless.

What Segar needed was a real winner, a drug that everyone needed. Amflex was his ticket to the major leagues. It would save the company and Segar's own fortune. He needed something that would make his shares of stock actually worth their $125 printed value.

The drawback was that he wasn't fully vested. He would have to wait another year until that happened. If the stock tanked during that time, his shares wouldn't be worth the proverbial paper they were printed on.

The success of Amflex would blunt a lot of the disappointment in their existing failed product. After all, hundreds of thousands of people had been afflicted with the bacteria in less than two weeks. It was a safe bet that millions of people would eventually be affected. Of course, the most massive consumer group would be the general public who would take the drug in hopes of *not* contracting the virus at all.

Amflex was the working name he gave the vaccine for the B form of spinal meningitis.

As Segar and the chemist stood talking, a diminutive man with thinning gray hair and heavy bifocals came through the door. Though it was warm in the room, he walked over to the two men wearing a long camel's hair winter coat. In his left hand, he carried a briefcase; and in his right, he carried a fedora.

"Gentlemen," the man said, "it is good to finally meet you. Let us sit down and talk about this problem of the bacteria. I have some ideas."

2 4

"And to think I voted for that son-of-a-bitch," Henry said in a loud voice over the phone to his son. "He's no damned different than any of the others."

While his father continued his rant, Nathan sat in the cab of his truck, warming his hands by the heater vent as the engine idled.

"The man thinks he's king, I tell you. He's a maniac with power," Henry continued. "We've got to protect ourselves."

Nathan didn't fully agree with his father, but he wasn't going to get into that discussion, particularly over the phone. He knew, too, that some form of martial law was going to be needed, at least temporarily. He knew that some quarantines were inevitable. People's travel had to be restricted for one thing, to try to contain the bacteria in identifiable locations.

Right now, Nathan's only desire was to be with his family. He wanted to hold his daughter. He wanted to tell Stella face-to-face that he was sick and that, as he knew might happen; he seemed to be losing his hearing. She would help him through this. She would be his strength.

But he also knew he could not risk infecting them. He would have to battle the virus' symptoms—the bouts of vertigo, the nausea, the constant ringing in his ears—alone.

The CDC was in full control of the epidemic now, so there was little Nathan could officially do in his role with the EPA, but he also didn't want to just stand by and do nothing. He would find a way to help.

When Stella had taught hard-of-hearing kids, he hadn't paid much attention to her concerns as to how the public perceived deaf people, but he certainly would now. If the hearing loss that he and others were experiencing turned out to be permanent, then everyone—deaf and hearing people alike—would have to start learning new ways to communicate.

"You remember where the cabin is, don't you?" Henry asked.

"Of course, how could I forget? It was my fort when I was growing up. I never even told Mom about it," Nathan responded.

"Well, whenever you get back here, that's where we'll be. I've got the handguns, the shotguns, plenty of ammo … and I've stocked up on enough food and water to last at least three months. Oh, and don't forget to keep that ham radio I gave you in your truck—you might need it."

"Dad. I like your plan, but I'm not so sure you need to prepare for World War Three. We have no idea how people will react. Besides, you don't live in a heavily populated area.

"Have you talked with any of your friends or neighbors out there?"

"Haven't had the time, son. I did talk with old man Marley on the phone yesterday."

"Has he seen any troop activity?"

"Nope. But he's not goin' anywhere anyway. He's too old and he's got nothin' to do. Why?"

"Just trying to get a handle on how the Guard is deployed there."

"Son, did you read the article about the President this morning? *He's* certainly not taking any chances. That coward is going into hiding, and he's taking all those fearless generals with him." Henry said, shutting the basement door behind him.

"What are you talking about?"

"He's going into full lock-down mode. You've heard of that bunker the government built to keep the President safe in case of nuclear war, right?

That's where he is, only he's not hiding from bombs, he's hiding from the people."

While the news was startling, Nathan understood the rationale behind it.

"Dad, he's not hiding from people—he's hiding from the virus."

25

August 18, 2010

"*W*hy is it so cold in here," President Jordan asked the Captain.

"We keep the temperature at a constant sixty-seven degrees because of all the computer equipment, sir. With that many mainframes going, they tend to heat up," the Captain answered. "Plus we have a lot of very sophisticated radar equipment. All of it needs to be kept as cool as possible.

"There are six main centers here at NORAD sir. We're in what we call the Combined Intelligence Watch Center."

The President surveyed the concrete rooms that would serve as his office and apartment for the foreseeable future—gray linoleum floors meeting the gray concrete walls, which climbed to the gray ceilings—the only color anywhere was the greenish white halos cast down from the evenly spaced halogen lights in the ceiling.

"Deter, detect, and defend. That's the motto here, isn't it, Captain?"

"Yes, sir. I guess we never thought we'd be defending ourselves against our own citizens though."

The President bristled at the young officer's comment.

"Captain, you aren't defending us from our own people. You're defending us against a deadly bacteria."

"I understand, sir."

"And you don't have to keep calling me sir. We're going to be here for a while and you'll be helping me quite a bit. So tell me a little bit about life down here, Captain. How far down are we?"

The Captain took off his hat, placed it on the table, and poured a cup of coffee for each of them.

"Well, sir," the Captain caught himself. "Well, Mr. President, you're a long ways down, close to the equivalent of a forty-story building. The mountain is solid granite and more than eight hundred people live and work here.

"The complex is capable of providing its own air—albeit a little chilly—water and power, with enough provisions to feed all eight hundred for more than six months. It was designed to withstand a direct hit from a fifty-megaton nuclear device.

"This is just about the most secure, safest location anywhere on earth, and we have complete control of the skies from northern Canada to Mexico City. We can track data, satellites, missiles, planes, and even space debris the size of a pea," the Captain explained.

In other sparse concrete apartments spread throughout the complex, the Vice President, Joint Chiefs of Staff, several NSA and CIA managers, four senators, and two congressmen were also taking up residence.

Building NORAD started in 1961, just before the Cuban missile crisis, and was completed in 1966. The mission had changed over the years, but they were the front line defense for any foreign attack for all of North America. Now, they would be the command center in another kind of defense.

Here, the President could communicate with anyone in the world instantaneously, provided they could hear him. The NSA had always felt they had the most sophisticated communications and listening devices. NORAD made that capability look downright impotent.

They could see deep into space or zoom in to take a full color photograph of your license plate from miles above the earth. They could listen to cell phone conversations, read emails, track Internet searches, read your mail if necessary, though they'd never been enlisted to do those types of things—spying on their own citizens. Only NSA had been given that power back in 2003, which eventually led to the dismantling of one major facet of the NSA and nearly caused President Bush's downfall.

As President Jordan began to pull several files from his briefcase, someone knocked on the door. Jordan crossed the room and opened it to see Madlyn Kramer.

"Come in Madame Vice President."

"Please, Robert. It somehow doesn't seem appropriate now to be so formal."

"You're right, Madlyn. Come in."

"I have the updates you requested."

"Please sit down," Jordan said, gesturing to a large couch and overstuffed chair. There were, of course, no windows in the room, but it was as comfortable as one could expect under the circumstances.

"Well, first of all," she began, as she settled herself into the overstuffed chair while Jordan sat across from her on the couch, "if you take all the troops from the Federal and State National Guard, there are only two hundred and forty-five thousand people. Many of these are in administrative positions, and quite a few are medical practitioners. I suppose you could call the remainder 'fighting personnel,' people who've been trained for riot control and civil disorder containment.

"However, and this is a big however, most of this training has consisted of only four hours of instruction. Ninety-nine percent of these troops are weekend warriors at best—most train just once a month. The rest are in Iraq and Afghanistan.

"Eighteen states are reporting widespread infection already. We don't know how it started, but we've pretty much pinpointed the town of Troy in Montana as Ground Zero. It would seem the quarantine you established there was not very effective against the spread of the virus.

"On that note, maybe related, maybe not, the Canadians have picked up two suspicious French Muslims who came across the border several weeks ago and ended up in Calgary.

"After accessing the contents of their laptop computer, the Canadian government contends they are terrorists, although they have yet to specify what the charges are or what they might have been involved with," the Vice President read from the three sheets of paper in her hands.

Jordan rubbed his chin as he considered her last words.

"It is a compelling coincidence that they crossed the border into Canada from that same area in Montana. Keep me posted on that one, will you?"

"I will. Lastly, the National Guard troops have all been given their orders; most will be in place in the nation's major cities within the week."

"Thank you, Madlyn. Anything else?"

The Vice President shrugged.

"Not really. The good news so far is that there doesn't appear to be any widespread panic, although there have been pockets of rioting and looting. Of course, that might change when the troops start pouring in. Right now, it appears that most people are just scared and are staying indoors. The ones who are getting sick are inundating the emergency rooms and walk-in clinics."

The Vice President stood up. "Mind if I have a cup of coffee, Robert?"

"No. Of course, Help yourself," Jordan replied, putting the papers he was reading back into his briefcase.

"How about on the medical side of things? What news do we have on the vaccine?"

"Well, as you know, the FDA was allowed to fast-track that San Diego biotech firm. It was decided to just go with one company, since the Russian doctor could only be in one place at a time anyway.

"It's only been a few days, so time will tell. But their CEO, a guy named Segar, seems to be very positive, though he wouldn't give us a timetable. We have a twenty-four-hour guard on Dr. Revchenko as well, but they say he's pretty harmless. He's eighty years old and nearly blind."

"I want to have a daily report from that company. They've got to move fast," Jordan said.

"I know, and the guys at the FDA say they've pulled out all the stops to help. They're allowing them to bypass all of the initial testing on animals and go straight to human volunteers. Hell, that's about eight years cut out of the normal process."

Jordan nodded thoughtfully. From the bunker buried hundreds of feet beneath the surface of the earth, he contemplated the challenging days that lay ahead.

26

Four weeks after the initial outbreak in Troy, Montana
August 19, 2010

"Oh dear God!" Sheryl gasped from one of the upstairs windows of her bed and breakfast in Troy. Hop had just left two days before and she suddenly felt very alone and extremely vulnerable. She was a widow and all the rooms in her inn were empty.

She had been glad to share everything that had been happening in town with the award-winning journalist, annual guest, and friend. She knew that through his column, he would tell the truth and people would know what was going on.

She did not know just how far the virus had spread—that Troy was just one of many towns and cities with a growing population of very ill people and that Hop's stories had been headlines in every newspaper in America for the past two days. There was nothing coming in and out of Troy, including newspaper deliveries, mail, or deliveries of any other essentials.

Her bed and breakfast sat near the quieter edge of town on Deer Lane and she could clearly see the confrontation unfolding from her window.

"Halt! Halt or I'll shoot!" the soldier yelled.

One of the National Guardsmen was standing in the center of the street, wearing a flak jacket and a steel helmet strapped snugly on his head. He had his AR-16 automatic rifle raised and tucked in tightly to his shoulder, pointing at a man who was getting in a car.

"Halt! I won't tell you again," the soldier yelled.

Sheryl couldn't see who the man was, only that he got into his car, shut the door and began to speed toward the barrier that blocked the exit from town.

The man revved the engine and then floored the accelerator as the back wheels spun furiously and kicked up a cloud of dust in the soldier's face. Sheryl knew the man was trying to leave. He only got about thirty yards when the crack of two shots pierced the night air.

She saw the back window of the man's car shatter and splinter into a shower of glass. Inside, the man slumped over the steering wheel, setting off the horn. The car slowed, veered to the right, and hit a tree on the side of the road.

He was now too far away for Sheryl to tell if he was alive. The horn continued to blare and lights began to come on in the windows of the homes nearby. The man had been killed instantly—one bullet through the back of his skull and out his right eye socket. The other .76-millimeter round was lodged in his heart. The entire inside of the front windshield was splattered with blood and brain fragments.

Sheryl bowed her head into her hands and began to cry. Sobbing, she tried to catch her breath as she picked up her cell phone and called Hop. The phone rang several times and then his familiar voice said to leave a message.

"Hop. Wherever you are, you've got to know. A National Guardsman just shot someone here. I think the man is dead. It looked like he was trying to get out of town. Call me. You know the number."

She closed the phone and slumped down on the edge of the bed.

Hop Brody had no real reason to hide anymore. It wasn't like the Colonel and some men from his guard unit were going to pursue him. The damage had been done. Everyone over the age of three knew that the country was facing an epidemic and that martial law had been established.

He'd received Sheryl's message that night, called her back, and was now at his computer in the Park City office furiously writing the story. He also knew that it was just a matter of time before the papers would be shut down. Already, the only thing coming over the airwaves, on radio and television, were civil defense instructions from the emergency networks.

The broadcasts were always the same. A deep and authoritative male voice, probably a little known actor, would breathe out the same message:

"Stay in your homes. Everything that can be done is being done. The best way to avoid becoming contaminated with this bacteria is to stay indoors and avoid contact with others.

"Teams of medical personnel are now accompanying National Guard units in most of the major cities.

"Stay indoors until you are contacted and keep your radios and televisions turned on."

Hop could smell the oncoming sense of chaos that would ensue. Already, gas stations and grocery stores were closing.

He had to finish his story:

Man Shot Dead By National Guardsman in Troy, Montana.

Today, the National Guard shot an unidentified man as he tried to flee the quarantined town of Troy. It is not known whether the man survived the shooting.

The story relayed the details as Sheryl had described them, then veered in the direction of editorial opinion.

Why would a man defy an armed soldier's order to halt? There are many reasons: He might have been afraid. He may have wanted to escape so he could be reunited with loved ones. He may have even been a rebel with a death wish.

Or maybe he just never heard their orders to stop.

Hop Brody was all too familiar with the challenges of living without the ability to hear—his daughter, Amanda, and his son, Casey, were both deaf, had been since birth, a genetic quirk that his wife had brought to the marriage. None of this would be new to them, and everything he'd learned about their world would now serve him well.

27

"Joanne, please don't argue with me. We don't have any choice. I'm taking you, Stella, and Jennifer away from here. It's not safe anymore," Henry told his wife.

"And you know someplace that is?" Joanne challenged.

"Yes. It's a small cabin that Nate and I built."

"A cabin? Where? Why haven't you ever told me about it?"

"It's a guy thing. We built it to have a place to sleep while we were out hunting or fishing up at the north end of the ranch. It's nothing fancy."

"And how long have you kept this a secret from me?"

"About thirty years. It was a place for Nate and me to get away, to bond a little. No women allowed—till now."

Stella walked into the kitchen having heard the tail end of Henry's sentence.

"Where aren't women allowed, Dad?"

"Stella, your father-in-law wants us to go hide in a cabin in the woods. He thinks we may be in danger here."

"It's the perfect place to wait this thing out," Henry explained. "It's stocked with food, water, bedding, clothes …"

"And guns, I suppose," Joanne interrupted.

"Not yet. I'm taking those with me. Now, I've already loaded up the pickup. You two just need to get your personal things. Trust me, we are much safer out there than here. When the troops start arriving, no one's going to go anywhere."

"Does Nate know where we're going?" Stella asked, her voice fluttering with anxiety and fear.

"Yes, dear. And don't worry. It's not such a bad place. There's a generator, a little fridge, even a small TV. Heck, you might even want to end up staying out there."

Half an hour later, the four-door Ford pickup was jostling down the dirt road that led out to the edge of the forest, the same area he'd cut the trees from forty years ago to build his ranch.

There was a small deer trail about three miles away from the house that took off to the north. It was narrow, but the four-wheel truck handled it with ease. They bounced their way along the trail for the next four miles, and then stopped at a small clearing beside a dry streambed.

"This is where we get out," Henry said.

"What? We're in the middle of nowhere, Henry," Joanne said.

"I know. That's the point, dear."

Henry walked over to a couple of large boulders, reached down in the crevice between them, and pulled up what looked like a clump of dead leaves.

As he made his way back to the truck, he began to unfold the mass of material, which was actually a large camouflage net. He made quick work of draping the net over the truck.

"There. Now, come on, ladies; we've got a little hiking to do."

"Dad. Are you sure about this? I mean Jennifer is only three. She's not really a hiker."

"She'll be fine, dear. I wouldn't bring any harm to my princess," he said as he walked over to her, leaned down, and gave her a big hug.

"Wanna go on an adventure, darlin'?" he asked her.

"Yeah, papa. Let's go on an adventure."

"See there? She's game. It won't be that difficult. I brought Nate out here when he was only three and he did just fine. Grab your stuff."

"Oh boy, Mommy," Jennifer said, "we're going to go camping."

"Yes, sweetie. We are going to go camping," Stella responded with an unconvincing smile.

They had barely walked a mile when a shot rang out. It felt like the crack of a whip close to Henry's ear. In reality, it had been fired over his head. Henry knew the sound instinctively. It was the rever-beration of a high-powered rifle. Jennifer and Stella screamed and Henry yelled, "Get down! Get down!"

Mere seconds passed before a booming voice yelled out, "Going on a trip, folks?"

Henry turned while simultaneously motioning for the women to stay down. About one hundred yards away the soldier stood with the butt of his rifle still tensed into his shoulder.

"My name is Lieutenant Williams with the 163rd Infantry, and I suggest that you all just stay right where you are. Under martial law, I am ordered to make sure that everyone stays where they belong. I'm guessing you folks live in that ranch house back there about three miles."

"Oh Christ," Henry muttered.

"Oh, and sir? If you'll kindly put that rifle down, I'd appreciate it."

28

"Dad, are you all right? Why aren't you answering your phone?" Nathan asked, speaking to his father's cell phone message center.

"I've got to talk to Stella. Call me when you get this. They've already started closing down the major airports.

"Last night, a United flight crashed into another plane on the runway at O'Hare. The other plane was about to take off when the incoming flight landed right on top of it. They say it was pilot error, that he couldn't hear the air traffic controller's warnings," Nathan said.

The lieutenant had confiscated Stella and Henry Bannister's cell phones, as well as disconnected the landline to the house, so Henry would not be returning his son's call. The Bannisters had become prisoners in their own home.

Though the National Guardsman had confiscated all of Henry's guns and ammunition, they'd left them the food and water and hadn't noticed the short wave radio under the folded blankets. Besides, Henry always kept one gun tucked away upstairs in the nightstand, a .45 Army issue Colt. He had two clips for it, each with seven rounds.

They had no way of knowing if Nathan was calling and, of course, they had no way of calling out other than the short wave. He hoped that his son had taken his portable with him like he'd recommended.

Henry walked over to the window next to the front door and pulled back the gingham curtains that Joanne had made. Looking down the long dirt drive, he could see two soldiers standing at the front gate. Another guardsman was sitting in Henry's truck smoking a cigarette.

Nothing made sense: one house being guarded by three soldiers; twenty-four hour surveillance. Disconnected phone lines. There was no way in the world, regardless of the imposition of martial law, that anyone else was being subjected to such extreme measures of security.

*   *   *

Hop Brody's last column before the National Guard shut down his newspaper was the result of exhaustive research. It was an expose on what the government would face in an epidemic where millions of people suddenly lost their ability to hear.

Hop found out that several years before, the Department of Health and Human Services had produced an Epidemic Plan and a Web site. He also found out that planning needs to begin in the homes, neighborhoods, and communities.

All Emergencies Are Local, Hop's headline read.

It doesn't matter what stockpile of vaccine the government has or might have—if it doesn't get out locally, it doesn't matter. State and local health agencies are perpetually understaffed and short of cash and always struggling to prepare.

As usual, the government's right hand doesn't know what the left hand is doing. There are 5,000 state and local health departments. However, in one county, they could be closing schools and banning sporting events to restrict the spread of the disease, while in another county, business as usual might be the order of the day. Since FEMA has not issued any definitive orders, every state and county is left guessing.

It's a good thing it's summer because, in some states, they are designating that only fire and police will be the first to receive the vaccine. If it was winter, it might be the snowplow driver.

FEMA officials are painting a grim picture. They estimate 50% absenteeism at work, travel restrictions, schools closed (no kidding!). Further, it says, the government is committed to expanding a stockpile of other anti-virals while they work to develop a vaccine.

Right now, the plan to manufacture and distribute a vaccine is in total chaos. The entire country is going to be only as strong as its weakest link—and here is that link—everyone from DHS to Health and Human Services is pinning all their hopes on the fact that a vaccine will soon be available.

To that, this reporter has a bombshell to drop before what might be our last press run. I have it from reliable sources that the CEO of BioGem, a guy named Daniel Segar, was under federal investigation for securities fraud before all this happened.

Apparently, the blockbuster drug they came out with that allowed them to raise millions during their IPO didn't do what they said it did—and he knew that. At least that's what my sources report.

Of course, now that he's been given the task of developing this vaccine, they've temporarily shelved the investigation. He's been fast-tracked to make this miraculous antidote. I ask you: Will you feel safe taking such a drug?

As it turns out, we may not even need the vaccine. According to news out of Termez in Uzbekistan, the Russian doctor who went there and treated the people admitted he wasn't sure if his vaccine had worked, or if the people just basically pulled out of the symptoms and got over it just like you get over a bad case of the flu. That is, they got over all the symptoms but one—no one can hear.

Dear readers, this is our real challenge. What if, like the good Uzbeks, our fevers run their course—but in the end, we can't hear one another?

The fact is that we don't have much time left. I know a little about this dynamic because my son, Casey, and my daughter, Amanda, have both been deaf since they were born.

You're going to be hearing a lot more about this in the coming days— and then again, maybe you won't be hearing anything.

That's all for now, and maybe for a long time, but I'll keep writing as long as the presses are still running and we can still sell newspapers.

Hop Brody

PS: I wanted to leave my readers with this one last thought. Freedom of speech isn't much good if you can't hear anything. Likewise, what good is freedom of the press if you can't read anything? I find that all very ironic.

All the major papers including the *Washington Post* picked up Hop's column. Nathan was reading it on his Treo and thinking it odd that his father's cell phone was automatically going to voice mail—he always answered it right up until he went to bed at night. *Maybe the battery was dead?*

He'd already read Hop's other article about the guardsman shooting the man in Troy and he just wondered how much longer writers could write and newspapers publish that kind of news or any dissenting opinions. He knew that sooner or later, the government would declare just about everything a matter of "National Security," meaning any dissent or differing opinions would be painted as grounds for treason.

As he stared up at the glittering carpet of stars overhead, Nathan was torn. Part of him wanted to drive back to Billings to check up on his family, while another part felt compelled to meet this Hop Brody. He liked his brashness, his honesty—it reminded him of when he'd been in Libby and he'd blown the whistle on the government and the asbestos fiasco.

Yes, the President had probably done the right thing, but then why were he and his staff hiding? It also bothered him that everything was so scattered and disorganized. *Who's in charge here?*

Nathan picked up the phone and dialed 411.

"Yes. What city, sir?"

"Park City, Utah."

"Name?"

"Hop Brody."

"I'm sorry, there is no listing in Park City for a Hop Brody. There is a Benjamin Brody. Would you like that number?"

"Yes. Thank you."

It seemed much longer, but Nathan realized that this whole ordeal—the first visit to Troy, sending his wife and daughter to his parents, the President going into hiding—had all transpired in a little over three weeks.

As Nathan lay there in the bed of his truck staring up at the stars, he remembered what the first man he'd looked at in Troy had said when he'd asked, "How long before the vertigo sets in?"

"A week, maybe longer," came the reply. "The ringing comes next, incessant ringing. It's like I'm standing next to one of those big brass church bells, or maybe right inside it. It's awful. Can't hardly describe it. After a few minutes it goes away, thank the Lord. But it always comes back. And, of course, you can't hear a damn thing for hours afterward."

Nathan remembered the encounter almost verbatim and it made him think. *This is all happening to me, but I have to fight it somehow.*

He lay there trying to envision what was coming, what it would be like if he and a large portion of the population went deaf. He knew from his wife's work with hard-of-hearing children that deaf people were often regarded as slow learners and half-wits. Stella would come home sometimes in tears relating stories of how difficult life was for them being forced to learn to speak. He tried to imagine what it would be like not to be able to hear and all the things he would miss—*so many things we all take for granted,* he thought. He wouldn't be able to hear his daughter's voice ever again.

But this was something far beyond just a few school children— this was going to wreak havoc in so many ways across the country.

He could easily imagine some people in Washington just relishing the chance to hold people down in the name of helping them, of protecting them from themselves.

He had to do what he could to keep that from happening, and right now he could think of only one person who really seemed to have his pulse on what the government was really up to; a man who thought like he did. He picked up his phone and dialed the number he'd just been given by 411 information. After the fifth ring, a faint voice answered.

"Hop Brody," was all the person said.

"Mr. Brody, my name is Nathan Bannister. I work for the EPA and I have a couple of questions I'd like to ask you."

"I'm listening," came the reply.

"One, have you been exposed to anyone carrying the virus?"

"Yes, why?"

"I need to meet with you, but I don't want to put your health at risk."

A lingering silence filled the line before Hop replied.

"Are your ears ringing?" he finally asked.

"Nearly all the time now. Why?"

"That seems to be the point where you're no longer contagious."

"I guess that's a relief of some sorts. Are you going to be in Park City for a while?"

"I don't have any plans otherwise."

"Good. One way or another, I'll be there in less than two days."

He clicked off the phone, then punched the pre-programmed number he had stored for American Airlines.

"American Airlines. How may I help you?"

"I'd like a one-way ticket to Park City from Billings

Montana. When is your next flight out?"

"Sir, we have only one flight left. It leaves at eleven forty-five tonight. After that, there will be no more flights. Can I have your name?"

"Wait. What do you mean there won't be anymore flights?"

"Haven't you been watching TV?"

"No. No I haven't been watching TV. What's happening?"

"The President has ordered all air travel to cease. Only military flights will be allowed after tonight. It's a mad house at every airport, so I highly recommend you get there as early as possible."

"Hello, are you there?"

"Yes, sir, I'm here. Can I do anything else for you?"

"Hello. Hello. Are you there?"

29

August 20, 2010

There was a heavy knocking on the door.

"Who is it?" President Jordan asked, peering over his shoulder from behind his desk.

"It's Eric Jennings. I have urgent news, sir."

"Come in."

"Christ, they keep it cold in here don't they, Mr. President."

"Yes, they do. What do you have? The President asked.

"Bad tidings," the head of the DHS answered, putting some files on the edge of the President's desk. "We've got reports in now from most of our precinct guys and the CDC."

"What reports?"

"The hearing thing, sir. Or, rather, the not-hearing thing, sir."

"Okay, Eric. Come over here. Let's sit on the couch. What's going on?"

"People all over the country are losing their hearing—the thing we feared most."

"Shit, this entire country will come to a standstill. I've already shut down air traffic," Jordan said. "And it looks like I'll have to do the same with banks and the stock market. We can't let panic ruin our economy overnight. Christ, Eric, this is happening way too fast. I seriously don't know if we are going to be able to cope."

As the two men sat looking at each other, neither offering an idea, someone knocked on the door.

"Yes?"

"Mr. President. I've got to discuss something with you. It's extremely important. I'm sorry to interrupt."

"That's all right, Ms. Weber. Everything is important right now. Mr. Jennings has just given me the bad news about the loss of hearing."

Halley Weber crossed over to the President's desk and dropped a file on it. She looked at the two men and said, "We're getting reports of pockets of riots in New York and Los Angeles, as well as Chicago. The only good news, if you can call it that, is that most people are staying indoors. With the troops in limited areas, if most people stay inside, we might be able to contain this thing. We just won't know for sure for a while."

"Isn't your daughter in Los Angeles, Halley?"

Weber came from behind the desk and sat next to the President.

"Yes, sir. She's with my parents, though, and I know they're doing the best they can. I'm just saying my prayers.

"Our problem is that we've initiated limited martial law to put a temporary lid on all this, but we haven't taken any steps to deal with the reality of many people suddenly losing their hearing. According to the latest CDC report, it appears that seventy-five percent of the population will be safe—for genetic reasons, they aren't getting it. We know that because the incubation period is about ten days.

"Also, while the people in Troy are getting over most of their symptoms—the vomiting, vertigo, and headaches—only a few of them are getting their hearing back.

"I know you shut down air traffic, but most of what's going on out there is all regional or local efforts. It's a mess, so disorganized. Each county is handling everything differently."

Eric Jennings stood up.

"Ms. Weber. That's what we were just discussing. Got any ideas?"

Halley Weber stood up and went back to the President's desk, picked up the file, and brought it back to the couch.

"Yes, Eric. As a matter of fact I do. As the President knows, I have a daughter who is deaf, so I've been dealing with this challenge for some time—nine years now."

"I'm so sorry to hear that, Ms. Weber," Jennings said sincerely.

"Don't be. She gets along fine. I've spent a great deal of time studying her challenge, studying the world of the deaf. It's not a death sentence for her because we started working on her early, when we first discovered she was hard-of-hearing, which means she has some hearing, but not much. It's difficult to tell just how well she hears. The audiologists say it's a narrow audio range and mostly muffled.

"It's been a long haul, but she's an excellent lip reader. The challenge has been to teach her how to speak. That's not easy if you've never heard anything."

The President stood up and offered both cabinet members a drink. Jennings took a scotch and Weber a Coke.

"Halley. What organizations have you been working with in conjunction with your daughter? Maybe we can start there and instead of just dealing with it one child or adult at a time, we can apply what you've learned to the entire nation. If people could at least learn to read lips, we'd be making some progress."

"Yes, sir. That's what this file is all about. One of the best organizations for getting help is the AGBell Organization, but they really don't advocate sign language. That's something I took on myself."

"You mean like in Alexander Graham Bell?"

"Yes, sir. Exactly. That's where it all began for me," she replied.

"Halley, one more question," the President said, pouring himself another scotch. "Won't it be easier working with people who have been able to speak all their lives? I mean obviously ninety-nine percent of the people in this country were not deaf and most of them can talk. They'll still be able to talk, won't they?"

"Not necessarily, sir. Of course, my daughter was born the way she is, but teaching her to speak was, and still is, a major undertaking. I won't bore you with it all now, but when hearing people suddenly go deaf, they often have a great deal of trouble speaking as well.

"The tones in their auditory track change. They often end up mumbling incoherently. The AGBell Organization recommended cochlear implants and that's what we did with her."

"I'm happy to hear that, Ms. Weber, but at this point, I don't think prescribing a complex surgical procedure to what may end up being millions of people is very practical."

Nathan had missed the last flight. It was hard for him to believe that the skies above the country, where normally hundreds and hundreds of planes would be criss-crossing the nation, would be silent, with the exception of some military flights.

It's likely that by now, the trains have been stopped as well.

For the moment, his priority was meeting with Hop Brody—the man who seemed to know everything. He would have to make the journey to Utah in his truck. He'd once driven from Billings to Chicago and made it in a single trek, but this would take two days and he'd have to try to stay awake.

When he arrived he had to ask a cab driver directions.

"Where are *The Park Record* offices," he asked the driver.

"The main building or the printing plant?"

Nate did not answer.

"Sir. Do you want to go to the printing plant or the main office?" he asked again; still no answer.

Nate yawned deeply trying to unplug his ears.

"Huh? What did you say?" Nate finally replied shaking his head.

The driver realizing Nate was having trouble, began to draw a simple map on the back of one of his trip tickets.

30

"Gentlemen. We need to have a discussion," Dr. Revchenko said to Daniel Segar and the scientist standing beside him. "Do you have a conference room?"

"Of course we have a conference room," Segar answered sharply. He didn't particularly like the little Russian man, but Segar's entire future was in the biophysicist's hands.

The trio walked down a long hall with polished marble floors and into a large conference room. An expensive teak table took center stage and around it in a giant oval were twenty high-back, leather chairs.

The three huddled together at one end as Segar began the conversation.

"Dr. Revchenko, I respect you and your work, but we haven't made an ounce of progress since you arrived. I'm sure I don't need to tell you that the very fate of this company is in your hands."

"Yes, Mr. Segar, not to mention the fate of your *country*, which is probably at least as important—wouldn't you say?"

"Yes. Of course," Segar said, feeling like he'd been caught stealing. "So what do you propose?" he asked the man with the thick glasses.

"It isn't working—the vaccine that is, at least not yet. The bacteria is so old, it's acting strange—a little like a virus—a little like bacteria. The small amount of vaccine I had left from Termez, which I thought would be enough to begin replicating, is running out. We've done at least a hundred experiments. I do not know why it worked before and it isn't working now."

"Well, that's just great, Doctor," Segar said as he quickly jumped up and began pacing in front of the floor-to-ceiling windows in the room.

"Let me tell you something. If we don't fix this situation fast, and I mean real fast, then you'll be going back to Russia and I'll be going with you. I figure it can't be as bad as prison.

"What you don't seem to understand, Dr. Revchenko, is that the only reason I'm still functioning here is because the government needs this vaccine. They already have enough on me for securities fraud to put me away until I'm at least as old as you."

Segar kept pacing and was now chewing on one fingernail. The scientist sat quietly, taking in the scene but offering nothing.

"Let me ask you this, Doctor. From what you've seen and know about this renegade meningitis bacteria, what will happen to people in terms of their hearing?"

"I can't be certain, Mr. Segar, but my best guess is that it would be permanent, just as it usually is with meningitis. My other opinion, based on Termez, is that there will be some percentage of the population that won't be affected simply because of genetics.

"We need to attack this at the molecular level with a highly personalized vaccine. By personalized, I mean the vaccine has to be designed to kill only those cells that have been affected by the bacteria. Otherwise, it will attack the normal cells as well. Manufacturing a drug like that isn't something you do in a few weeks."

"Wrong answer, Dr. Revchenko," Seger fumed as he got up and stormed out of the room.

"And don't forget to send me a postcard once you get back to Russia," he threatened, his voice echoing through BioGem's cavernous hallways.

Same day

"Stella, can you show me how to use that thing?" Joanne asked.

"Sure, Mom. There's nothing to it," Stella replied, opening her laptop computer.

"Easy for you to say. I've been after Henry for the last year to buy us a computer. He told me it was too expensive, but then I asked him how we could afford all that ham radio equipment and he just shrugged.

"I wanted to get on that AOL thing and window shop. Marian, one of the women in my reading group has been using one that her son gave her two years ago. She says it's easy, too."

"We can definitely get onto AOL. Let's check the government alert site first. I look at that twice a day for any new information."

"So, how do you start it?"

"Just push this power button and wait a minute. There, see it's lighting up. Now it'll make some sounds, you'll see some messages, and voila! There's my homepage."

"What's a homepage?"

"That's just a place to start. There are literally millions of pages like this on the Internet. See, I'll type in an address. Every page has an address, just like every house has an address."

Joanne watched as the government's site page loaded. There were all the obligatory official symbols—eagles, shields, etc., and then the day's date popped up in a panel across the top.

The first panel was headed: *Vaccine update* in red letters. The copy below that read: *No vaccine updates as of 8-21-10.*

Below that, Homeland Security had posted some generic information as to how important it was to stay indoors. Mostly, the news and commentary was all fluff without much substance. Stella knew the government didn't want to alarm anyone. At this point, it was better to have no news than bad news.

"Okay. So how do I get on AOL, dear?"

"Easy, Mom. Just click here."

Stella stayed with Joanne until she tired of looking at the screen. Then she shut down the computer and they returned downstairs.

Taking a seat near the front window, Joanne took notice that the guard who had been in Henry's truck was now out with the other two, guarding the gate to the ranch.

"Well, dear," Joanne said to start a new conversation, "it would appear that your communications background is going to come in handy."

"I suppose so. But we're all still hoping for a cure, aren't we?"

"Of course. That goes without saying, but from what the President just said, it doesn't look good. You heard it. They estimate that there are already over two million people who have lost their hearing. We're lucky to be out here, away from it all."

Stella slowly stood up, went to the kitchen, and poured herself a cup of coffee as she continued talking to her mother-in-law.

"You know, Mom, being deaf isn't as bad as everyone thinks. It's not the *end* of the world."

Joanne gave a quizzical look to her daughter-in-law as she reentered the room.

"Oh, I don't know about that. I think I'd rather go blind than lose my hearing. I can't imagine not being able to communicate, to hear music, or to listen to the birds in my garden. God, the thought is just awful to me."

Stella sat back down and tried to change the subject. "Where is Henry?"

"Oh, he's back down in the basement with Jennifer. He's trying to see if he can raise anyone on that short-wave radio of his."

"Stella, I really am interested in what you have to say about the deaf. Please, tell me more," Joanne urged.

"Well, Mom, you remember that class we talked about, the one I quit last year?"

"Yes. We were talking about that the day you arrived. You said not to call them handicapped."

"That's right. The sad fact is that they are often pitied as being defective human beings, and that is absolutely *not* the case. They aren't defective at all. In many ways, they are more adaptable than we are. When they learn the right way, they become bilingual. How many of us communicate in two languages?

"I got so furious that by the end of my year teaching there, I could barely stand talking to the administration. You see, just about all government agencies, school districts, and various powerful organizations, look at the deaf almost as if they're not completely human."

"Oh, Stella, I didn't realize. I guess we're all a little that way when we encounter someone who's handicapped."

Stella never realized that her mother-in-law was as uninformed as the general public. It was hard to blame her.

"Mom, can I tell you a story?"

"Certainly."

"Imagine if you can, a museum. A museum unlike any other—no art hanging on the walls—no paintings or statues. Instead, this museum would be dedicated to the deaf experience through the ages.

"On one wall, there would be a large ear trumpet—do you remember those from the movies, Mom?"

"Yes, dear. Those ridiculous things that old deaf people stuck in their ears so they could hear. Did they really have those?"

"Oh yes. They were invented in the seventeenth century," Stella said.

Joanne was fascinated as she moved closer to Stella. "Go on, dear."

"On another wall, there would be images of young children being operated on by eighteenth century quacks who liked to think they were doctors. They would be shoving some obscene instrument in the ear canal, not knowing what in the world they were doing."

"Oh my," Joanne said.

"Yes. Then there would be old black and white and sepia photographs of other 'doctors' forcing children's mouths open with heavy, sharp chrome instruments, trying to bring forth sounds from their mouths—which, of course, never came.

"In the back of the museum, there would be more photos. These would be pictures of small children, forced to wear ridiculously large sets of headphones. More photos would depict surgeries much closer to the brains of the children—all in an effort to get them to talk, or to 'fix' their eardrums or whatever other misguided efforts they used to 'save' the freaks who couldn't hear or talk."

Joanne was rendered silent for a moment.

"Stella, I'm sorry. I had no idea. Please tell me more about your experience with the deaf. What do you mean they are bilingual? I don't understand," she said.

Just then, they heard Jennifer screaming down in the basement.

31

"*J*esus! Do you realize what this means?"

"Oh yeah. It's all I've been thinking about for the last week. Do you mean to tell me you just thought of it?"

Three people, two men and a woman, were sitting at a large conference table on the twenty-fifth floor of a building in Manhattan, New York. One of the men, Aden Bartholomew, was the CEO of DataCom, the world's largest manufacturer of cell phones. The other was his Vice President. The woman was the head of R&D at SatCom, the world's largest cellular phone company. She sat at the opposite end of table.

"It means we're going to be going out of business very soon if we don't start putting our thinking caps on," the CEO said.

Each of the men wore a heavy, worried scowl.

"Excuse me," the woman said, "but sometimes there's more at stake than just the bottom line."

The two young executives looked incredulously at each other. The CEO stood up and said, "I would remind you that you have a stake here as well—not only your salary, but the stock you own. Don't you realize that if only half the people in this country go deaf, we'll be out of business within the year? Who in the hell is going to be buying cell phones?"

"I understand that. I'm just saying that in this situation, where many people are getting sick and losing their hearing, we should be wondering how our technologies might be able to help them cope. *That's* the question we should be asking ourselves," she said.

Both men were stunned. The woman had never been one to speak her mind. She was a brilliant scientist who had helped bring the firm from an "also ran" to the leader in the industry. She was the one who had thought up ring tones and text messaging, which in 2001 had set the entire industry on its ears. It took most of the competition the better part of a year to catch up.

"I've got an idea," the woman said. "Obviously, those people who do lose their hearing, and who do own a text-capable phone and text messaging account, will still be able to communicate with others, albeit a little slower than actually talking and listening; but nevertheless, all is not lost.

"Okay, we've pretty much figured that out. What's the new idea?" The Vice President said.

"We introduce a service that makes our phone and our pagers more useful for the deaf to communicate with their hearing friends and family."

"We're listening," the two men said in unison.

"What we do is we set up a bank of operators. When a deaf person wants to call a hearing person, they text the operators, who in turn call the hearing person and relay the message. Then, that person can tell the operator to send back a text message to his deaf friend."

The two men looked at each other with nearly the same thought. "I've got an even better idea," The CEO volunteered. "Why use operators? Why don't we just make the phone itself be capable of doing what you just described? The deaf person types, which the phone reads aloud to a hearing person. Then the hearing person speaks, and the phone translates their voice into text for the deaf person!"

The Vice President chimed in. "Now that's an idea, a good one, which gives me another idea," he said. "What if we start adding news and weather as text alerts on those new phones—at a small additional cost, of course."

As the woman listened to the two men she thought, *God, we are nothing but a nation of greedy capitalist fools.*

3 2

"My God, Stella. Where have you guys been? I was so worried. I've left at least ten messages on Dad's cell phone, and the phone at the house is dead."

"Nate. I've got bad news."

"Stella, how could things be any worse? Is Jennifer all right? God, don't tell me something happened to her. Are any of you sick?"

"None of us is sick, but your father had an accident."

"What kind of accident?" Nate said, suppressing a lump in his throat. "Is he okay?"

"Yes, he'll be okay," Stella said as the two National Guardsmen stood on the porch watching her. In the driveway, an ambulance was pulling away, pushing a large cloud of dust up into the hot August air. The temperature was over a hundred and the humidity was hovering around eighty-five percent "They sewed him up with about a dozen stitches, right here in the house.

"He was down in the basement. I guess he was trying to get something off a shelf and a full can of paint fell on his head. He has a real bad gash on his forehead. Jennifer was screaming and there was blood all over the place. But he's okay. The soldiers brought in an ambulance …"

She said the word so casually that Nathan almost didn't catch it.

"Wait a minute. Soldiers? What soldiers?"

"Nathan, they've been here for days, guarding us."

"Oh Jesus."

"Where are you, Nate? I've been worried sick about you."

"I know, sweetheart. And I've been worried about you. I'm in Utah."

"Utah? Why Utah?"

"I came here to meet a reporter. He's the one who broke the story about the secret quarantine in Troy."

"Didn't see it. The only information we're getting is off the Internet, the radio, or your dad's ham set. They took our cell phones and cut the lines to the house."

"Cut the lines to the house?" Nathan sputtered. "Are you serious? Why would they do that?"

"I don't know. We just assumed this is how they're treating everybody."

"Wait a minute. If they took your phones, how are you calling me?"

"When your father hurt himself, the three soldiers who guard the house came running. Each had a rifle and they were pointing it at me. I was screaming that I had to use their phone to call the EMTs. So one of them handed me his cell phone.

"They're still standing at the front door staring at me, but they can't hear what I'm saying." Stella told Nate to hold on a second, then yelled out, "Mom. It's Dad's doctor in Billings. He says to keep Henry off his blood thinners for a couple of days."

Hearing that, one of the guards pressed his face to the screen door, "Uh ma'am, I've gotta have my phone back. If anyone finds out I let you use it, I'll be toast."

"Okay, soldier. Just give me one more minute, please."

"That's it, ma'am. One minute."

Nathan was confused. "Stella, why did you just make up that story about me being Dad's doctor?"

"I'm not sure. But something tells me that if the National Guard isn't cutting everyone's lines, maybe they only cut ours so we couldn't talk to each other."

"That doesn't make any sense," Nathan argued. "Why wouldn't they want us talking to each other?"

"I don't know. Nothing seems to make sense anymore."

"You're telling me. So anyway, I'll be here in Utah for a few days with this reporter, trying to figure some things out."

"What's his name?"

"Brody. Benjamin Brody, but everyone calls him …"

Hearing the name caused Stella to bolt upright in attention. "Hop?" she finished for him. "You're with Hop Brody?"

Nathan was now more confused than ever.

"How do you know who Hop Brody is?" he stammered.

"Believe it or not, I had his daughter Amanda in my class last year. He's got a real story to tell. Both of his kids are deaf, you know."

"That's one of the reasons I'm here."

With that, the guardsman opened the screen door and asked for the phone. "Sorry, ma'am. I can't take a chance."

"Goodbye, Doctor. I've got to go."

"Sweetie, tell Dad I'll call him on the ham. I love you."

"Thanks for that, Doctor. I feel the same way."

The phone went dead in Nate's ear.

Montana had been held under tighter government scrutiny than any other state. First it was Troy, then Libby, then Billings, and then the rest of the towns from one border to the next. It was almost as if the entire state was conducting a sweeping manhunt.

In Utah, it was different. The Mormons were a powerful force to reckon with and the President chose wisely to go along with the Mormon governor's wishes. It was almost business as usual in Park City.

After talking with Stella, Nathan knew that Montana had become a virtual military state. But in Utah nothing much had seemed to change, at least not yet. For some reason, only one in ten of the people in Park City showed any signs of the disease. Those who did were quarantined in the city's hospital. People were allowed to move around freely, with the sole provision that they couldn't leave the city.

Since his paper had been shut down, that evening Hop Brody had set up his own Web site and started a Blog. The Internet was still wide open—it had to be, it was the best way for the government to reach people other than the open-captioned television broadcasts.

"Yes, Mr. Bannister. I know your wife. What an odd coincidence," Hop said as he motioned for Nate to sit on the couch in his office.

Hop looked just about like Nate had envisioned. He had thick auburn hair, which framed a square-jawed and heavily freckled face. Like Nate, he wore cowboy boots, jeans, and a tan canvas sports coat.

He had an easy smile and energy Nate could feel the second he stepped into his presence.

"Is your father okay? You said he took a gash in his head?"

"Yeah. It was an accident. He's okay. Thanks for asking," Nate replied.

"Now that I know you know my wife, I should tell you that she's connected to one of the reasons I'm here."

Hop's eyebrows arched with slight suspicion. "Is that right? When you said you were with the EPA, I assumed this was an official visit of some sort."

Nathan looked down at the ground and sighed. "Not really. It's more about the lasting symptoms of the virus."

"You mean the deafness," Hop deduced straightforwardly.

"Yes, the deafness. You see, I … I seem to …" he could not make his mouth say the words.

"Seem to be losing your hearing?" Hop asked as casually as if Nathan had said he was losing his hair. "Not to brag, but I kind of already figured that out. I mean, you did warn me that you'd been infected."

"I did at that, didn't I?" Nathan answered with a sniffling chuckle.

"And after reading my articles, you think I'm the guy who's got some good advice on how this country should mainstream a few million deaf people back into society."

"I should have known you weren't the type to mince words."

"Got that right. Learned that from my kids. Make every word count."

As he listened, Nathan took the opportunity to make a quick scan of Hop's office.

The room was sparse: an old leather couch, a laptop computer sitting on a gray Steelcase desk that had to be at least fifty years old, one entire wall of books, and a dim lamp sitting on the desk.

On the far wall were two framed pieces: One was a photograph that Nate couldn't quite make out and the other was a certificate, or award of some kind.

Nathan smiled. "You sound like my wife. She's always saying things like that."

"Your wife is a very bright woman, Mr. Bannister."

"Nate. Call me Nate. And thank you for the compliment. You two would get along great."

"I'm sure we would," Hop smiled mischievously. "We have a lot of the same ideas when it comes to deafness."

"And that's what I really came to talk about. I think there's something the three of us can do to help.

"I'm all ears, Nate. So to speak."

But as Nate began to lay out his plan, he felt another wave of nausea coming over him and he became lightheaded again. Then he felt a surge of vertigo, as if the walls were spinning around him.

It was the strangest feeling he'd ever had, and he felt completely out of control as he clung to the arm of the couch, as if that would save him.

"Nate, are you all right?" Hop asked.

"No, Hop. I'm afraid I'm not."

33

*H*enry Bannister sat in his living room, his forehead heavily bandaged. The cut had taken twelve stitches to close and he had a horrible headache. Stella and Joanne sat on either side of him, fixed on the latest emergency radio broadcast.

It was the middle of another sweltering day.

"Dammit!" Henry bellowed. "Why do they keep talkin' about this stuff? It just incites people—gives them crazy ideas that they hadn't even thought of yet."

The news broadcast was describing the looters stealing everything from canned goods to plasma TVs from stores in downtown St. Louis.

Joanne added her own feelings on the matter. "What I can't understand is why they're looting. Is a free television going to make someone forget that they're sick?"

"I think they do it because they're scared," Stella offered. "They fear that life is changing forever for the worse, and they may as well grab whatever bit of the past they can."

Listening to the broadcaster describe how various parts of St. Louis were under siege, Stella wondered how long it would take before all major cities were enveloped in mass hysteria.

"You know, when I was in college, I took a series of psychology classes and one of them dealt with just this phenomenon. It was called 'The Psychology of Crowds,'" Stella said, as she grimaced while the broadcaster described a policeman who was continuing to beat a looter, even after he'd given up.

145

"When an individual joins a crowd, whether that's a street mob or an audience listening to a speech, the person's 'awareness of self' can disappear. What happens then, particularly in the case of a street mob, is that people lose their sense of judgment ... their sense of society. They become increasingly more suggestible," Stella explained.

"That's a bunch of horse shit. They're all just turning into animals," Henry said. Henry loved his daughter-in-law, but he often found her liberal attitudes irritating.

"Half of them already *were* animals. To hell with social norms; these people are just plain, violent crooks. There's always the type that'll take advantage of any weakness. That's what I think."

"Ladies and gentlemen," the reporter continued as sirens screeched in the background, "all of this city's emergency rooms are overflowing, and not just with those that are being injured in the riots and fires, but those who are rapidly losing their hearing.

"The doctors can only treat the injured and so there is mass pandemonium here in St. Louis. It's difficult to explain. I tried to interview a man this morning, not realizing that he'd contacted the bacteria. All he could do was point to his ears and shake his head, in essence saying he couldn't hear me.

"We were at one emergency room this morning, and half the people in the waiting areas were hurriedly scribbling notes on any piece of paper they could find to communicate with the nurses and doctors.

"It's very difficult to describe what is going on here: desperation, complete disorganization, and abject fear all stirred together in a devil's stew of violence."

The Bannisters sat in shock, holding their collective breaths. That was the turning point. Even Henry now realized that martial law had been the only viable plan of action.

Stella's mind raced off in several directions at once: *Is Nate going to make it back? What will he find out from Hop Brody? How will we ever pull ourselves out of this, as a nation, if most of us won't be able to communicate?*

The rioting was borne of just that, an inability to communicate combined with a primal fear of the unknown. As long as people were this afraid—not to mention unable to hear anything—she knew it would be catastrophic for the country.

As the three sat in stony silence, the radio broadcaster announced an upcoming message from Halley Weber, President Jordan's Secretary of Education.

How odd, Stella thought. *Why in all this chaos and violence would the Secretary of Education be talking to the nation?*

34

NORAD Bunker

August 31, 2010

*M*ore than twenty-five men and women were seated around the enormous oval table, chattering away among each other. They consisted of the Joint Chiefs of Staff, most of the President's cabinet members, and various other government officials deemed necessary to run the country given the circumstances.

The room went silent as Robert Jordan came through the door, walked silently across the cold linoleum floor, and stood at the head of the table. All those present stood and the military personnel saluted. Jordan wore the familiar green heart against the American flag pendant in his lapel, the insignia of the Independent Party—a symbol he was proud of.

"Please, be seated," he said as he lowered himself into his own chair. "This evening, I've received updated reports from the FBI and Homeland Security as well as the CDC in Atlanta. As I'm sure most of you would guess, none of it is even remotely promising.

"First of all, we still have made no headway with the vaccine. Secondly, there is sporadic rioting—fires, looting; in some cases, guardsmen shooting citizens.

"On top of that, most of the emergency facilities are overflowing and as the populace, particularly the police, fire, and emergency crews begin to lose their own hearing, communications are rapidly deteriorating.

"This morning, I was notified on my private line that President Marquez of Mexico is reluctantly closing the border with the U.S. I find that missive filled with irony; given how stringently we've tried to protect our borders. I suppose we won't be having that problem for the foreseeable future."

The President took a deep breath and paused, then poured himself a glass of water from the pitcher on the table. Every eye in the room was on him as he methodically raised the glass to his lips and gulped the entire contents.

"In addition, Prime Minister Alexander of Canada has sent the same message. To be honest, I certainly can't blame either one of them. Prime Minister Bradley of Great Britain, President Custeau of France, and President Hansjurgen of Germany have expressed their willingness to help us, but I'm not sure in what fashion—and neither are they. They have mentioned having their scientists work on a vaccine as well, which certainly wouldn't hurt.

"For all intents and purposes, the United States of America is now an island."

Jordan paused again and stood up, walking past each seated member, touching him or her on the shoulder. He was clearly stressed, his eyebrows furrowed, his shoulders taut.

On the opposite wall of the drab, gray room was a ten-foot-long map of the United States with hundreds of various colored pins stuck in strategic cities and areas.

Some indicated the estimated number of people stricken with the bacteria, others were indicators of flash points or riots, and still other indicated emergency facilities—nearly seventy percent of the map was covered.

"People, we are beyond FEMA or DHS or any other organizations to contain this unprecedented challenge to America. That's why we're all here together.

"This is an open, free forum for dialogue. Together, we must begin to get some answers. For starters, assuming that we don't get a vaccine for quite some time, and further assuming this is an epidemic, how are we going to communicate with each other, with the world, if so many people can't hear?

"Secondly, we need a plan to quell the rioting, and we need it now.

"Let's start with you Madam Secretary Weber."

Halley Weber cleared her throat with a nervous cough.

"Mr. President. I know nothing about riot control or emergency readiness. My background is education and, as you and many others here know, my daughter is deaf. For the past nine years, I have dealt with the issue of how best to help non-hearing people live in a hearing world.

"Though most of you probably haven't heard of it, there is an organization that can help us. It's called AGBell, which stands for Alexander Graham Bell."

Weber was in her element on this subject. She'd long been an advocate for Bell's organization and was one of the many federal recipients of lobbying money for that organization.

As the secretary became more comfortable in the midst of all the high-ranking people seated at the table, she stood up and began walking around the room.

"It's my feeling that a great deal of this rioting is, for lack of a better term, the result of a cultural panic attack. People are scared, and there's no one out there telling them not to be afraid.

"I feel that one of our primary focuses must be on calming people down with respect to their hearing loss. We need to let them know that they have not been handed a death sentence.

"What is really important, though, if we are to look beyond the immediate, is to ask this question: Assuming that most people survive the illness, the seizures, and all the attendant other ills of the bacteria, what if, God forbid, a vaccine is not developed and some significant part of the population does go permanently deaf?" Weber said as she continued to walk about the room twisting a pencil in her hand. "That, my fellow colleagues, will be the issue long after this virus has become old news."

President Jordan interrupted. "Excuse me, Ms. Weber, but we may be getting a little ahead of ourselves here. Although I'm sure we all appreciate your expertise with the deaf, our primary interest now is controlling anarchy."

Just then, a man named David Riley, head of FEMA, raised his hand.

"Yes, David," the President said, "what's on your mind?"

"Well, this will sound a bit drastic at first, but if you give it a moment to sink in, it may be a good option."

"Go ahead," the President said as all eyes turned toward the slightly balding man in the dark blue suit.

David Riley had been the head of FEMA for three presidential terms. He was the man who could have become emergency president during the Reagan era when the secret executive order granted FEMA broad powers in the event of a crisis or widespread dissent. The powers, of course, were never used, but that was because the Iran-Contra fiasco went away and President Bush managed to put a lid on the Iraq dissenters.

Now, it was a different story. Everything they thought might happen back then, seven years ago, *was* happening. The only ones in the room who knew of it were the President, the Joint Chiefs, the head of the FBI and CIA, and himself.

"Well, sir, I'm sure you remember Executive Order 23997."

Suddenly each of the five Joint Chiefs jerked their heads in Riley's direction and the President took in a deep breath.

"Yes, of course, David, but I don't think we're there yet!"

"I'm not so sure of that, sir. Think about it for a moment. We don't know how many people have the virus or not. But one thing we do know for sure is that all those people who are losing their hearing definitely *do* have it, right? And that number, at this moment, is a manageable three million.

"And, if Secretary Weber is even remotely correct, that a lot of the dissent and fear and rioting is the result of those people, then we could kill two birds with one stone, so to speak."

"You're not thinking what I think you're thinking, are you Riley?"

"Yes, sir, I am. Internment camps for the deaf. There, I've said it."

A collective gasp erupted in the room before all twenty-five people began murmuring loudly amongst themselves. The President sat, taking it all in, waiting for the clamor to stop. Then Riley spoke again.

"Sir. It's not beyond the realm of imagination. The initiative and the executive order still exist in theory. Not only would isolating the deaf help to stop the spread of the bacteria, it would quell the rioting.

"And, of course, it would be only a temporary situation; just until the virus ran its course or a vaccine was distributed."

The room fell silent as the cabinet members actually started seeing the sense of Riley's plan.

Riley sat down, quietly reveling in his statement and idea. He hoped some in the room; those who weren't Libertarians at least, would delight in the same way he was.

After all, he was protecting the people from themselves, the more than three hundred million with their irrational impulses and self-indulgent actions who didn't understand the yellow from the orange on the terror-alert thermometer.

Robert Jordan, being the student of history that he was, remembered the Japanese internment camps during WWII. That, of course, was a dehumanizing disaster of cosmic proportions—but this didn't have to end up like that.

Even Jordan, in his 180-degree differing view of America, could see that this could be humane and it would certainly go a long way in reestablishing order. The more he thought about it, the more he liked the idea, the more he convinced himself it made sense. The only part he didn't like, as he recalled, was that the original order would have given the head of FEMA emergency presidential powers—and that wasn't going to happen.

Jordan remembered that on February 19, 1942, soon after the start of the war, Franklin D. Roosevelt signed Executive Order 9066. The evacuation order commenced the round up of 120,000 Americans of Japanese heritage to be sent to one of ten internment camps. They were officially called "relocation centers" and were located in

California, Idaho, Utah, Arizona, Wyoming, Colorado, and Arkansas.

Of course, the already existing prejudice against the Japanese was only fueled by their attack on Pearl Harbor. That one event was all that Roosevelt needed, in terms of public opinion, to use the Executive Order. Eventually, more than two-thirds of the Japanese population living in America was put into the camps.

If they could do that then, they could certainly do better this time. The deaf population, according to the pins on the map in the room, was growing daily and was now estimated at about three million people. *Nevertheless, it could be done*, Jordan thought. *But how will we segregate those who are already deaf, but don't have the bacteria, from those who really have it?*

Actually, it wouldn't make any difference. They would all have to go into camps, regardless. We don't have the capacity to check everyone. And, after all, there can't be that many deaf people out there anyway, can there?

Combining the police, armed forces, National Guard, and maybe even fire fighters into a "relocation" force would not be that difficult, given the fact that they were already deployed throughout the country.

Humane housing would be the most important objective and that could probably be accomplished through FEMA's already formidable inventory of manufactured homes and trailers left over from Katrina.

The room was still buzzing when Jordan spoke again. "Let me ask you something, Riley. You know better than anyone. How many of those manufactured units do you have in inventory, and where are most of them?"

"Well sir, I couldn't give you an exact count right now, but I'd say there's at least four hundred thousand of them in about ten locations."

"That's a start. How long would it take to gear up to make another hundred thousand?"

"Hard to say, sir. Especially given the fact that there are fewer workers now who would be able to build them. Still, I'd say no more than a month or two."

Jordan looked to his cabinet member Hayden Marsh, who had been a constitutional law expert before joining Jordan's team.

"Hayden. What would be the legal challenges?"

"Not something we'd have to worry about now, because under martial law, you have the power to do just about anything. Essentially, as you know, the constitution has been suspended.

"However, afterward, when things calmed down again, there might be problems. As I recall, two important legal cases were brought against the United States concerning the Japanese internment in 1944. The defendants argued the government violated their Fifth Amendment rights. In other words, they argued they weren't given due process."

"What happened to those cases?" Riley asked.

"The Supreme Court ruled in favor of the government—of course."

"Ladies and gentlemen, the more I think about this, the more I like it," the President said. "I'm beginning to think we might be able to get a handle on this thing."

"Okay then," Jordan said. "Let's get on with this. Riley, as head of FEMA, you're going to be the point man on this. I want to know how many camps we'll need, how much housing, how we're going to feed all these people, and what it'll take to get them into the camps. You've got five days. Oh, and don't call them camps, sounds too much like World War II. Let's think of some other term. Any suggestions?"

Jordan looked around the room. It was silent.

"Habitats," Secretary Weber said, with a self-satisfied smile.

"Hearing Habitats," she added. "If we promote the idea that these habitats are where their hearing will be restored, who *wouldn't* go?"

"I like it," Jordan said.

35

"Nate. We have to get you to a doctor. You don't look good," Hop said as he began to ease Nathan down on the couch.

"No, don't do that. That makes it worse. I've got to sit up and hold on. I feel like the room is spinning around me. Christ, this is horrible.

"Give me a minute. Let's see if it subsides. When I was first meeting with the people in Troy, they told me the vertigo would come and go fairly quickly.

"Oh geeze, here it comes again," Nathan said as he clenched his fingers deeply into the leather. "Never felt anything like this."

Hop felt helpless. He couldn't imagine how Nate must feel and he knew there was nothing he could do but wait.

Within a few minutes, Nate began to take slower breaths and finally release his death grip on the couch.

"It's going away. Thank God," he said. Then slowly, he sat completely upright, wiped his mouth, and took a deep breath.

"Maybe I shouldn't have come here. I don't have much time before I lose my hearing like the others, I'll be deaf and dumb."

Hop let out a loud laugh, stood up, and walked over to his desk. He turned and faced Nate and laughed again.

"What's so funny?" Nate said.

"You are so typical—your choice of words—what you don't know about the deaf would fill a book."

"What do you mean?"

Hop walked over to the bookcase, pushed back two volumes and pulled out a bottle of bourbon. Three framed pictures sat on one of the shelves. One was a typical family shot with a man, a woman, and two children in a contrived pose, as if done for a family gift.

The one next to that was a picture of a man with his arm around a woman seated in what looked like a booth in a restaurant, and the last was of a man with a small boy and girl all sitting on horses. From where he stood, Nate couldn't see much detail.

"Care to have a drink?" He asked.

"Naw. Not now. My stomach's still queasy."

"Well, I will."

Hop poured half a glass of the brown liquid and took a large gulp.

"Dumb; the word dumb. You used it to describe people who can't talk. How *dumb* is that? And, what makes you so sure that you can't talk when you can't hear? Actually, some deaf people speak fairly well.

"I'm really surprised at you, pardner. Your wife used to teach deaf kids, she's teaching communications now, and you don't know the first thing about either one?"

Hop was feigning irritability.

"Actually, speaking is the least of your worries. I'm surprised that Stella never taught you ASL. She's an expert."

Nate began to slowly stand up. "The ringing's back. Can you speak up? What in the world is ASL?"

"Oh boy. We've got a lot of talking to do, and a lot of listening. Come over here and sit down. Are you sure you don't want a drink?"

"On second thought, yeah. Give me a small version of what you're having," Nate answered.

"Do you feel like you should see a doctor?"

"For what? There is no vaccine, no cure. Life as I've know it is about to end, don't you get that?"

"Pardner, you've got a lot to learn. Sure, things will be different for you, but you've got a whole *new* life ahead of you. Just because you lose your hearing, that doesn't mean you automatically become 'dumb' or are less of a person. It's not going to affect your thinking processes. You'll just have to start adjusting to your new data flow rate."

"Huh? What do you mean data flow rate?"

Both men took a sip of whiskey and Hop began to tell Nate the story of his two children.

"My daughter, Amanda, and my son, Casey, are staying with their mother right now. All three are okay. My daughter, the oldest, and my son were both born deaf. Actually, that's not technically correct. Casey is deaf, meaning he can't hear *anything* and Amanda is hard of hearing, meaning she can hear a little, but not much. It's hard to know just how much because, after all, I can't experience what she hears."

"It must've been hard raising them."

"Quite the contrary. They are both very healthy happy kids. In fact, if you were to ask them if they wanted to hear, I'll bet you they'd both say no—at least Casey would say that."

"I can't believe that. Isn't it difficult for them to learn? They can't hear music or your voice. That's gotta be hard."

"Well, I have to admit, it was hard in the beginning, when Amanda was first born. We didn't even know she couldn't hear until she was about two months old.

"Frankly, my first reaction was total terror. I actually felt like a part of me had died. I was devastated. My wife was beside herself—we didn't just have a handicapped child, we had a child who couldn't hear, at least not very well. It felt like our world was crashing down.

"Thank God, we found your wife, Stella. She completely changed our lives *and* Amanda's."

"Really? I'm beginning to feel like I don't really even know my wife."

"Nate. Come over here. I want to show you a picture and then tell you a story."

Nate followed as Hop limped across his office next to a bookcase on the opposite wall. Hanging there was the large color photograph

Nate had noticed when he first entered the room. Next to that was what Nate thought was a certificate.

The certificate was framed in gold, a typical 8-inch by 10-inch border. At the top of the parchment paper, in an ornate scroll like you would see on a college degree, it read: Pulitzer—just that one word. Nate was impressed, though he didn't say anything for the moment.

In the photo next to the Pulitzer Prize were two people, facing each other underwater; both were wearing full scuba gear. It appeared to be a swimming pool. One of the divers was gesturing with his hands to the other.

"Can you make out who that is?" Hop said, pointing to one of the figures.

"I'd say it's a woman, but, of course, I can't see her face," Nate answered.

"Look closer," Hop said.

Nate peered in closer to the photo.

"What the … Is that my wife? It is, it's Stella! What in the world are you two doing in a pool together?"

"We weren't on vacation, if that's what you're thinking. Stella was teaching me ASL. Didn't she ever discuss her work with you—her work with the deaf class?"

"Yes, but I never heard the acronym ASL."

"It stands for American Sign Language."

"Oh. Yes, she talked about sign language a lot, even taught me some."

"That's not the same thing. ASL is a completely different mode of communicating from what most people know as S.E.E., or Signing Exact English," Hop said emphatically. "Imagine watching two men, one an Asian and the other a Russian. Neither of them speaks the other's language, but there is something immediate and extremely important that one of them has to convey to the other. What will they do?

"In all likelihood, they will resort to gestures, kind of like two people playing charades. They can't even jot down notes for each other. They will have to point, draw pictures in the air, and touch some parts of their bodies—anything to try to communicate that important thought quickly. That's kind of what ASL looks like. It's very animated and lively, not at all like S.E.E."

"Boy, now you've got me confused," Nate said as he walked back and sat on the couch. "I don't get it. Is it signing or not?"

In the split second before Hop answered, Nate's mind jumped to another thought—*this man has put his Pulitzer Prize notice, one of only five framed pieces in his office, on the wall next to a picture of him learning ASL underwater?*

"Nate, most of the time, when you see two or more deaf people signing, they are using ASL."

"I'm still not getting the difference."

Hop laughed and gave Nate a pat on the shoulder.

"Do you have a couple of hours? I can explain it to you."

"As a matter of fact I do."

Hop came over and joined Nate, sitting across from him in a large leather chair.

"After we found out that Amanda was hard of hearing and we'd gotten over the initial shock, the first thing we thought about was, we've got to learn sign language and lip reading, but, of course, so would our daughter. Otherwise, what good would it do us?" Hop asked.

"But she was only a baby," Nate said.

"I know. It seemed like an impossible task and, as it turned out, none of it worked out well at all. In fact, all the problems we encountered and the guilt I'm still carrying around, later led us to Stella. She had just started working with ASL."

"Why do you feel guilty?"

"I made a big mistake. I forced her to undergo surgery. That was brutal and I'll never forgive myself."

"What kind of surgery?"

"Some yahoos at a hearing organization convinced me that she had to have a cochlear implant. It was awful. They told me it was the only way she'd ever hear or talk. Imagine this: She was under general anesthesia for more than three hours. Of course, they didn't tell me that it would take that long before they started the surgery."

"That's a long time for a young girl to be under a general."

"Exactly. Then they made a broad crescent-shaped incision behind her ear to open the mastoid bone leading to the middle ear. A part of her temporal muscle was removed. Then they drilled into her skull and reamed out a place to make room for the internal electrical coil. Then a section of the mastoid bone is removed as well to expose the inner ear.

"God it makes me sick going back over it. She was only four years old."

Just then Nate pressed his hands over his ears and made a strange face.

"Nate. What's the matter? Are you okay?"

"Yeah. I'm okay. There's a pressure on my ears that I can't make go away. Usually, I can just yawn real hard until they pop."

"Do you want to lie down? Can I get you anything?"

"No. I'll be fine," Nate shook his head and pulled his hands away.

"Tell me more about the swimming pool."

"That was way later, after we met Stella. By that time, Amanda was nearing five years old, time for kindergarten, but she wasn't near ready. If we'd sent her to school, she would've been light years behind the other kids."

"What about the implant. Didn't that help?"

"Not nearly as much as we'd hoped. By that time, I was desperately playing catch-up with a situation I didn't think I had a prayer of getting in front of. And another thing the organization didn't tell me was that the surgery was irreversible.

"That's when I saw an article about Stella and her work with ASL. The newspaper article was talking about all the battles she was having with the school district.

"I called her the following day and, to my surprise, after I told her my story, she invited me to come up to Helena, which I did."

"Guess I must've been off on one of my interstate probes. Jeez, looking back, I sure spent a lot of time on the road. I had no clue what she was doing."

"Don't torture yourself. That's water under the bridge now. Speaking of water, that's why I was in the pool. Your wife had been experimenting with something called Emotion Recognition Software. It has to do with the very subtle facial expression we all use unwittingly when we interact with other people."

"This is fascinating. Now I remember her reading me a magazine article a few weeks ago about this. It had something to do with the Mona Lisa painting. So how did the pool idea come about?"

"Well, she realized that the brain is really only good at processing one kind of signal at a time—either sight, sound, smell, taste, or pain. Confronted with a visual stimulus, the brain tends to close down the other circuits in varying degrees to focus on the sense of sight. Similarly, confronted with a strong auditory stimulus, the brain tends to focus on hearing.

"One of the challenges of teaching ASL to a hearing person is the distraction of noise.

"She told me that the underwater method could teach me ASL twenty times faster than in a classroom.

"Stella explained that by going underwater where there is zero auditory, the brain is forced to go one hundred percent visual. She also pointed out to me that although deaf people are obviously visually oriented, most hearing people are not. Hearing people are prone more to auditory signals until the brain decides that a visual signal is more important."

"I get it. So, underwater your brain starts focusing completely on signing, or visual communications."

"Precisely. Only ASL isn't really signing in the way you're probably thinking."

"It isn't? Then what is it?"

"Well. I'm getting a little ahead of myself. How do you feel?"

"I'm better. It comes and goes."

"Good. By the way, you never said why you came here to talk. You said you had an idea."

"Well, I've got a completely different take on things now. I had decided to come here to talk to you about your Web site. I like what you're saying about the government, what they might be covering up, how the two of us could work to inform the public about what is really happening.

"Then, when I talked to Stella yesterday and told her I was coming here, she recognized your name—told me she'd had your daughter in her class. I had no idea you knew so much about the deaf. I think the three of us should work together."

"I'm up for anything, pardner. I read about your run-in with the Feds a few years ago over that asbestos thing in Libby. Good work, man, good work."

"Come with me. I've got a short wave radio in the truck. Stella's staying with my parents outside Billings. I want the three of us to talk."

36

September 8, 2010

A week had passed since President Jordan assigned the Hearing Habitats' project to FEMA director David Riley. In that time, he'd put together a team that consisted of his lead man, Gordon Boggs, the President's Press Secretary; General Pap Renkins, the second in command of the Army after the Chief of Staff; HUD Chairman, David Briscomb; and seven others, each bringing his own expertise to the table.

The lead man, or at least the voice of the administration for now, would be Gordon Boggs. He was the one with the most experience, the one who'd come into the administration from the media, and the one who would be the face of the "bad news."

Riley couldn't paint this massive internment with the President's face or voice. It had to come from another individual, someone who could take the heat, at least in the beginning. He would be the one appearing on television and radio. That press conference would be preceded by the enormous thrust they'd set up to go public on the government Web site a day in advance.

Not many newspapers or magazines were being published because there was no easy way to distribute them, so the Internet, television and radio announcements, or billboards were the only means of mass communication.

Fortunately for the administration, it was estimated that more than eighty-five percent of the population had, for the most part, been staying in their homes. Most were petrified of contracting the disease, and many of those had Internet access. Those who didn't, mostly the elderly, were relying on TV and radio.

Even close neighbors didn't venture out much to discuss the disease, the sporadic rioting, or anything else. If they did, it was from a distance—across a yard or across the street.

In the towns that had been fully quarantined, there were other problems. Some of the residents in those communities had the disease and others didn't, so there was an immediate panic among those who were still symptom-free—they were trapped in tight quarters with very contagious neighbors.

When a victim did venture out of the home, those who were still healthy closed their windows, doors, and drapes.

National Guard troops were acting not only as a police force, but as delivery boys, at least in some counties where their presence was strong. Once a week, convoys of two-and-a-half-ton trucks would rumble down neighborhood streets, dropping off boxes of essentials on the corners of every other block in residential areas.

The large boxes were filled with rice, beans, bottled water, sugar, cooking oil, and other staples. Those brave enough, mostly men, ventured out to receive the rations. One by one, each man would walk up to the containers, grab whatever he could carry in one armload, and then walk back home. The others would stand nearby, but not close. They made sure they kept at least thirty feet between themselves, no one fully sure of who might be the next to contract the disease.

The process would be repeated until the container was empty and all the men returned home.

In other communities, things didn't work that easily, especially those urban areas where homes were spread out over much further distances. In those cases, the Army would use a school or church and make a much larger drop of supplies. Community leaders, such as the clergy, mayor, doctors, and others, would organize distribution to the rural areas.

Not every community responded the same. In Park City, life was still relatively normal, or as normal as it could be considering the circumstances. In other areas, like farmlands in Iowa, anyone driving by could still see farmers working their fields of corn or tending to their pigs. Some people had the attitude that the virus would or would not affect them no matter what they did, so they went on with their lives as if nothing was different.

In stark contrast, New York, particularly Manhattan, looked as if aliens had landed and taken all the inhabitants away. Stores, for the most part, were untouched. Marquees were turned off and there wasn't a soul in Central Park. There were no homeless people living in cardboard boxes on the sidewalks and the subway, which had stopped running a week before and was now eerily silent.

Occasionally, an Army helicopter would swoop down between the skyscrapers and buzz down Broadway or criss-cross over Times Square, but there was never anyone outdoors.

Inside the high-rises, however, people could still be seen peeking out windows, watching the government television station, or surfing the Internet—trying to maintain some semblance of normality.

As the disease continued to spread across the country, and as more time passed, those who hadn't contracted the bacteria began to feel a little more confident that they would be spared—but only if they maintained their distance from others.

It fell to General Renkins to spearhead the "relocation" of the deaf. He hadn't offered to the President that he had a nephew that was hard of hearing, feeling it wiser for the time being to remain quiet about his knowledge.

Of course, as second in command to the Army Chief of Staff, he had a great deal of experience in "relocating" people, usually enemy combatants into various new compounds, jails, or communities. This was different. He wasn't the head of a National Guard unit who *did* have extensive knowledge in those areas—they were the ones who went into civilian areas of the country or who worked large-scale riots.

In fact, the General had to turn to precedent in order to design his plan. The only other situation in his country's history where people were "rounded up," essentially arrested, and placed in large-scale camps was the wholesale relocation of Japanese Americans during WWII.

He quickly resorted to his knowledge of history and his own personal library and began to research how that had been accomplished. In one city, San Francisco, which had a larger Japanese population than most other U.S. cities at the time, he turned up articles from the Virtual Museum of the city of San Francisco.

There was a reference to the War Relocation Authority in Washington, D.C., on May of 1943.

"During the spring and summer of 1942, the United States Government carried out, in remarkably short time and without serious incident, one of the largest controlled migrations in history," it began. The General liked the words, "remarkably short time and without serious incident ..."

The article continued, "This was the movement of 110,000 people of Japanese descent from their homes in an area bordering the Pacific coast, into ten wartime communities constructed in remote areas between the Sierra Nevada Mountains and the Mississippi River.

"The evacuation of these people was started in the early spring of 1942. At that time, with the invasion of the west coast looming as an imminent possibility, the Western Defense Command of the United States Army decided that the military situation required the removal of all persons of Japanese ancestry from a broad coastal strip.

"In the weeks that followed, both American-born and alien Japanese residents were moved from a prescribed zone comprising the entire state of California, the western half of Oregon and Washington, and the southern third of Arizona."

The General's time would be similarly limited. There would be the challenge of where to set up the camps, how to get the temporary housing built or sent there, and how to best transport that many people.

Busses and trains seemed the best bet, mainly because the trains hadn't been carrying passengers now for two weeks. He would have to plot train routes to large rural areas most likely in states like New Mexico and Nevada, but beyond those monumental logistics, there was the thornier issue of how to handle the announcement—how to tell three million people you were going to arrest them and send them to some desolate camps in the middle of the desert, even though they hadn't done anything wrong or illegal.

That would be up to Boggs. He was the PR guy. He and the General would have to sit down together and come up with not only the logistics, but also the story—one that would literally convince people it was for their own good, but more importantly for the good of the country, to willingly take up residence in the camps.

The internees, or "visitors" as Boggs had decided to name them, would be of every descent, age, religion, or political persuasion. Whereas the Japanese were an easy singular target, this would be quite different.

General Renkins knew at that moment that he'd be pitting the people of the country, who had contracted the virus, against those who hadn't—or at least not yet.

37

September 9, 2010

Sergi Revchenko sat at the far end of the conference table. Daniel Segar, CEO of BioGem, sat at the other. There had been no progress in the development of a vaccine and Segar was fuming. He blamed the Russian scientist for what might very soon be an impending prison sentence. He also blamed him for creating the bacteria in the first place.

Oddly, Segar thought, *this little man has single-handedly created the reason I might have become one of the wealthiest men in the world, while almost simultaneously dashing all my hopes.*

Segar stared at Revchenko, his eyes squinted, his pupils focused tightly on the man who, despite the early September heat, was still wearing a long camel's hair coat indoors.

Suddenly, Segar jumped up and brought his fist crashing down on the heavy oak table.

"*Goddammit*, man. You managed somehow to save all those fucking illiterates in Uzbekistan. Why can't you re-create the vaccine here? After all, it's why you're here. It's why you're a free man," Segar yelled in anger.

"And now I've got to contend with all these other countries that are trying to jump on my bandwagon. Germany, Japan, and Russia are all testing vaccines. That's all we need, for some fucking other country to get all the spoils."

Revchenko sat quietly and patiently, waiting for the CEO to calm a bit, at least enough to interject a few words that might be heard. After another thirty seconds of tirade, Segar sat back down and slumped deeply into his chair.

"Mr. Segar, may I speak?"

Segar looked around the room as if giving it some thought.

"Yes. What the fuck is it?"

"The bacteria is very old. The small sample of vaccine I had was very old. The Termez solution was pure luck. This is an entirely different situation.

"I have determined several things, however."

Segar perked up, turned his chair toward the scientist, and said, "Yes. And what are those things?"

"Most importantly, based on the information coming from the CDC and other government scientists I've been speaking to, the virus does not appear to be fatal."

"Okay, fine. But that doesn't help me."

"Next, since the incubation period is less than two weeks, the disease has had time to run some of its course. That means the majority who have contracted it have exposed about as many people as they are going to, since so many have stayed indoors or otherwise have been isolated. It has been three weeks since the end of the first incubation period in Troy.

"According to the scientists at the CDC and FEMA, many of those people are now getting better. The vertigo is disappearing, the seizures are diminishing, and the vomiting is entirely gone. The only permanent symptom seems to be the loss of hearing. In other words, the other physical symptoms will eventually run their course on their own and won't have to be dealt with."

"Oh. That's just peachy. How in the hell does that help me? Don't you see that I've got billions on the line here, not to mention a prison sentence pending, if we don't come up with some kind of remedy?"

"My point exactly."

Revchenko stood up, walked over to a chalkboard at the far end of the conference room, and began drawing a formula. He didn't say another word until he was done.

"There, Mr. Segar. There is your remedy."

"What in the hell is that?" Segar asked.

"That, my dear man, is the solution to your problems." Revchenko put the chalk down and began to walk out the door.

"Wait. Wait a minute, Dr. Revchenko," Segar said as he picked up the pace to follow the little man. It was the first time he'd ever referred to the Russian as "doctor."

38

"Mr. Boggs, it's your responsibility to figure out a way to bring this to the people. It's my responsibility to get them there and to contain them," the General said to the Press Secretary.

"I think we both know this isn't going to be easy—in fact, there is the distinct possibility that we'll have more riots on our hands. This isn't like World War II. Things were different then. We were fighting the Japanese and they were almost universally hated here in the U.S.

"Which could not be more different than the situation this time. These people are our friends and relatives, our fellow workers and schoolmates."

"Absolutely, General Renkins. I couldn't agree more. That's why I've come up with a plan; a good one I think, based on what Secretary Weber said the other day. It's all about perceptions. Perception, for the most part, is reality. We need to stick to the script that the government is working round the clock on an antidote that will restore their hearing, and that the Habitats will be the place where they will receive this antidote."

Renkins frowned.

"But just to make sure I'm understanding you correctly, there really isn't any antidote coming?"

"Who knows? Maybe there is and maybe there isn't. That's not the point. The thing we have to stress is that the Habitats will be the *most likely* place for them to restore their hearing. Hence, the name 'Hearing Habitats.'

"At any rate, my orders from the President are to proceed as planned."

Boggs reached into a pile of papers in front of him and handed a bound document to the General.

"We aren't to say anything about the possible vaccine at first. The President is working on a plan to use the Hearing Habitats as the 'centers,' if you will, where the government will provide many different types of support for the deaf: sign language instruction, lip-reading classes, that kind of thing.

"Also, Secretary Weber has a connection with a large organization that is willing to provide hearing aids to every person who wants one. Apparently, she has a deaf daughter and she's been very active with the organization for years. That's only a start, though, because we don't even know if the hearing aids will work.

"I've told her that teaching people to use sign language is a much more realistic short-term plan than distributing hearing aids, and that we'll need as many instructors as we can get out hands on. She doesn't really agree, but I think I'll have the President's ear on this."

"The same President who said we need to be proactive, open, and honest with the public about what's going with this epidemic?"

"Hey, we're being proactive and open, aren't we?" Boggs said in defense of the plan. "At this point in the game, I'd say two out of three ain't bad."

39

"No, I haven't heard from him for days. No need to anymore, I suppose," Avery Beckman said to the FBI agent on the line.

"No. I have no idea where he is. The last time we spoke, Bannister was going to try to go to see his parents. I told you that. That's why you sent the guard out there. If he comes back, you'll have him.

"By the way, what do you want him for? He doesn't know anything that I don't."

Avery nodded, listening to the agent ramble on.

"Yes, Agent Radcliff. I understand. It's a matter of national security. Where have I heard those words before?"

The phone went dead.

40

A week later. September 17, 2010

Gordon Boggs and Halley Weber sat in the briefing room at NORAD; he was using her for a sounding board for his advertising ideas. Before going into the media, Boggs had been employed at a large New York ad firm as a senior copywriter. Some of the firm's most memorable jingles were his.

Boggs' last effort for the agency was the famous milk campaign. He'd won several awards as a result of that work. His concepts now, of course, were far more important than selling dairy products. Somehow, he had to convince millions of people to get on trains and buses and travel to unknown destinations around the country.

After being identified as carriers of the bacteria, they would have to want to be cured, or at least to learn how to speak clearly and read sign language and lips.

Deep down, he was hoping that vaccine would become a reality soon, then he wouldn't have to lie, although as an advertising executive, he'd done that well for many years. He knew he had one thing in his favor for sure. He was well versed in author Malcolm Gladwell's books *Blink* and *The Tipping Point*. He'd also studied Emotion Recognition software, though he had little working knowledge of sign language, nor could he read lips.

From his knowledge, he knew that people's brains tend to focus on one stimulus at a time. If you put on a headset that cancels out noise, the brain will tend to focus more on the visual stimuli around you. That is why it is often said that people who lose one sense, tend to make up for it in another.

For those reasons, he assumed that the people who were now going deaf would automatically be more visually oriented. His campaign would rely heavily on open-captioned television, bill-boards, and posters in public places. The President had given him carte blanche on his budget, and he'd use every penny of it.

In fact, he was thrilled that for the first time in his life, he had a decent budget to work with. If this wasn't successful, he'd have no one to blame.

The briefing room had plenty of computer equipment for him to work with, a high end MacIntosh, a thirty-inch-wide full color Epson printer, and a top-notch scanner; and camera equipment along with a T-2 high speed Internet connection.

Good God, he thought as he downloaded a one-gig photo file in less than four seconds, *I wish we'd had this kind of speed at the Agency.*

Boggs had come up with what ad people call *comps*—four or five comprehensive layouts for ideas: One was a billboard, one was a poster, one was the broadside of a bus, and others were visuals for the government's Web site. He hadn't yet developed the television ideas.

Wilbur Mulrooney was one of the well-known celebrities used in several of the print ads. Mulrooney had one of the highest Q scores in Hollywood. His pudgy face and walrus-like white mustache made him look a little like Santa Claus without the costume or beard. He had the same twinkle in his eyes.

Mulrooney had been in dozens of movies over the years as a character actor, but his career actually didn't take off until he started becoming a spokesperson for various products or services.

Mulrooney was always careful to choose the products he pitched—he always made sure they were honest and were quality products made by good companies. He couldn't afford to taint his words by pitching some lame device that wouldn't work. People just automatically believed what Wilbur said.

"Okay, Ms. Weber. I'm going to show you five ideas—one at a time. Look at each carefully for fifteen seconds. Then, I'll put that one face down on the table and put another one up. Don't make any comments until you've seen them all, please. That's very important. Try to reserve judgment until you've seen the last one.

"You might be a little biased because of your daughter, but try to keep an open mind. Try to imagine what it would be like to go deaf yourself, today."

"Okay, Gordon. I'm ready."

Boggs stood up and away from the table. To his right was an easel with the 30-inch by 24-inch posters facing away from Weber. He took the first poster, turned it to face her, and then rested it on the table on its edge. She looked at it but did not make any expressions.

After fifteen seconds, Boggs placed that poster face down on the table and picked up the next one, setting it once again in front of Weber. Again, she scanned the picture, but gave no hint of expression.

On the third poster, as Boggs set it on edge in front of her, her eyes lit up, she gave a huge smile, and said, "That's it. I don't need to see the others. That is absolutely brilliant, Gordon. Brilliant!"

Though he was flattered, he was a little annoyed. "Ms. Weber, please. I asked you to wait until you had seen all five."

"All right, then. Let me see the other two."

Boggs completed his presentation, then sat and took a deep breath.

"Okay, Ms. Weber. Is it still number three?"

"Positively. No question about it. Good work, Mr. Boggs."

41

September 19, 2010

Presidential briefing room: NORAD

Those present: President Robert Jordan; Secretary of Education Halley Weber; General of the Army, Pap Renkins; FEMA Director David Riley; Presidential Press Secretary Gordon Boggs.

"Mr. President," David Riley began, "we have three orders of business this afternoon. First, the briefing on our overall national status. Second, the status of the internment projects' and third, the CDC's assessment on antivirals and the vaccine.

"I'll cover the general national status, General Renkins and Mr. Boggs will report to you on the internment project, and then Madame Secretary Weber has information for you as well with respect to the internment process," Riley said as he stood up from his seat.

"On a national scale, estimates now have projected that over three million people have become ill. Of those, roughly thirty percent have lost their hearing. The CDC says it is like trying to contain an epidemic of the flu. In short, nearly impossible, even though all air travel has ceased and there are no longer threats of new, outside sources coming in, or any Americans taking it out. Since the epidemic began here, air travel isn't a big factor in the ongoing new cases.

"The government Internet site seems to be working well. Nearly seventy-five percent of the country is online at some time during the day. We can continue to use that resource, though now we have the problem of that reporter, Brody, and his Blogs. He's putting out information daily and encouraging others to come on board and say what they have to say. As you can imagine, no one is singing our praises.

"He's already started to question the Hearing Habitat projects. My opinion, since we can't shut him down entirely on the Internet, is that maybe the FBI ought to pay him a visit, though that could be very dicey as well.

"The state control of the epidemic is still a huge mess. Each county is still treating everything differently. The good news, though, is that a lot of people are just staying home. The few hearty souls who are still operating seem to be those 'community-minded' types who own Mom and Pop grocery stores, or small community clinics to care for those in the early stages.

"Other than those types, most offices have closed. The National Guard is trying to keep up with food distribution, but it's getting worse by the day. MRIs are running extremely low.

"On another note, one I don't think any of us anticipated: There has been a run on the bank, of sorts. Health insurance and life insurance companies are reporting record claims. In fact, some of the smaller firms are threatening bankruptcy. They say there is no way they will ever be able to pay all the claims."

The large, cold granite and concrete room was absolutely still. None of the members at the table had a comment, each staring into space, trying to visualize the chaos on the outside.

President Jordan sat at the head of the table deep in thought, making notes on a pad in front of him.

"Thank you, David. This is truly a grim scenario.

"However, this country has undertaken things of far greater magnitude and accomplished tasks that everyone thought were impossible at the time. Remember the months following Pearl Harbor? Nearly all of our Pacific fleet was devastated, and we had very little war capabilities at the time; but somehow, within a year, we were assembling one hundred and fifty B-29 Bombers a week.

Riley just nodded. He knew the President's comparisons weren't even close. Nothing like this had ever been attempted anywhere. *As horrendous as it sounded, the internment of the Japanese was the closest they'd ever come to a massive relocation like this.*

"Every able bodied man, woman, and child in this country was working in some manner related to the war effort. No, David. We can do this. We have to, which brings me to General Renkins and Mr. Boggs."

Jordan looked at the General first and then his press secretary. The General stood up and walked across the room. He pulled down a projection screen and then walked back to the table where he turned on a laptop with a Power Point presentation.

"Sir. As you can see, these are the prototypes of the centers. Each is strategically located around the country. No group will have to travel any further than eight hundred miles. Mr. Riley and I calculate that in three weeks time, we'll have them all up and running to one degree or another.

"My estimates right now are approximate, but FEMA trailers will accommodate about half of the total camp populations. The rest will be a combination of Army tents and quick-tilt barracks with plastic roofing. The one thing we have in our favor right now is the dry weather, which should remain fairly static for the next two months, anyway.

"The armed forces will operate food and medical facilities at each camp. We've calculated that the cost of food will be about ninety cents per person per day, but then costs aren't our problem right now. Most of the camps have been located near Con-Agra agriculture sites, so that will help.

"We even anticipate having the internees working the farms near the camps, much like they did with the Japanese during World War II.

"Each center will have four medical facilities, six mess halls, and enough bunking for two shifts; one shift will work days, the other nights. Otherwise, we won't have the facilities to handle them all.

"Likewise, each camp will use the mess halls when a shift isn't eating, for 'education' as Secretary Weber and Boggs call it. She'll expound on that, I'm sure.

"We also plan on patterning the management of the camps after the prison system where some internees will be used as 'trustees,' so to speak. They will help with most management tasks outside of the security system, of course. They will also help with the further, ongoing construction of housing. The barracks and mobile facilities are only going to be a stopgap measure for the start.

"The good part of this plan, after the most difficult part, which is, of course, going to be convincing these people to go and the transportation itself, is that each camp will require only a hundred troops for security, management, and other logistics. Like you said, sir, and I agree: It can be done. Sir, I will go over the rest of the particulars in our private meeting this evening."

"General Renkins," President Jordan said, "not to interrupt, but how will security be constructed. What will keep them in?"

The General looked at the President as if to say, *Now that's a dumb question.* "Concertina wire sir. Good old barbwire, what else?"

As soon as he'd said, "What else?" he knew he'd incurred the President's displeasure.

"General, are you saying like in Guantanamo?"

"Precisely, sir. Anything else would take too long."

The President swiveled his chair around—facing away from the group—cleared his throat, and seemed to be taking several deep breaths. After a moment, he turned back.

"Well, I guess that brings me to the obvious. How does that marketing plan of yours work? Mr. Boggs, how are we going to convince all these people that they *should*, no wait, make that they *want* and *need* to go to these happy camps, or Hearing Habitats? You're the marketing and media whiz. You've shown us a couple of posters, but I don't see how the whole thing lays out."

"Thank you, sir," Boggs said as he stood up to use the same laptop the General had turned on.

"Well, it's not as difficult as it appears. Actually, it all began with the name. Now sure, some people will see through that, as it appears this reporter Brody has. Habitat has a sort of warm and fuzzy sound to it. I borrowed it from the Habitat for the Homeless organization.

"Please look to the screen, Mr. President," Boggs said as he began to unveil what amounted to an advertising campaign.

"When I was in the media, we had what was known as Q scores. Those were numerical ratings of the 'likeability factors' of various celebrities. The higher the score, the more believable, honest, and appealing that particular actor or celebrity was perceived to be. All kinds of Hollywood people and marketing types used those Q scores for various reasons; like whom to cast in a certain movie or who would be a good spokesperson for some product."

Boggs clicked his handheld mouse and another slide appeared. It was the by now familiar picture of Wilbur Mulrooney.

"I'm sure you'll recognize Wilbur Mulrooney with his walrus-like mustache, pudgy face and amiable disposition," Boggs said.

"Mr. Mulrooney's Q score is among the highest in the business at a ninety-three. That means he is perceived by ninety-three percent of the population as likeable, but more importantly, he is perceived as truthful and dependable. In other words, people think he has integrity. They believe what he says and they buy lots of the products he sells. Of course, whether he does or not isn't important. It's only vital that he is *perceived* that way."

"Very interesting," Jordan said. "Please continue."

"Yes, sir. I won't take up this time now to show you the other people who will be involved. At this juncture, it is sufficient just to say that you know them all, they are all celebrities and they all have very high Q scores. Each of them will be a spokesperson. They will be what I call the traffic controllers."

"Boggs, what do you mean by that?" the President asked.

"I mean, they will appear on posters, Internet sites, television, et-cetera, et-cetera. They will be our promoters. They will convince the people they need and want to go to the Hearing Habitats."

"And just how will they do that, Boggs?"

"Well, we don't have the time right now, sir. I can go into detail tonight in our private session, but I can tell you all this: It's really all marketing one-o-one. How do the cigarette companies convince people to smoke something that they know is going to kill them?

How do the makers of fine scotch convince people that they are more sophisticated than others, if they drink that particular brand?

"Sir, certainly you know from running a presidential race, just how important perceptions are?"

Just then there was a knock on the door and a voice from the intercom: "Mr. President. It's urgent. I'm going to unlock the door. You need to come with me immediately."

"Okay, people. This meeting is adjourned. Ms. Weber and Mr. Boggs, I'd like to see you in my quarters in two hours."

The evening of September 21, 2010

"Ladies and gentlemen. I present Gordon Boggs, the President's press secretary," the news announcer said.

It was six o'clock prime time and Gordon Boggs was about to deliver the most important message of his career. He knew that from this day forward, he would either be the face of a great solution, or an incredibly inhumane government action—another wholesale incarceration of innocent American citizens. His name would forever be linked in the minds of millions upon millions of people as either a hero or a despot.

Yes, he stood in front of a large American flag and the symbol of the executive branch, an eagle with two crossed arrows; but it was his face, his name, and his voice that everyone would remember. Besides, he was hoping that it would all work out, and he could get a great deal of the credit someday. In his mind, it was certainly a roll of the dice.

He doubted there was a household in the country that wasn't listening or watching his message, either over the radio, television, or via a live stream on the Internet.

"My fellow Americans," he began, as they always do. "Tonight I come to you with hope. Hope not only in my heart, but also in my mind, for *I* have *great* news for those of you who have contracted this insidious disease, a plague that threatens our entire way of life."

He emphasized the "I" just slightly.

"If you have this disease, or know someone who does, then you will understand more than any of us, the importance of communicating.

"You will be experiencing a life-altering impairment, a handicap far beyond what most people will experience in their lives. You are deaf, or soon will be. My heart goes out to you and your loved ones."

Boggs paused for effect and the television cameras scanned the press corps. Some were now beginning to dab Kleenex at their eyes; most were visibly emotional.

"Today I am here, along with General Renkins," he said as he pointed to the General seated nearby, "to bring good news to you, my fellow Americans."

At that point, Boggs turned and a curtain pulled away behind him to reveal a large color poster with a logo bearing the script, Hearing Habitat. Surrounding the words were graphics of green pastures with large oak trees and big puffy white clouds hovering in a crystal blue sky above.

"I present to you, Hearing Habitats."

The press corps gazed at the poster as if in a dream state and sighed, although they also didn't know what was coming.

"Fellow Americans, it is now estimated that three million of *us* have already lost our hearing, and there will most certainly be many more. We are at a crossroads in history. Our President, against all his better wishes, instituted a prioritized system of martial law. Some of you have been affected more than others. Whereas before, we only had limited options, we now have a choice. We are rapidly developing Hearing Habitats where, on an immediate basis, you will be able to go to learn sign language and lip reading. There will be classes taught by experts from the foremost deaf organizations in the country. You will be fed and even receive medical treatment as needed, and every individual will receive free hearing aids. Of course, we are working on a cure to reverse the insidious effects of this disease, and that cure, when it comes, will be distributed through the networks of Hearing Habitats.

"As you can see by this visual, Wilbur Mulrooney was intimately involved in these new ideas. In fact, he will be sitting on the board of directors who will be managing the Habitats.

"It will be costly for your government, but it is imperative that you be given the opportunity to be able to communicate, to once again join normal people in normal lives. It has now been estimated that somewhere between sixty and seventy percent of the population will not contract the disease, just because of their genetics. Of course, there is no way of knowing who those people will be.

"In a moment, General Renkins, the second in command of the Army, will address you with more of the particulars. Also, please go to www.hearinghabitat.gov./for more complete details. Thank you for listening, and may God be with you all and with the United States of America."

42

*H*op and Nate sat in front of the television. They were both stunned. Neither could speak as General Renkins began to lay out the plans to transport people in the western states to Nevada and New Mexico using Amtrak trains, busses, and the Southern Pacific railway cars.

According to Renkins, the transportation and the "accommodations" at the Hearing Habitats were all free, compliments of the government, which of course, helped to keep it looking more like an invitation than an order.

The advertising campaign had all been brilliantly conceived. It had been designed to make those who had any hesitancy to actually feel left out if they didn't join in.

It had been planned so that it appeared that the most believable celebrity in the country was the innovative and benevolent creator of the entire concept.

It was a combination of deception and peer pressure.

Boggs had enough experience in advertising and the media to know the six criteria that people use to decide whether something is true or not, at least by American standards. Most people "filter" their information through these criteria, which are: consensus, consistency, authority, revelation, durability, and science.

Of the six, science was the most neutral, at least if it was based on rigorous testing.

Boggs had covered all the bases. His message was consistent across the country. There appeared to be a consensus, at least that's what the government and Mulrooney said, so that certainly lent authority to the messages. And then there was the science—the promise that there would be a cure that the best minds in the country were working on it feverishly.

Those who were located in the Midwest would be given transportation to Hearing Habitats in Oklahoma and Arkansas, and those from the South and Northeast would travel to Kentucky. The migration would begin in two weeks as soon as the Habitats were fully equipped with medical centers, housing, and classrooms.

The advertising visuals, of course, intimated that those going to the Habitats, would be "visitors." They even implied that their host would be Mr. Mulrooney; and finally, the underlying message, though subliminal, was that all of this was going to be extremely pleasant and that the "visits" would only be temporary.

Hop knew otherwise.

Nate had caught up on his wife, daughter, and parents over the short wave. His father's wound was healing nicely. So far, they were still safe, and none of them had contracted the disease.

Nate had reintroduced his wife to Hop over the ham radio last night before the broadcast. They'd sat in Nate's truck for half an hour. Hop relived some of his experiences with Stella, and she told him she had been starting a new communications class until all this happened.

The three decided to communicate once a day, after each day's news announcements. Hop wanted to brainstorm with Stella prior to each of his Blogs. He was now writing a lengthy update on government activity, news about the vaccine, and anything else he felt like sharing about martial law, the government, and the deaf.

One thing the three immediately agreed upon was that the Habitats were a scam. That people would not be leaving them anytime soon and that it was doubtful that the government's "education" plan would even work.

From his many years as a syndicated columnist, Hop had contacts everywhere, though admittedly, sources had dried up over the last week, if only because there was no public transportation and those who could drive their own cars mostly stayed put indoors.

Landlines and cell phones were still the best communications tools, as long as his sources could still hear. Some of them in local governments had already contracted the disease.

His source in the Pentagon was now avoiding him, but he still knew a few people at the CDC and the FBI, as well as some local law enforcement officials.

His primary source, though, seemed to be sharing information with other writers across the country that were in the same situation he was. Some of them had also started their own Blogs—*writers must write—reporters must report,* he thought.

Boggs and Renkins had certainly caught him by surprise—they'd caught everyone by surprise. Who could have conceived it would come down to this? Not even Hop had given this idea any thought.

Most people were too young to remember the war and the internment camps. It was an ugly piece of history that belonged in glass cases, not to be dwelled upon—but not to be forgotten, either.

On another note, waiting for calls from his sources, Hop finished up his daily Blog:

September 24, 2010
Hop Brody Network Blog

'My fellow Americans.' How many of you are sick to death of that introduction? Raise your hands. I don't have the bacteria. If I did, I still wouldn't be climbing onto an Amtrak train to New Mexico. Hummmh, let me see, what image does that conjure up? Millions of people innocently climbing onto railroad cars?

What in the world is a Hearing Habitat? I don't know about you, but doesn't that smack of ad talk, marketing mumbo jumbo? What in the world is a Habitat? For those of you who watched on television, did you see that pristine pastoral setting on their poster? I don't think there are any pastures like that in the New Mexico desert.

I just want to alert you to stay tuned, because I'm going to investigate this further and let you all know what's really going on.

On a side note, my sources tell me the Canadian Mounted Police shot and killed two Iranians they suspected of terrorism. No details other than they had been pursued after a routine crossing at the Canadian border up near Montana (strange coincidence). Autopsies showed they both had the bacteria. Canadians are already very spooked about all this and, of course, completely closed their borders weeks ago.

The only evidence they found to suggest terrorism, other than their nationality, was a note one of them had written in Farsi. It simply read: "We will turn Americans against themselves. There will be total chaos."

Well, dear readers, the plot thickens. I don't know about you, but that sounds like a terrorist threat. Just remember, all of this started in Troy, Montana, only 90 miles from the Canadian border.

End of September 24, 2010 Blog. Hop Brody.

43

"You know what, Nate? I think you and I had better stay close together. I wasn't having any problems when I first started my Blogs, but I've got a feeling that won't last too much longer—now that I'm blasting the powers that be over this Hearing Habitat bullshit. I also don't think we should stay here any longer."

"I agree, Hop. What do you suggest?"

"One of my fishing buddies has a cabin about ten miles out of town. There's no phone or electrical coming in; he uses a generator. That should be perfect—no way to track us. I can drive back in close to town in the mornings to log onto the Internet wirelessly and send my Blog.

"We'll grab a bunch of supplies this afternoon and use your truck. We'll still be able to use your ham radio as well."

"Sounds like a plan to me. We better stock up on Pepto Bismol, too. Could be a rough week or so from what I've seen. My only worry is it won't be long before I won't be able to hear, either. We better buy a lot of note pads and pens as well. You'll have to eventually talk to Stella for me."

"Hey pardner. This is all gonna work out. Trust me. I'll take care of you."

Next day, September 26, 2010

There were only three people working at *The Park City Record*: Tom, the editor; Wilma, a clerk who had nothing better to do at home; and Randy, the janitor who already lived in the basement.

As the two men, both in dark suits approached Wilma's desk, she smiled.

"Hello, gentlemen. What can I do for you?" she asked.

Both men looked around the room suspiciously, then one spoke up, thrusting his badge in her face, "Agents Siskind and Harper, Miss. FBI. Can we speak to Mr. Brody?"

"Yes, I can see that," Wilma said looking at the badge. "Sorry. Mr. Brody's not here. Only Tom the editor is left and, of course, me and Randy."

Wilma wasn't necessarily surprised that there were two FBI agents looking for Hop. He had always been steering up something, enough so that he'd had visits before.

"Do you know where he went, ma'am?" Siskind asked.

"Can't say that I do, Agent Siskind. He might just have gone home."

The agent looked at Wilma then pulled a small notepad out of his jacket pocket and flipped it open.

"Would that be the Aspen Drive address, ma'am?"

"Yes. That would be. He's just on the fringe of the main street, down about ten blocks that way," she said, pointing north.

The two agents turned to walk out then one turned to Wilma and said, "Oh ma'am. By the way, have you ever heard of a man named Nate Bannister?"

Wilma thought for a moment. "Nope. Can't say that I have."

The agent walked back toward her and held out a photograph.

"Does this man look familiar, ma'am?"

Wilma glanced at the photo, instantly recognizing Hop's visitor.

"Nope. Can't say that he does."

"Okay then. Thank you, ma'am," the agent said and the two men disappeared through the doorway and out into the street.

By sundown, Hop and Nate were already out at the cabin bringing supplies inside from Nate's truck: bottled water, canned foods, the short wave, laptop, and Nate's files. It would be enough for a couple of weeks at best. The only reason to move would be Hop's early morning trips to the edge of town to be close enough to the Star-bucks receiver to transmit his column.

By now, Hop had become suspicious enough that he no longer used emails to contact his fellow writers or other sources. Six years before, President Bush had tapped into so many domestic phone calls and emails that he knew someday, they might come looking for him as well.

For the same reason, he'd abandoned his regular cell phone calls. Instead, he used the satellite connection stored in his cabin for just such potential occasions. Hop had his very own dish for his satellite calls.

It would take far too long for any government agents to track him through his Blogs. They'd have to go to his provider to get him shut down; and he knew they wouldn't do that, at least not right away. The Internet was his salvation. Hop knew that was the one thing the government couldn't afford to shut down and there weren't any ways to really control it, at least not in the short-term.

Ahh. What a wonderful tool technology has become, he thought as he pulled out the satellite dish. Eventually, they'd be able to track this, too; but, for now, too many people were too caught up in managing the epidemic to bother with that. He still wasn't that big of a threat, although *that*, he knew, would soon be changing as well.

When the two men finished unloading everything, Hop said, "Well, pardner. This is going to be my last regular cell call. After this, we use the satellite phone. Here, let me show you how to use it. It's pretty simple, phone works the same, but you have to punch in these numbers on this console before you make a call. I'm going to let Tom know where I am."

With that, Hop dialed Tom's office number.

"Tom. It's Hop. Like I told you, we're out at the old cabin. I'll be using the satellite phone from now on, so better that I just call you if we need to talk."

"Hop. There were two FBI agents here a few hours ago looking for you *and* your EPA buddy."

"Shit. I knew it. What did they say?"

"Not much. According to Wilma, they asked for you, then Nate, then they showed her a picture of Nate."

"What did she say?"

"Nothing. You know Wilma. She's had a crush on you for years. She told them she didn't know where you were. She did confirm your home address, though."

"Good. No one's there anyway. She knew that. Give her a kiss for me. I'll get in touch with you soon."

Hop pushed the button on the console and turned to Nate.

"Well, my friend. The Feds came to see both of us a few hours ago."

"Really. Both of us?" Nate said, surprised that he was of interest.

"Why in hell would they be looking for me?"

"Haven't a clue. What did you do?"

"What do you mean, what did I do? I'm just trying to make sense of all this. You know I came to you to try to connect you and Stella."

Hop began putting cans of chili and spaghetti into the cabinets.

"What were you doing before that?" Hop said, sounding as if he were suspicious of his new friend.

"Hop, you know I came to you for help. Before that I was camping in the middle of Nowhere, Montana. The last move I made was to drive here non-stop to meet you.

"What was I talking to Beckman about?" Nate said out loud as he began to pace the cabin floor.

"Let's see. We talked about the CDC taking over. He was giving me grief about the Libby thing again. Hummmh. Wait a minute. I remember him saying, 'I won't preach to you, Nathan, about what you're up against. Just watch your backside.'

"He must've known something—but what? At the time, I just thought he was talking about my reputation as a pain in the government's ass. Maybe not. Shit, I really don't have a clue."

"Nate, don't worry about it. I trust ya."

"Wait a minute. I thought it was odd that the National Guard had sequestered my family in my parents' ranch. At the time, I thought they'd done that to most of the people out there because this whole thing started in Montana. Maybe they were actually looking for me, but why?"

44

Late at night, September 26, 2010

"Mr. President," Secretary Weber began.

"We're alone. Call me Robert and I'll call you Halley, if you don't mind."

"No. That's easier."

President Jordan and Secretary Weber sat in the President's personal quarters down the hall from the briefing room. It was as nice as the circumstances allowed. The Air Force personnel weren't accustomed to having dignitaries in for extended visits.

There was a queen size bed, dresser, couch and chair, and a few lamps alongside a small desk. The President's staff had added the large screenTV, the computer, radio, and various other touches—mostly emergency equipment, including the "football," as the briefcase was called. The football was the emergency phone the President or a Secret Service agent carried at all times when the President wasn't in the White House. It contained the codes to launch nuclear weapons—the true weapons of mass destruction.

Weber sat in the large chair and the President sat across from her on the couch, a small table separating them. In front of her was a briefcase filled with papers. She pulled one out.

"Robert. The General talked about transportation being the most difficult task. Mr. Boggs said it was the marketing, or getting them on the trains. I say it's the training—or the retraining, if you will."

"Go ahead, Halley."

"Well, we don't know how long the hearing loss will last—perhaps it's permanent. We've gotten no feedback from BioGem, and I don't think we will for a while. We don't know ultimately how many people will be affected.

"What we do know is that all of this is beyond most of our abilities to comprehend. We've never faced a situation like this. This is far beyond a simple epidemic where a lot of people get sick or die.

"This could be the end of the way this country exists.

"And the costs are nearly incalculable. It won't be long before there will be a run on the international bank, as well as the rest of the insurance industry.

"Already, our infrastructure is nearly at a standstill. Even if the initial phases of the epidemic are cured or just pass through like a plague leaving some segment of the population standing, but deaf, then we have to design a way to continue to live. We have to learn to communicate with the deaf and they with us if we are to live any semblance of normal lives. My friends at the organization feel that hearing aids are our best bet, at least to start.

"Our financial markets will need to be rebuilt in terms of how they communicate. Lord, I can't even begin to conceive how air traffic and emergency services are going to ever run again.

"However, we do have to take all this a step at a time."

"I agree, Halley. That's why you're here. You're the only one in my administration who has any knowledge or background with the deaf. You're right. We have to figure out a way to run the country, a country where millions of the citizens are deaf, without voice communications. All of us, deaf or not, will have to learn a new way of life."

"Precisely, Robert. So let me tell you what my initial plan includes. I spent a great deal of time with the organization. Everything I learned with them, in struggling to teach my daughter to speak, I have brought to the table for this discussion.

"Of course, teaching a deaf one-year-old to speak is quite a bit different than teaching an adult who has been hearing and speaking all of his or her life. However, there are enough similarities in the challenges," Weber said.

The President stood up.

"It's late, Halley. Want a drink? I've got scotch and white wine."

Jordan walked over to a small portable refrigerator.

"I'll take a glass of white wine, thanks."

For the next two hours, Weber laid out her plan. The President was both fascinated and dismayed. He had no idea the world of the deaf was so complicated, so many competing interests—*not unlike the federal bureaucracy*, he thought.

He heard terms he'd never heard, like: oralism and audism. He now knew there were such people as "Language Planners," the people who make language choices and policies. It was a whole new world unto itself. There were, in fact, entire cultures with subsets and offshoots—all with audiological, linguistic, political, and social dimensions.

Weber knew she could control the new bureaucracy that was about to spring up, because neither the President, nor anyone else in their NORAD command center understood any of it. She would only give him the information she wanted him to have. This would give her the opportunity of a lifetime.

"You know, Robert, there are going to be people who will disagree with what I'm telling you. In fact, disagree is a benign way of saying it. The world of the deaf is a complicated arena with many competing ideas and agendas."

"Frankly, Halley, I never realized this world existed. It's nearly as complicated as Congress and it sounds, just as acrimonious. If I have this right, the big picture is this: Soon after the internees arrive, those that want them will be tested for hearing aids. Then the counselors, as you call them, will begin to assess how well they work. *If* they work."

"If you'll allow me, Robert, I can come up with a detailed plan on how to handle the internees and how we can begin to train them."

"That makes sense to me. The sooner these people can begin to communicate, the better. How long will it take the average person to begin to sign and read lips?"

"We could probably teach you to sign some basics in a few weeks. Lip reading is highly individualistic.

"An average citizen might take longer. It also depends upon how motivated the person is. I'm guessing that these 'visitors' will not be happy in the beginning. They won't be as receptive as they would be in any other setting. Eventually, though, as they begin to realize there is no other way, and that this is their ticket to freedom, they'll come around.

"Halley, we'll talk more about that tomorrow. For now, I like where you're going. I feel like we might be getting a handle on some of this.

"By the way, where in the world are you getting all those hearing aids?"

"A company called Starkey. In fact, they've just introduced a technology called, nFusion. It's fascinating, I have to admit. It involves the use of software that learns. That's all part of my report, sir."

Early morning, the next day, September 27, 2010
FBI Headquarters in Washington, D.C.

Four men were seated at a conference table in front of a window looking out across the city. Agents Siskind and Harper sat with file folders in front of them. This was their weekly briefing with their station chief.

"Gentlemen, we have two orders of business this morning. First, that reporter and the EPA guy. Second, this Segar guy, the BioGem CEO and that Russian scientist. Siskind, what's going on?"

"Sir. We were in Park City yesterday. No sign of Brody or Bannister. Checked the newspaper and Brody's house. No signs of them. Not many people out in the city, either. It's starting to quiet down. There was only a skeleton crew at the newspaper offices.

"We went through Brody's files, but there wasn't anything there really. As far as BioGem goes, that's a cluster fuck. This guy Segar is talking out of his ass. He's all pie in the sky about the vaccine, but can offer no progress reports. I'd say, our best bet might end up being with a foreign country. We'll see.

"We did talk with the little Russian guy, though, and he says they've been barking up the wrong tree all along. I don't know; he's weird. Who knows?

"I had an agent check out the Bannister ranch yesterday as well. All quiet there, too. The captain of the National Guard unit is reporting directly to us now.

"*Goddamnit!* We've got to do better. I know Bannister is involved in this somehow. Why else would those terrorists the Canadians caught have been contacting him?"

"I don't know, sir."

45

It was late at night at the BioGem lab where Dr. Revchenko was working with two other scientists; one a biochemist, the other a specialist, like himself, in nano-technology.

The lab was a large room on the second floor of the BioGem lab in San Diego. There were five rows of stainless steel countertops that covered cabinets below filled with equipment. Each cabinet was 25-feet long and each had four lab stations complete with microscopes, beakers of liquids, and various types of electronic devices for measuring or mixing, or analyzing compounds.

The room smelled of strange unidentifiable odors as vapors drifted out of the beakers of chemicals. Along another wall was a mainframe IBM computer with more than 250 servers stacked in rows. The sounds of the computer fans and the air conditioning system provided a constant drone in the background.

Along another wall were several walk-in refrigerators filled with compounds, drugs, chemicals, and blood samples.

There were no windows in the room and each scientist wore an electronic security badge around his neck with which to open the large steel entry door.

The three men in white coats were busy chattering and viewing a petri dish. Dr. Revchneko seemed more excited than he'd had reason to for the last several weeks.

"Okay! This is phenomenal, gentlemen," he said. "At least now we know we can deliver it."

"Yes, doctor," one of the other men replied. "Our only challenge now is to test it and see if it does affect the cochlear pathways and the amagdyla region of the brain."

"Yes. We know our little nano-nurses," [as Revchneko called them], "can get to the sites, and we know they'll be able to deliver the specific chemical to the specific cells—now it's just a matter of finding out if the cells in the brain respond to the chemicals," one of the scientists said.

Dr. Revchenko's work in nano-technology was finally bearing tangible fruit. For personalized medicine to work, you needed the nano-delivery device, you had to know what receptor sites to attack, and you had to have the actual chemical on board to kill the specific offending cells of any particular disease—in this case, the meningitis bacteria—without attacking any other cells. The reason being, the chemical used to attack the meningitis was extremely powerful and would be toxic to any other cells or tissue.

Dr. Revchcenko had used the Japanese model for building his nano—delivery device. Way back in 1999, the Japanese engineers had already produced a working car the size of a grain of rice. Of course, not many people believed it until they saw it actually operate.

However, Dr. Revchenko's "vehicle," as he called it, had to be much, much smaller than that. It had to be even smaller than a molecule of water. It had to be delivered easily and quickly in a large scale. That's when he'd struck on the idea of producing it in aerosol form. That way, he'd killed two birds with one stone: An aerosol or a mist can be squirted into the mouth onto the cheeks where there are millions of capillaries. That way, he'd bypass the stomach, which normally absorbs more than half of everything we ingest before it ever gets into the rest of our systems, let alone our brains.

The aerosol idea also made great sense because it could be produced quickly using existing pump bottles like people used for breath sprays, or small existing aerosol bottles like the ones people used for car deodorizers—either vehicle would work in the mouth.

These could be distributed rapidly to all parts of the country and could be in use immediately. There would be no need for mass inoculations, which would take much longer and pose many more distribution problems.

Revchenko's version of the miniature Japanese car was a robot whose diameter was less than 1/1,000 the width of a human hair. Millions of them could disperse the vaccine in a single spray and be taken up in the brain in less than a minute.

The fuel for his tiny robots was the same stuff that powers human cells, ATP. Each molecular dose this robot delivered would only attach to the specific diseased cells in the inner ear and in the brain. Once attached, the theory was that they would kill the diseased cells, just as antibiotics killed virus cells, only on a much more specific and infinitesimal scale—and far faster. That was the only facet of the entire experiment the doctor wasn't sure about—they'd had no chance to test it.

So the doctor had a proven nano-device, a specific way to deliver a vaccine, but an untested vaccine. That was at least a start. He hadn't shared the good news yet with Segar and he wouldn't, not just yet.

46

*G*ordon Boggs' campaign was in full swing almost immediately. HAZMAT crews were sent out in trucks and soon, broadsides were glued to the sides of thousands of buildings, often pasted over whatever was already there.

The government's Web site was rife with the same types of images. None of the television or radio broadcasts ever went on without several mentions of the Hearing Habitats. Although there weren't many people driving, billboards were also covered—practically every visual media was projecting the same messages, and there was Mulrooney's large, sincere smile each time, assuring the populace that everything would be okay.

Boggs knew that repetition would be a key element in the campaign. It was important to indoctrinate people slowly to new ideas, especially radical ones. People tend to be more afraid of losing something than they are motivated by the advantages of giving it up. In other words, people don't tend to change their routines or behavior patterns in the short-term, but they will in the long-term as opportunities arise.

Boggs called it the "How to boil a frog" story or theory. When asked the question, "How do you boil a frog?" Boggs would answer, "Slowly. If you want to boil a frog you don't put him into a pot of boiling water, because he'll just jump out.

"Instead, you put him in a pot water that is comfortable, about room temperature. Then as he becomes contented and begins swimming around, you turn up the heat ever so slightly, and you continue to do that until the frog is boiled."

The whole idea is that the frog becomes acclimated to the higher temperature so slowly, it doesn't realize it.

The previous administration had used the same tactics on American citizens. They'd use the threat of terrorism and national security as the springboard to internal spying on American citizens, phone taps, email traces, and other techniques. Eventually, each new erosion of civil rights was a small turn of the knob until the gas was as high as it would go, the water was boiling, and no one complained one bit.

President Jordan had reversed all that, but now he and everyone else were faced with a truly devastating epidemic—*a threat of complete chaos and the collapse of the government and the law*, Boggs told himself. That was how he rationalized what he was doing.

He would convince people slowly, cleverly, with frequent repetition, that the Hearing Habitats were vital. That it was not only imperative they "visit" but it would actually be a pleasant experience.

He would boil some frogs.

47

September 29, 2010

*H*op had awakened at five o'clock. He was upstairs in one of the four bedrooms of the 2,200 square foot cabin. Nate had taken one of the downstairs rooms.

It was already seventy-five degrees out and he knew it would be another sweltering day. There wasn't a cloud in the sky so it would be perfect for broadcasting his Blog using his satellite hook up.

Hop came downstairs, saw Nate's door closed, and immediately went outside to start his transmission. He set up a small stool next to the satellite dish in a clearing surrounded by giant pine trees about fifty yards from the cabin and was programming coordinates into the feeder when he heard a loud but muffled scream from inside the cabin.

Immediately, he jumped up, ran back to the cabin, and pushed open the door.

Nate sat on the edge of the bunk with the short wave microphone in his hand. Tears were streaming down his cheeks, as he screamed again, "No My God no! Please tell me it isn't true. *Please!*"

Hop ran over to his friend and stood beside him, shaking his head as if to ask what was happening. His eyes were riveted on his friend as Nate dropped the microphone and began to weep into his hands.

"What's happening, buddy?" Hop asked.

"It's Jennifer, my daughter. She's been shot!"

"What? Is she okay?"

"No. Maybe. I don't know. I've got to go," Nate said as he began to rise.

"Wait a minute, pardner. You can't go back there. They're looking for you. Let's just take a deep breath and slow down for a second. How did she get shot?" Hop said, gently pushing Nate back down to the cot.

Nate took a deep breath and pulled his hands away from his face and looked up at Hop.

"That was my father on the ham. I guess the FBI went out there looking for me. I still don't know what the fuck that's all about," he said, trying to catch his breath again.

"Two guys in suits came to the door and said they were looking for me. They threatened my dad and told him if he didn't tell them where I was, they would take the whole family in and lock them up."

"Oh shit. Then what happened?"

"Then he said Stella came out with Jennifer to talk to them, to try to calm them down, try to convince them they didn't know where I was. That's when my dad got his .45 from upstairs and brought it down.

"I guess when they saw him coming, they drew down on him and one of the Fed's guns went off by accident. It hit Jennifer. Oh my God, I've gotta get back there."

"Nate, you can't go back there. The FBI's waiting—somewhere."

"I'll have to take the chance."

"Man, you're sick, too sick to drive five hundred miles."

"I don't care. I can manage."

"All right then. Jesus, you're stubborn. But you can't go without a plan. Even if the Feds aren't waiting, there are the guardsmen."

"I'll figure it out on the fly. By the time I get there, I'll know what to do."

"Okay, but you've got to take my cell. Here's my number on the satellite phone. Stay in touch all the way. Also, you're gonna need gas. Probably won't be any stations open between here and Billings.

"Take some of the MRIs as well, and I'll load up a few gallons of water. That'll get you there and then some. If I think of anything, I'll call you. God bless you, man," Hop said as Nate began gathering up his things.

48

First Journal Entry

I hadn't traveled more than 100 miles when it started in earnest. I was losing my hearing. It wasn't like it was a surprise. I had just been ignoring the inevitable, which had been easy under the circumstances what with everything that was happening to and around me.

Though I knew it was coming, there was a reprieve of sorts. Thank God for small favors. The nausea was gone, I hadn't experienced the vertigo in two days, and my fever had subsided. I no longer felt any of the physical symptoms.

All the way through the rest of Utah, I kept turning up the radio, at first not realizing what was happening. My world resided entirely within my mind as I crossed through the northern part of the state, not even glancing at the stunning landscape that was passing.

Jennifer. My daughter was all that I could think about. Although Stella finally convinced me that she was going to be okay, my imagination was running wild and I tried not to envision just how bad her injury might be.

The thought of killing the FBI agent, although I knew I wouldn't actually do it, was my only diversion—strangling the bastard helped me to keep my mind off Jennifer.

By the time I'd crossed into the southern tip of Montana, my hearing was completely gone. At first, for maybe an hour, there was a slight ringing, but nothing else. During that hour, I panicked. The thought of being deaf, of never being able to hear my wife's voice, my daughter's voice, music, the birds—everything—caused me to break out in a sweat.

I could feel my heart starting to race, my blood pressure going up and my breathing becoming shallow. For the first time that I could remember *since I was a kid, I was really scared, but then even all that diminished as my thoughts drifted back to my family.*

It's easy and unemotional now to recount it. At first, I banged my fist on the dashboard of the truck. I turned the volume on the radio all the way up. Nothing. It was a very strange feeling. I honked the horn several times then shouted to myself in the cab with the windows rolled up—nothing, with the exception of the vibrations I could feel inside my skull as I yelled.

By the time I was 70 miles inside the state, I realized I hadn't seen any troops. I hadn't seen anything but the serene, tranquil country that is Montana and that sky you can't find anywhere else on earth.

Without the purr of the engine droning in the background; without the sounds of country western music whining out of the radio; without the familiar loud hum of the large knobby off-road tires dancing with the pavement at 80 mph, I began to calm down considerably. In fact, I was beginning to like the fact that I didn't have those distractions. I began to realize just how much static there is in the world. My thinking began to clear up as I sucked in the astounding landscape with only my eyes—a brilliant moonlit night was passing almost in slow motion before me without the disturbances of sound.

I looked down at the seat and smiled as I saw the cell phone sitting there—obviously, now it was worthless. I would have to wait to have Stella put in a call to Hop.

As I continued to glance back and forth from the oncoming highway and the cell phone, I even began to laugh, to think how important that damned thing had always seemed to me, to so many people.

The more I thought about it, the more I realized I didn't really have anything to say to Hop—not now anyway. If Hop had anything to say to me, I would know he'd called by the "missed call" message on the phone's screen. I even began to console myself about my new deafness by thanking God that I could still see. As long I had sight, I told myself, I would be fine—I'd get by somehow.

Then I realized the ringing was gone. Now there was nothing. It was as if I'd been locked in a recording studio where no sound came in or escaped. In this case, however, it was even more silent, because I couldn't hear my own movements; my own breathing even.

At that point, I noticed I was coming up on a sign. I slowed the truck down to about 40 mph. It read, "Yellowstone National Park, Next Four Exits."

Exhausted, I pulled into a cheap motel to get a few hours of sleep. That's when I decided to keep this journal. It would be a way to capture the beginning of my new life. I was afraid I wouldn't be able to share anything with Stella, Jennifer, and my parents unless I made notes about my journey and my feelings.

I had gone from Utah, through the western parts of Wyoming, nearly due north, the entire trip. Now I'd be entering the Grand Tetons, the stunning forests of Yellowstone, then up through Cody, Powell, and finally to Billings, and still I had not seen a living soul. Nevertheless, I kept vigilant, especially as I drew closer to Billings. Soon, there would be National Guardsmen; there would be some sign of life. I slowed the truck down to 50 mph. The Feds would have a description of my Ford and my plates.

Before entering Billings, I pulled off the road into the woods, then got out of the cab, took the binoculars out of my backpack, and climbed up on a ridge overlooking the city limits. There, I crawled the last few feet to the edge and peered down through the high-powered glasses.

There was no movement. I scanned from side to side as far as I could and still no people, no guardsmen. Looking down Highway 240 as far as I could see onto the horizon, there were no cars, no horses.

I decided it was safe to continue, at least to the first rise on the highway, at least until I could again scan the distance for any signs of the guardsmen.

I continued in that manner to the east all the way until I could see my parents' ranch and then, suddenly, there they were—not a guard unit as I'd guessed there would be, but two black Fords—government issue. From a hill about half a mile away, I could see several men standing on my father's porch. Some of our horses were out back and out on one of the grazing meadows there were still some cattle munching grass.

I guessed—actually, hoped—that my family was inside. Was Jennifer still there? Had they come with an ambulance? It just all seemed too quiet, even beyond my own deafness. It also seemed odd that these two men were the only signs of life in the last 200 miles.

Hop had given me his .357 magnum. It was loaded and sitting next to the cell phone on the seat. I pulled myself up onto a large rock and finally decided that Hop was right. I needed a plan. Now that I'd arrived, what would I do? How many of them were there? Were there more men inside the house?

I realized as I sat there that I would have to say something to Stella, to my parents. I'd have to tell them I couldn't hear. I'd have to get them to go along with whatever plan I had.

I wondered how I sounded. After all, I'd gone deaf, but that didn't mean my vocal cords weren't working. I began talking as if I were talking to Stella. I mouthed words dramatically with my lips as if that would make them clearer.

Testing, testing, one, two, three, I said, as if I were doing a mike check. Of course, I could hear nothing. I could feel a vibration deep inside my head, but I had no way of knowing what I sounded like.

I'd seen plenty of deaf people in movies struggling to talk normally. Sadly, they were very difficult to understand with their guttural mumblings, with their words all smeared together into a sort of vocal stew. However, those people usually portrayed people who had been deaf all their lives. They didn't have the benefit, as I did, of 41 years of hearing, so I might sound okay. My brain would still have a memory of the sounds and would, I guessed, send the right signals to my facial muscles to move my mouth correctly, to force out just the appropriate amount of wind so that I was neither yelling nor whispering.

In truth, I had no idea. It was all a crapshoot at this point as was any action on my part. Then, I began thinking of my father, how he'd always told me from his Marine Corps stint to "Overcome, improvise, or adapt." I decided to do all three.

I would drive the truck up the dirt drive to the house as if nothing in the world had happened, as if I were delivering a pizza. They wouldn't expect me to come here and they certainly wouldn't expect me to just drive up as if everything were normal.

I would tuck the .357 in my belt above my back pocket and I would approach the two men on the porch. If they did not draw down on me in their surprise, as I hoped, then I would pull out the magnum and tell them to put their guns down on the chair—assuming they would understand whatever came out of my mouth.

And that is exactly what I did. Driving deliberately and slowly up the drive, I could see one of the men in a dark suit, pulling out a cigarette and then glancing nonchalantly at me. The other turned slowly, a cigarette already in his hand.

As the truck slid up to a halt and the dust spit out around the tires, the two perked up slightly, dropping their smokes on the porch and mashing them out with the soles of their black leather shoes.

I took several deep breaths, pulled on my sunglasses, touched the magnum, and got out as calmly as if I was a visiting neighbor bringing some hot apple pie over to the neighbors, which gave me an idea. As I got out of the cab, I immediately reached around into the back of the truck and pulled out the small Coleman ice chest in the back and held it up in front of me.

Drawing closer, the two men squinted into the sun, trying to identify me.

"Cold drinks, gentlemen," I said. Their expressions remained the same. I couldn't tell if they'd heard me or not.

"Cold drinks from town," I said again, trying to force more air out as I spoke.

The two men seemed unfazed and one even smiled as they began to approach me. It occurred to me that they didn't know what Nate Bannister looked like. To them, I could have been a neighbor. Who knew how long they'd been there at the ranch. I was dressed in my usual cowboy boots, flannel shirt, and jeans, which to most people are a friendly, casual look.

As they got within 20 feet of me, I realized they hadn't a clue who I was. I was just about to set the cooler down and reach for the gun, when Stella appeared through the screen door. Oh Christ, I thought. Don't say a word. My eyes darted from them to her mouth then back. It all happened in a split second. I could see her lips begin to form my name as I pulled out the heavy chrome revolver and pointed it at the two men.

"Don't move," I mouthed.

I still had no way of knowing if I was making any sound, but realized the sight of the gun would be sufficient to stop them in their tracks.

Just then, Stella burst through the screen and came running out, her arms flailing in the air in joy, a look of surprise, fear, and delight all mixed into one expression.

Quickly I said, "Stella, can you hear me? Can you hear me?" Then I pointed first to my left ear and then to my right and shook my head, my first attempt at sign language. I was trying to tell her as quickly as possible that I couldn't hear.

As I kept the gun on the two men, I watched her lips intently for any response.

"Of course, I...."

I couldn't make out the rest of what she was saying, realizing that some words don't require much lip movement.

Then I turned back to the two men. Neither looked more than 24 years old.

"Okay you two, put your guns on the ground—slowly." I couldn't believe what I was saying. I was acting out a scene in a grade B western movie.

Each reached into his suit jacket, eyes as wide as silver dollars, slowly pulled out a revolver, and then just as slowly, bent over and placed it gingerly on the dirt.

My guess was that they were rookies, probably sent out to this hot steamy spot to hang around on the very outside chance that a Mr. Nate Bannister would one day show up.

Stella ran over to me, threw her arms around me, and began kissing me all over my face. I could feel her talking, but could not hear her voice.

Knowing they could all make out what I was saying, I quickly told the two men to kneel down in the dirt. I didn't want them making a sudden move on me. Then I turned to Stella and said, "Sweetie, I can't hear. I'm in the final stages of the disease. We've got to get out of here. How is Jennifer? Tell me she's okay, please."

Stella took my face gently in her hands and made sure she was squarely facing me and then she used a silent gesture I knew immediately to mean, "I love you." Then she mouthed the words slowly, knowing I would struggle to understand her lips. "She is okay. The bullet grazed her arm," she said, as she gestured with her hands on her own shoulder.

"She was more in shock than anything. Your father nearly killed the guy with his bare hands, but they subdued him. I was screaming, your mother was screaming ..."

I cut her off in mid-sentence. "Slow down, honey. Slow down."

She smiled knowingly then began to use more dramatic lip movements. She also began to sign instinctively. Some of what she signed as I tried to follow both her lip movements and her gestures, I could understand—they were obvious motions.

"It was all horrible, but we're okay now. After that, the guardsmen and the two original FBI guys left and were replaced with these two. Why are they looking for you anyway? I don't get any of it," she said.

"I don't know, Stella. All I know is that we've all got to get out of here. I've got to take you someplace safe. How's Dad?" I asked.

"He's all right, but still plenty mad."

That afternoon, I tied up the Feds and left them in the kitchen. We grabbed as many supplies as we could load into the two pickups—Stella, Jennifer, and me in mine; and my father and mother in the other.

I had Stella call Hop on the short wave before we left. She told him we'd be there in a couple of days, that we'd join him in the cabin. It would take longer to get back, because we would have to stay off all the highways and take as many back roads as possible. The two agents would untie themselves eventually and alert others what had happened.

Jennifer sat next to me with her favorite stuffed bear in her lap, her arm bandaged up and me with my arm around her shoulders until my arm finally went completely numb. I kept looking in the rear view mirror to make sure my mother and father were right there with us.

PART

III

49

Three months later
Thanksgiving Day, 2010

The giant Southern Pacific diesel engine grunted and squealed to a standstill in the northeastern New Mexico desert; behind the engine, thirty-five gleaming silver passenger cars extended to the horizon; the final car another General Electric diesel engine.

In each of the twenty-five double rows in each of the thirty-five cars, faces were pressed to the windows seeking a hint of some oasis among the brambles, sage, and cactus but otherwise barren sand that extended as far as the eye could see in all directions.

The engineer pushed a button that set off an obnoxious air horn signaling their arrival to the guards at the Portales Hearing Habitat.

In reality, the camp wasn't in Portales, a small city near Clovis to the northeast, nor was it in Roswell, a city to the southwest known for its alleged alien visitors and home to a supposed secret government cover-up of the visit, as well as a tourist site to mark the exact spot where the extraterrestrials supposedly landed.

The camp was located 175 miles from both towns and 300 miles away from anything else resembling civilization in the other two directions. The faces pressed to the windows straining for any sign of habitat could not see the compound, for it laid directly in front of the engine and covered the equivalent of twenty football fields laid end to end.

Outside the train, National Guardsmen walked alongside holding up large signs that read: *Visitors welcome to the Portales Hearing Habitat. Please disembark through the front doors of your cars.*

There was no one barking out orders through a bullhorn, no intercom announcements on the train. Inside, it was as quiet as the bleak desert outside.

All of the travelers were deaf.

From this point on, they would follow orders through a combination of simple, obvious, hand gestures and written signs posted everywhere. At first, none of the visitors stood up. There was no rush to get to the doors and out into the chill late November air. Each visitor sat with a single suitcase in his or her lap—all that they were allowed to bring.

Eventually, one brave soul stood up, picked up his case, and began walking to the front of the car. As he approached the steps and gazed out across the tan expanse and past the Habitat greeter, others slowly joined in, each shuffling in acquiescence toward the door.

One by one they eased themselves down the three steps onto the desert floor.

The first man had dark skin and wore dreadlocks, the next man was slight with a stoop and he wore a yarmulke. After him, an Asian woman appeared, wearing a housedress and sandals; then several Caucasians—males, females, young adults, seniors—they represented the mosaic that was America.

Now that they were deaf, regardless of their ethnicity, gender, or age, they all shared a common bond; they were relegated to the fringes like any minority.

In his mind, the man with the dreadlocks now had the proverbial three strikes against him—he was black, old, *and* deaf—a minority trifecta. He was used to discrimination; used to being marginalized, but this was a new sensation.

His name was Brandy, because that's what his skin color reminded his mother of as he entered the world. Brandy Jones.

Approaching the end of a long sluggish train ride, he thought his heart would be tumbling in his chest as he was confronted with his new circumstances.

Instead, he felt a void of emotion—a resignation of sorts—and that left him lifeless, unable to fight it all, neither in his mind nor on the ground. Perhaps he was just weary—at least as a black man, or African American, as some of his friends wished to be called, people knew without asking questions that he was a man; he was a person of color; he was tall, those appearances were unavoidable and really, the default mode of the viewer—certainly nothing he had to explain.

Now, however, at least by those who would preside over his future—the guards, the government, whomever was hiding behind those chain link fences, those who could and would control him— he was "disabled" and that would eventually have to be explained, if and when he ever got out of here, for he suspected there really was no cure.

Eventually, like holding his breath underwater, he would have to come up for air, exposing the fact that he wasn't a fish, but a less water-*abled* human. He could remain silent when approached; he imagined he could simply walk the other way, at least at first, but ultimately, out in society, his deafness would be visible and he would have to explain a part of himself.

The visitors came mostly from the Los Angeles and Phoenix areas. The Portales Habitat served five western states and soon there would be thousands more just like these first 3,500; from every race and ethnic group, they filed slowly off the train. Their compliance had begun the minute they realized they were being sent out into the vast and featureless desert. They didn't need to wait to see the so-called Habitat to know they were being interred—imprisoned because of their poor fortunes to be among those stricken with the disease—for no other reason than the fact that they could no longer hear.

The only saving grace, most thought, was the promise and the hope for a cure the government had conveyed in all their marketing efforts. Brandy had a feeling that was all propaganda right from the start. He was sullen, bordering on angry, but he reminded himself that this was nothing new. He understood the need to sever the lineage of the disease by isolating those who had it, but he also knew that disconnection would last far beyond the critical stages of contagious.

Being deaf would ultimately just put him one rung lower on the social ladder.

As the first of the visitors were shown the way, they stepped upon a wooden path made of old railroad ties that led nearly two hundred yards away from the train to the façade of the camp. Each of the camps had been constructed and assembled within three hundred yards of an existing railroad line. Each looked similar, though only two were constructed in desert areas. Some were developed in the mountains, some on the great plains—but all were well out of everyday view and none offered much possibility of escape—if for no other reason than it was just too far from populated areas to consider walking away without water or food.

The front gate and the fencing that encompassed the camp were made of chain link. The fence was fifteen feet high. On either side of the massive gates were life-size posters. On the right side was a picture of a grinning Wilbur Mulrooney. Below his picture it read: Welcome visitors to the Portales Hearing Habitat. We love having you *hear* with us.

On the other side of the gate was a photo of President Robert Jordan, waving his hand as if he were the Grand Marshall riding in a New Year's Day parade. Below, it simply read, "Welcome, my fellow Americans."

The government did not want to spook any of the visitors upon their arrival, so no concertina wire was used on the front gates or fencing. That was reserved for the three other perimeters of the camp. In addition, the facing gates and fencing had all been painted a pleasant greenish blue.

At 100-foot intervals, a guardsman would be standing, smiling, holding a sign with an arrow that read, "Proceed to the front gates for further instructions." A large black arrow was painted at the bottom, pointing to the right or left of the wooden path.

The guardsmen did not carry any weapons, nor were they wearing their normal uniforms. Instead, they were all issued jeans, a pair of western boots, and western shirts with white T-shirts underneath.

Once the Portales' visitors walked in, they didn't walk out.

The façade of the camp stretched a quarter of a mile in both directions and the side perimeters were nearly a mile long. Inside, there was a combination of FEMA trailers, mostly shipped in from Purvis, Mississippi, where they had been stored since Katrina; Quonset huts that the Army had been able to assemble quickly; and the rest were temporary plywood structures, like the ones many school districts used while new classrooms were being constructed.

Since there was no bedrock, only sand on which to raise this "community," most of it was built upon quickly poured, crude concrete pads; and the walkways in between the various structures were compiled of plywood, railroad ties, or other castoff materials.

It might have technically been a habitat, but it certainly illustrated no sense of community. Several of the larger structures, the visitors would soon learn, were classrooms. Every hundred yards or so, there was a communal mess hall for meals and all the toilet facilities were construction site Porta-Potties lined up side by side in various locations in the camp—sometimes twenty-five in a row.

As Brandy approached the gate, he turned back and gazed at the line of souls, two by two, who trudged behind him. He noted his own passivity, of which he was now acutely aware, as well as the insufficient demonstration of will from the others—how easily they had been brought to this place without a fight and no revolution in sight or mind.

That's when the two ladies caught his attention. The line of visitors stretched back nearly two hundred yards to the train and about a third of the way back he noticed the two elderly ladies in flowered dresses gesturing wildly with their hands and arms. At first, he thought it might be a disturbance, some renegades, or a fight; but upon further observation, he realized they were signing.

Brandy made a mental note to get closer to the two women and, if possible, be assigned the same quarters.

Suddenly, he was at the entrance gates and just as quickly, he was guided with signs to the nearest structure, a Quonset hut made of tin. He quickly glanced back to keep note of the two women as he walked into the dimly lit quarters.

It was getting close to sundown, perhaps another forty minutes until he would have to rely on the 75-watt light bulbs hanging every twenty feet from the domed ceiling of his new home.

The floor was made of plywood and down each side of the arch of the walls of tin were bunk beds, just like the ones he'd slept in while in the Marine Corps.

Above each top bunk, there was a small plastic window and next to each set of bunks was a vertical steel cabinet for clothes and personal items. As his eyes traced the interior, all he could think was, *No one ever fell in love in this room, and no one ever will.*

At the entry, a sign simply read, "Choose a bunk," which Brandy did. He dropped his suitcase at the foot of the bunk and sat on the bottom mattress hoping that the two women would end up in the same hut. After the first forty-eight people had settled in, the women in the flowered dresses appeared in the doorway—the forty-ninth and fiftieth, respectively. All the bunks were now filled and the two ladies continued their very animated communications.

Brandy couldn't help but noticing that unlike he and the rest, the two women were smiling as they gestured to each other. It struck him as a magical sort of ballet.

As he continued to watch, completely drawn into their private discussion, a guardsman walked down the center aisle tossing note pads and pens onto each bunk—this is how the guests would initially convey their questions, thoughts, or displeasures among themselves or to their "hosts," as they were asked to think of them.

The two women signed, barely aware of the other people in the room.

"I wanted to be hearing."

"Really? I didn't."

"I have friends who didn't as well."

"For me, though, I wanted to leave my deafness behind at an early age in the worst way."

"What changed your mind?"

"I discovered I really wasn't running away from deafness, I was fleeing the deafness that the hearing world had created for me," the taller of the women signed.

"Interesting," the other woman replied, as she began to unpack her things as if she'd just checked into a Hilton Hotel.

Six bunks away, Brandy felt odd, as if he were eavesdropping, but then not really since he didn't understand their gestures, which, at first glance, appeared quite unstructured and random. Upon continued observation, however, he began to see that their gestures were very precise hand shapes and movements, many of which he could see repeated.

Brandy patted the tight wool blanket covering his mattress. He was fascinated with their seeming ability to understand each other in depth with a minimum of effort, almost like talking, only with a beautiful tempo and symbolism about it.

I have to get to know those two women, he thought to himself as he rolled over and closed his eyes; *the sooner, the better.*

"Ladies and gentlemen," the first slide in the PowerPoint presentation began, "Most of you are newly deaf. However, there are those among you who know how to communicate by reading lips, using a hearing aid, have cochlear implants, or know how to sign."

The woman at the head of the makeshift classroom stood in front of a large white screen where the slides were being projected. Her student/visitors could obviously not hear her, so she had to start someplace. Odds were good that most of the people brought to these camps could read, though the government wasn't sure how many of them read English, so the slides were presented in Spanish as well since the Portales Habitat was accommodating mostly people from the southwestern states. And then there was the matter of those who were illiterate. There was no plan for them, as the government was going, as always, on the philosophy of what was best for the largest percentage of people—the doctrine of the greatest good.

That was also one of the guiding philosophies of deaf education in the public schools—English only, which when taken to the extreme, meant the deaf.

The teacher who was assigned this section of the camp had been a long-time friend of Halley Weber, who had contacted her as soon as the government had made plans to build the camps. She, like many others like her, had attended conferences set up in various regions of the country to learn the curriculum—the plan to "fix" the newly deaf by using hearing aids and the teaching of speech and speech reading.

The teacher, Gail Hunnicut, was an "oralist," as was the Secretary of Education. She was also an advocate of English-only education so it irritated her that she even had to use the Spanish language version of slides.

During President Bush's last two years in office, beginning four years before, in 2006, illegal immigration had become yet another hot topic and a problem for the President and the Republicans who were split on how to handle the southwestern borders of the U.S., particularly.

During those congressional battles that also led to many demonstrations and finally full on riots, the English-only movement began to pick up many new supporters.

Those who for years had advocated an English-only society, became more vocal and more powerful.

Within the education system, there had already been many advocates of English-only and, in particular, many of those who taught the deaf were strong advocates of English-only, which included many of the oralists like Hunnicut.

When Congress passed the English-only legislation, even though it was largely ceremonial (some emergency facilities and printed materials had to still be printed in several languages), it provided people in education and in the organization more fuel for their agendas. If you're going to live in America, speak English (meaning, no signing, either). They meant it literally because their schema was to force the deaf to speak, to fit into mainstream America.

Hunnicut clicked her remote control and the next slide appeared. It read, "The government has generously provided Blackberry devices for any of you who wish to use them while you are here. These can be picked up at the mess hall anytime."

Click. The sound of the remote alerted the room to the next slide.

"Until we can begin to make some headway at learning how to communicate, we have provided all of you with pads and pencils. Starting tomorrow, each of you will be issued a hearing aid as well."

Just then, one of the women in the flowered dresses stood up and raised her hand, as a child in elementary school would.

Hunnicut didn't know exactly what to do until she saw the woman signing to her. Hunnicut recognized the gestures as American Sign Language, a language she did not advocate nor understand.

"I'm sorry, ma'am. Do you read lips?" Hunnicut mouthed in a stage dramatic manner.

The woman signed, "Yes," but then also nodded her head. Before Hunnicut could continue, the woman began to sign again, "Yes, I read lips, but don't you understand ASL?"

Hunnicut was becoming visibly irritated.

"I'm sorry, ma'am," she mouthed back almost grotesquely, as if making her lips move in a larger, more dramatic fashion would make her any more understandable. "I do not understand ASL."

The woman in the flowered dress sat down with a sign of disbelief, and began to sign with her friend seated beside her.

"Can you believe it, Maude?" she signed.

"This woman is going to try to teach all these people how to speak. She doesn't even understand American Sign Language. We're all in big trouble if this is the government's plan, at least for these poor folks who can't sign or even read lips.

"We've got to figure out a better way than this feeble, misguided effort, or we'll all be stuck out here for years—maybe longer."

December 5, 2010

Not wanting or having the time to reinvent the wheel, the government modeled the Hearing Habitats' personnel structure after the Japanese internment camps of the 1940s.

An internal security force was set up comprised of a contingent of guardsmen, one non-military government representative, and several "visitors" or guests as they were beginning to be referred to—something the guests themselves despised.

There was a Project Director assigned to each camp who oversaw everything, much like a prison warden or CEO of a company. The director acted as the chairman of the board as well, a board comprised of guardsmen, who served as judge and jury over any camp infractions—stealing, fighting, trying to escape, etc.

Consumer enterprises were eventually set up such as a canteen or barbershop. In addition, there were recreational rooms, a small hospital, classrooms, and a place to worship among the vast array of structures.

When the camp was finally filled, the "community" of Portales had a population of nearly 20,000 people, one of a hundred habitats across the country.

Once a week, instructors or teachers such as Gail Hunnicut reported to the Project Director. In that meeting, the instructors would pass along assessments of the progress or lack of it for her students. She or he would in turn receive updated orders and instructions, which came directly from the President's committee at NORAD.

By December of that year, if no cure was found, Dr. Revchenko, the CDC, and Centers for Health jointly agreed that whatever loose ends of the contagious stages of the disease managed to slip through the nationwide "round up," the disease would run its course within nine months. However, that only included the obvious physical signs of sickness—the vertigo, nausea, etc. There had been no assessment of whether or not the loss of hearing would be cured and, if so, how long that would take.

In essence, the camps were at first meant to slow the progress of the disease and keep it to a minimum of the population. Once that was contained, if a cure was not forthcoming, the camps would make for very convenient learning centers. No matter what happened or what the final outcome of the physical symptoms were, President Jordan knew that the United States could not function fully with a worst-case estimate of thirty million of its citizens unable to hear or speak.

The deaf were already there, a system was in place to educate them, and it was a very convenient way to transmit the political policies of the administration to a captive audience and persuade that population to be compliant to whatever needs the administration chose.

Horatio Amburgy was the Project Director at Portales. He had a background in security and administration, but none in education, and he knew practically nothing about the world of the deaf, other than what his instructors told him.

Gail Hunnicut was the first to meet with him. She arose at five-thirty in the morning, along with the rest of the camp, got dressed, and began the hike nearly a half-mile to the Project Director's office.

It was a cold, windy morning, with a bite in the air that only the desert offers up in winter. As she walked down the combination of plywood boards and railroad ties that formed the semblance of a street, the wind blew sand and brambles across her shoes.

"Come in, Ms. Hunnicut; so glad to see you. Please sit down," Amburgy said as he motioned to a stiff, steel chair alongside his Army-issue desk.

The Project Director's office was only slightly nicer than any of the other "civilians" at the camp. It was one of the original FEMA trailers. This one was a double wide and was outfitted with air conditioning, a desk, file cabinets, a tattered cloth couch, a folding steel chair, and a water cooler.

The other side was the Director's living quarters.

"Thank you, Mr. Amburgy. Since this is our first meeting, I need to give you an assessment of our first week here."

"Yes, Ms. Hunnicut. But since you are my first meeting of all the instructors, before you get too specific, can you help me understand a larger picture?"

"Uh, yes. Yes, sir, of course. What do you mean by the larger picture?"

"I mean tell me what we're really faced with here. What are our biggest challenges, other than the obvious?"

"Well, sir, that might take more time than we have," Hunnicut said, trying to make herself more comfortable on the chair. "However, I can give you the short version to start with."

Amburgy grabbed a yellow note pad and pen from his desk, pushed himself away, and walked over and sat on the couch.

"Go ahead."

"To be quite candid, sir, the government has not planned well for this. I understand that time was of the essence, but generally, the President's thinking was to isolate these people to keep the disease from spreading and then to follow the advice of his Education Secretary, Halley Weber."

"I'm aware of that. My assignment here is based on those goals," Amburgy said.

"Yes, sir. I understand. Those are good goals. I agree. We've even started testing people for hearing aids. Our primary next step is to continue to teach these people how to speak again and how to read lips.

"I am in total agreement with Ms. Weber as to our objectives. The only problem is, we don't have a curriculum or orders on what to do about everything else."

Amburgy made a notation on his pad and then slowly peered over his reading glasses at Hunnicut.

"And what might that 'everything else' *be*, Ms. Hunnicut?" he said as he put his pen down and leaned toward the woman.

"Well, sir, there are so many other issues."

"Issues? Like what?" Amburgy said in a slightly louder voice.

"Well, sir, like the children; like the people here who have always been deaf; like the ones who became deaf because of the disease."

"I'm sorry, Ms. Hunnicut, but I don't understand what you're getting at," Amburgy said.

"Sir, this is a large and complicated challenge. There are children here that are with their parents who were always deaf. There are children here with their parents who are newly deaf. There are children here who aren't deaf but have parents that are, and then there are children here who are deaf, but whose parents aren't.

"And then there are the babies."

"I don't think we're concerned about babies, Ms. Hunnicut. Stick to the adult population. We don't care if babies learn to lip read."

"Okay. Then there is the case of all the people who are illiterate completely. Not only are they now deaf, they never could read English or any language for that matter. It's a real quagmire, sir."

"What difference does it make if some of them can't read? All you're supposed to do is teach them to speak and see if we can't get them to hear something with the aids."

"Like I said, sir. I don't know if there's enough time to go over all of this in one meeting."

"Let me remind you of what our mission is here. There are many people here, as in the other camps, that are very important—doctors, scientists, and even celebrities.

"It is our mission to make these people productive in society once again. If they can't hear, they won't be productive. And, if they can't talk, they won't assimilate back into society."

"I understand sir, but …" Hunnicut was interrupted.

"Ms. Hunnicut, my nephew was born deaf, so I'm not entirely out of the loop here. I remember how mortified my brother was envisioning his only son trying to get along in school and having to sign—looking like a fool or a clown throwing his arms and hands around. It's not what any of us wanted for the boy.

"These people are no different. They aren't going to want to go out into public and begin flailing around like spastic mimes. They are going to want to be normal again, like the hearing people they were. They aren't going to want to stand out; and if they don't want to look like sore thumbs, they aren't going to be productive. That is our mission, plain and simple according to Ms. Weber's goals."

Christmas Eve, 2010
Presidential briefing at NORAD

"Look, I know it's only been a month, but don't you think we ought to be making some progress?" the president asked Secretary Weber.

"Do you mean with the vaccine, sir, or the hearing thing?" she asked.

"The hearing thing? Is that what you call it?" he replied.

"Well, I guess non-hearing would be more appropriate. I really don't like the word deaf very much, sir."

"But your own daughter is deaf, Halley."

"Yes, sir."

"And please quit calling me *sir*. Jesus, we've all been stuck down here for months now. We're past the suit and tie stages. Just tell me that we're making some progress in the camps—er, the habitats, I mean."

"Well, I'm sorry to report that our hearing aid program, what I was hoping would really help us get this started, is not going well, although we do expect, with some more instruction, it will work better overall."

"Do you mean the hearing aids aren't working?"

"No. They're working fine. They're state of the art technology. It's just that most of the hearing loss is too far-gone. We've been monitoring the supervisors in each of the camps and they're reporting less than a five percent improvement in hearing in less than three percent of the visitors.

"However, we were never going to try to rely on those entirely anyway. Our instructors are having more success with the lip reading and many of the people are learning to speak better, though, of course, that doesn't help much, if none of them can hear, other than the teachers."

"Jesus, Halley! Are you sure this organization of yours is right. I mean they only advocate speaking and hearing aids. I'm beginning to think this isn't the right approach."

"I think we just need to give it a little more time."

"What about the implants they advocate?"

"A good solution in any other scenario, especially for the adults, but not in this case. Hell, the operation costs thousands of dollars and, of course, there aren't enough doctors in the country. No, that's only on a case-by-case basis, not for millions of people."

Jordan stood up, obviously irritated and frustrated as he snapped a pencil in half. He paced and then went over to the couch and sat.

"Damnit, Halley, we've got to do better—much better!" he said loudly. "What about this newspaper reporter's Blog—this Hop guy? Boggs says he's forming groups of students who know American Sign Language. What the hell is that all about?"

"Pay no attention to that, sir. He's a nut and ASL isn't the answer. Trust me."

"I don't know, Halley. I just don't understand how spending all this effort to teach people to speak normally again is going to help our problem. Who cares if they can talk but can't hear?"

"Sir. You want people to be as normal as possible, don't you?"

"Do I take that to mean that you feel talking is more important than listening?" the President asked.

The President's question made Weber squirm in her seat. Everything she'd learned through the organization was being put to a test even more severe than raising her own daughter, but it was all she understood—oralism—striving to be normal—fitting into society—learning to speak. That is what had been ingrained in her. She never wanted her daughter to be stigmatized; to appear to be disabled, even though, in her mind, that is precisely what she was—to some extent, a cripple.

When her daughter had been born deaf, the only difference to Weber was that her disability wasn't readily identifiable—no lost or bent limbs, seeing eye dogs, or wheelchairs to give it away—as long as she could be taught to speak and, hopefully, as the organization had promised, with the help of devices, as they called them—implants or hearing aids—she could hear to some extent, she could lead nearly a normal life—though no one in the organization could promise that.

Weber had become so enamored of the work the organization did, that she used her position as Secretary of Education to further that work and that philosophy whenever she could at speaking engagements at schools and parent organizations.

As Secretary of Education, her views carried a lot of weight among teachers, educational groups, and parents of the deaf. She also used that power in a quieter manner as well, helping the organization to funnel campaign funds to those in Congress with like opinions—some legal, some maybe not so legal.

Even when the cochlear implant didn't work as well as she'd hoped, or been encouraged to believe, she pressed on, buoyed by the philosophy and the indoctrination of the organization, but more so from her own ego.

It was just inconceivable to her that her daughter would go through life the butt of so many cruel jokes; the kind the torture and pain only school children can bring to bear when another child is different, worse yet, disabled.

She'd seen other children signing and to her, they might as well have been carrying large signs pointing to themselves that read: Look at me. I'm defective.

The whole signing "thing" was a joke, as far as she was concerned—the children's hands and arms flailing about, struggling to make some sense out of some archaic three-dimensional dots and dashes—not only were they advertising their disabilities, they were acting like clowns.

Halley didn't want to send her daughter to a deaf school, they would only encourage her to sign and, of course, that would send out all the wrong signals to her friends and neighbors, but more importantly to those groups she spoke to. It would destroy her image of herself as an ambassador for the deaf on the road to recovery.

No, it was paramount that her daughter go to a public school and to appear normal—to act normal.

As all the options raced through her mind, Weber realized she'd left the President just sitting there, waiting for an answer.

"I'm sorry Robert. What was your question again?"

"I asked you if you thought talking was more important than listening."

Weber fidgeted again.

"Well, sir," she said, trying to buy some time, "not exactly. I think they are both important. I mean we can't really communicate clearly without hearing and speaking, can we?"

"No. I guess you're right. We can't."

51

I *was feeling the buzz of the wine and so was probably more "talkative" than normal. Being newly deaf, I was probably—no, make that definitely more opinionated than the others in the room.*

The topics ranged from child abuse, to the politics of deaf culture, to the politics of the country in general. We even managed to mix in some religion and sex—the latter, only after the kids went to bed, of course.

Obviously, I understood very little of the specifics. I could do some lip reading, and Stella's expressions and gestures were familiar to me since we'd been married ten years, but the actual signs, strokes, words and sentences were a blur. I didn't know if I was ever going to be able to learn it all, or at least I knew it was going to take some time. Tonight, I cheated and tried to pass notes to the others, but they wouldn't have it.

Even with all that had transpired since July, since the quarantine in Troy—I had to hesitate for a moment and catch my breath—had it been only five months since this all began? Seemed lifetimes.

There were three generations present, my parents being the elders. Then, there was me, Stella, Hop, and our new friends, Gracie and her husband, Bradshaw, and finally, their boy Jacob.

Jacob, like Hop's boy, had been in Stella's class. They were also some of the original escapees from the internment camps—more accurately, they weren't actually escapees in the technical sense that they'd gone to the camps and then departed. They just never went.

They estimated, and we could surmise from the incoming comments to Hop's Blogs that there were close to 50,000 like them—runaways if you will, or as we preferred—Bogg Dodgers—a title we'd come up with just that evening after the alcohol began to soften our inhibitions.

Not unlike the draft dodgers from the Vietnam war, Bogg Dodgers scattered when the powers told them to pack their things and get ready for a trip. It hadn't been long after the initial camps began to fill that some of us figured out the marketing scheme behind the camps and who was ultimately responsible for it all, and the fact that they were indeed camps, not Habitats. Bogg Dodgers seemed as good a term as any and it was easy to say.

Some went to Canada, just as their predecessors had done in defiance fifty years prior. Some went to Mexico, but many of them fled to the mountains, forests, and very rural areas of the country.

Hop had met Gracie and Bradshaw through Stella and now here we all were, one big family.

Even with four bedrooms and 2,200 feet of living space, Hop's friend's cabin was no longer so roomy as when the two of us had arrived, although we did all feel relatively safe and still as hidden as we could hope to be short of living in a cave. Each of us had our chores in addition to providing Hop material for his Blog. I was beginning to feel like I was living in a commune in the sixties.

The fact that it was New Year's Eve and we'd all been working on more than one vintage bottle of wine together made for one of our more spirited discussions.

Jacob had been born deaf just as many around Gracie and Bradshaw had predicted—they couldn't hear, a genetic predisposition, so there was a better than 80% chance their children would be born deaf as well—something for which the two of them suffered.

Even some of their friends who were deaf castigated them for trying to have children; knowing that would likely be the outcome, both had been strong. They'd grown up learning ASL and both were bilingual, so they knew better.

Hop, of course, could hear, as could Stella and my parents. I was the only newly deaf one in the group, so Gracie always argued that we represented a cross-section of the "new" culture—newly deaf, always been deaf, hearing adults, including seniors as well as the very young. Bradshaw always argued that we probably also represented a higher level of education than the general population, but considering his take on things, I didn't always agree.

The one thing we did all agree upon was how poorly, how abysmal, how shamefully, how ineffective the internment camps were being run.

Four months after BioGem had started working on a vaccine, they still had nothing to show for it. America was most definitely an island—an angry, impotent island of varying philosophies and opinions that made the past political and social structures seem downright simple and consensual.

But tonight, we were not impotent—none of us. We all had strong opinions, as you are prone to under the influence of alcohol and the holidays. Ultimately, there was nothing to celebrate coming into 2011, but being free, in a manner of speaking.

This evening, with the wine flowing, we were truly an animated and lively group. Hop and Stella spoke and gestured almost simultaneously. My father and mother were only catching on slowly and a bit reluctantly given their age. Me, I was just beginning, but my heart was in it to the hilt.

I could remember my hearing world. I was 41 years old and had gone through years of education. I was bilingual—English and Spanish as far as my reading skills went—and—I could devour a book a week. This evening, as we all sat sipping our wine after the kids were in bed, our "conversation" centered on the camps and Hop's Blogs. I was the odd man out. It was also obvious that Hop and Stella were speaking simultaneously to their signing, mostly for the benefit of my parents.

Not only were they teaching me gradually, they were reinforcing their own skills, but more importantly than that, I would often catch them signing only, without speaking—and as the days in solitude in those mountains drifted by, I realized they were actually far more expressive using their signing skills than Stella and I had ever been just talking to each other—they seemed able to say more in a shorter timeframe than if they were actually speaking sentences.

It was all becoming quite fascinating and I was beginning to lose my fears and embrace this new mode of communication. Though Stella and Gracie told me it might take as much as a year or more to become proficient, I only took that as a challenge.

From the time I'd been a young boy, my parents had taught me self-reliance. From that independence, I learned I often had to make do with whatever I had at hand—everything from the simplest task of starting a fire in the wilderness without matches, to surviving weeks on end in the forest on just my wits.

"Okay, here's the latest," Hop had signed, and this isn't word for word but ...

"You're gonna love this. I just received an email from a Hannah and Maude (sounds like they're both over 60 with names like that). They are in the Portales camp. Apparently, the government issued Blackberrys to anyone who wanted to use them and these two ladies were among only a few who took them up on it; God, what a sad state of affairs. Sounds like they've already got everyone brainwashed, with the exception of these two grandmas.

"Here's the interesting part of their text—they've all started devising and using their own language—a sort of rudimentary sign language.

"I'll be damned."

52

January 3, 2011

"It's time for me to call in the reinforcements, Dennis," Halley Weber said to the man on the other end of the phone. She'd returned to her own quarters and was pacing the floor for ideas.

"What can I help you with, Madame Secretary?" came the reply.

"Oh, Dennis, we go too far back for you to call me Madame Secretary," Weber said, pacing the room with the awkward satellite phone she'd been given by the Air Force captain.

"I know, my dear. Just having a little fun. What can I help you with?"

Dennis Rohrbacher was the president of the *organization*. He was an overweight, balding man; a rigid conservative, politically, and in just about every other facet of his life.

He'd risen through the ranks from his earliest beginnings in the Texas Chapter to be the most powerful person in the organization— one who had managed to commandeer a strong following among many political and educational groups through its generous donations.

The organization for the deaf and hard of hearing had been started in the late nineteenth century. Their charter was fairly simple: They advocated independence for the deaf and hard-of-hearing through the use of various aids such as hearing aids, amplified phones, cochlear implants, and more recently, infrared televisions and text telephones.

They felt that the deaf and hard-of-hearing have the *right* to speak and become fully integrated into society—a successful member of the larger world.

Most importantly, they promoted the idea that deaf children have the ability to listen and to speak. As odd as that sounded to most people, over the many years of their existence, they had become quite effective at indoctrinating a great many people—particularly parents—hearing parents of deaf children—those individuals who were the most scared. As it turned out, most deaf children were born to hearing parents and so it had been just that much easier for them to press their agenda.

When Halley Weber's daughter was born deaf, she'd gone into a tailspin and her fear had made her ripe for an "organization approach," which meant certain people within the organization contacted her outside the normal mainstream communication avenues—theirs was more of a clandestine political approach where they could not only appeal to her fears about her deaf daughter, but that her daughter would be labeled as a "retard," disabled, and less than normal. And, of course, they also played on her political aspirations as well.

The organization had been around a long time and they knew how to get what they wanted without being very public about it all. Rohrbacher was the constant fuel on that fire—a man driven to obsession about the organization and its agenda. To him, there were no other viable alternatives and he rarely even pretended to entertain any of that dialogue. What made him truly insipid was that he didn't really even prescribe to his own group's philosophy; it had, over the years, evolved into a position of power.

Even he knew that it was imperative never to let "them" see behind the curtain. It was essential never to let the deaf or the deaf advocates see the feeble little man pulling all the levers.

His biggest nemesis, though little known outside the world of the deaf, was a small liberal arts university in Washington called Gallaudet, the only university for the deaf in the world, certainly not much to worry about in the grand scheme of things, as far as Rohrbacher was concerned.

Rohrbacher was beyond arrogant. He was what had come to be called a Corporate Criminal Narcissist with no emotions outside his own vanity.

"You can help me with a better answer," Halley continued with Rohrbacher.

Weber had peaked Rohrbacher's interest. He pushed the speaker button on his phone, stood up, and walked to the window of his office.

"A better answer to *what*, my dear?" he said, genuinely confused.

"The President just asked me if I thought speaking was more important than listening. He caught me off-guard, completely."

"Well, what did you say to him?"

"After I'd recovered, I said that I thought both were important."

"Great, my dear. You're right. That's what the organization is trying to get across. It's extremely important to be able to speak and to hear. Are you forgetting what we've been discussing all this time?" Rohrbacher asked.

"No. No. I guess I just needed someone on my side. I needed to hear the gospel once again. Thanks, Dennis. I'll call you again soon."

"No problem, my dear. And listen; before you hang up, I've just had a meeting with one of the most powerful men in America at this juncture. I think he's going to form a joint venture with us. It'll be good for us and the country."

"Oh, and who is that," Weber asked.

"It's Aden Bartholomew."

"Who?"

"Name's not important dear, but it's Bartholomew. He's the CEO of SatCom, the world's largest cell phone company. Believe me, he understands our cause. He's pointed out how we could form an even more powerful alliance."

"And how's that, Dennis?"

"We advocate devices to aid the deaf, correct?" Rohrbacher said in a condescending voice.

"Yes."

"Well, his company invented text messaging. Actually, *he* contacted *me*. I never realized just how big that had become with the young. My God, some of these kids pound out more than a thousand messages a day. Hell! They hardly even speak to each other anymore. They're the generation that will make carpal tunnel syndrome a household word."

Weber realized she'd been out of the loop herself. The text messaging technology had exploded nearly overnight but she'd had more important things to deal with.

Since around 2006, Blackberrys, Sidekicks, iBooks, and Instant Messaging were actually beginning to supplant vocal conversations, even over cell phones. It was becoming a full-blown addiction, just as Bartholomew had predicted and, of course, encouraged and pushed.

The world, according to Bartholomew, was becoming a "160-character nation," the maximum length of a text message. Everyone, particularly the young, were actually losing their public speaking skills.

According to Batholomew, forty-two percent of North America's cell phone subscribers were now active "texters," as they were being labeled.

Now Rohrbacher was getting excited. He could imagine a day, not far off, when most of the population would be texting each other, rather than talking.

Bartholomew had told him that prior to the camps, back in 2007, there were 500 billion text messages sent and received worldwide, as reported to the public through rival Verizon Wireless. By 2012, the number would surpass five trillion and, of course, that was even before the prognosticators knew about the current epidemic.

Both Bartholomew and Rohrbacher were salivating at the prospects, albeit for two different reasons.

53

Two months later.
March 15, 2011

*O*ut in "the real world"—as those who had been fortunate enough to avert the disease, but of course, not the politics or the emotions of the epidemic, called it—there were new factions and loyalties being formed.

"The real world" consisted of those whom the Bogg Dodgers referred to as, the "Leftovers." Bogg Dodgers living in the hills and forests, out of sight of the government, sympathized with those who'd been tricked, marketed, and coerced into going out into the wilderness—at least to some degree.

They didn't blame the elderly or the children for giving up and giving in, but they had less tolerance for those who were younger, more robust physically and mentally, who trotted like sheep onto the "Habitat Express," as they referred to the trains that took them into desolation and out of the consciousness of the rest—the preponderance of those who never contracted the disease for whatever reasons.

In all, they were ambivalent.

Society had broken into new factions—ones that never existed before the epidemic.

There were the people who never got sick, and then there were those interred in the camps. Then there was the minority, the Bogg Dodgers, followed by the underground government and its enforcers, the National Guard and other military troops who still held reign over most of the larger cities, though it wasn't really necessary to enforce martial law anymore.

Once the government had initiated its powers, it was hard to give them back, at least not all at once and right away. There was much to be said about the control they exerted and the relative calm that ensued after the epidemic passed through.

The official government position was to keep air and rail travel closed, with the exception of "military flights" for purposes of national security. However, the flights deemed militarily important ranged from junkets to joy rides. Likewise, newspapers and other media were strictly muffled; the predominant form of communication now being the Internet, which the government dared not to shut down.

The official position also strictly prohibited anyone in the general population to visit a Hearing Habitat, again for reasons of national security, and the official government edict was to round up the evaders, as the government referred to the Bogg Dodgers, though they never used that euphemism.

In the general population, there were sympathizers, those who had family taken away to the Hearing Habitats. There were those who aligned themselves quite closely to the underground government at NORAD, which were still afraid to come up for air. And there were plenty who believed, as the government kept telling them, that they were still very much at risk, which was the main reason they complied with all of the televised propaganda messages, stayed close to home, and did not involve themselves in any inquisitiveness or curiosity, at least not vocally.

The risk involved what the government admitted were perhaps millions who had not come forward voluntarily and were not necessarily evaders, who might still be moving at will among the population. Still, no one knew if the disease had run its course, or was about to surge into the beginnings of a pandemic—a worldwide epidemic.

There were still plenty of communities under quarantine and the government even went so far as to stage EMT retrievals of people in the quarantine areas who were clean, who did not have the disease and to take them away, just to keep those neighborhoods compliant and fearful.

Occasionally, they lied in less dramatic fashion as well, broadcasting reports of deaf individuals being captured randomly across the country, living among the general populace. Of course, those people apprehended might have already been deaf and never contracted the disease, but that wasn't important. Through its deceptions, the government was able to equate deaf with dangerous, or at the very least, contagious.

In her office at NORAD, Halley Weber smiled as she read the Joint Chief's weekly assessments. She liked the fact that "they" were doing a good job of isolating those who could not speak or hear from the normal folks.

The President still trusted her, even though a month before he'd seemed a bit apprehensive. After her call to Rohrbacher and several others, she had once again found her courage and was now convinced more than ever that she was right—that the organization was right. Regardless of how it was being accomplished, she had to take care of these people—these poor disabled people. She and only a handful of others truly knew what the proper course was.

54

*T*wo months had passed since Stella, Jennifer, and the rest had joined Nate and Hop in the cabin. Nate had made great strides with ASL. He was by no means fluent, but by now he understood the underlying beauty of it all.

The conversations around the dinner table were particularly lively. They often cooked outdoors and ate the bar-b-cued chicken or ribs with their hands. It was messy, eating and talking with your hands at the same time, but no one minded.

Nate often watched in amazement and even some envy when one of the others made a joke and then gazed as the laughter cascaded like fallen dominoes from one to the other through a series of hand movements and smiles.

Nate became more and more observant, carefully watching as thoughts moved from one person to the next and then a reply went in the opposite direction—new questions and statements bounced back and forth like waves intersecting and careening off each other.

Nate likened it to a symphony, but instead of sounds coming from the various instruments, beautiful fluid gestures flowed one into the other and back. Although, at times, it appeared very abstract, Nate was learning that this visual concert was actually composed of complex and very expressive thoughts—it truly was a language with a distinct grammatical structure. In fact, he was astounded to discover that using ASL, he could be capable of conveying subtle ideas and complicated emotions—he could discuss philosophy, music, literature, humor, or wit.

As he became better at understanding and speaking in ASL, he understood his wife who had told him that the visual nature of ASL was much like a smile. You don't have to hear anything when someone you like or love smiles at you. That one simple visual says volumes and warms up your soul like words are hard pressed to duplicate.

At times, he was even embarrassed, once he understood just how much he conveyed to the others in every twitch of his muscles, with every slight raise of an eyebrow, with every body movement. It was as if they were able to eavesdrop on his every thought. He could hide nothing. Even his unconscious movements and facial expressions told the group what he was thinking. At times, it felt like a permanent lie detector machine was hooked up to his body.

Nate learned to slow down, to be more methodical in not only his conversations, but also his chores—he made fewer mistakes that way. Oddly, he was becoming more visual than he'd ever been, realizing that his eyes enabled him to tackle many things at once with just a glance—not something that could be said about hearing.

That night in March, he found Hop working late. He was answering questions or making return comments to the things that had posted to his Blog. Hop set aside three hours late every night, for this was his chore.

Sometimes there were important questions about *sign language*, which Nate had learned was a confusing issue to hearing people. Most people who signed in the U.S. at this point and even before the epidemic used American Sign Language. However, there were those that had been taught something called S.E.E., or Signing Exact English. The two were about as far away from each other as most distant stars in the heavens.

S.E.E. was a very rudimentary signing of exact letters and symbols. It carried with it no emotions, no subtleties, and no love. One could not, for instance, use a double entendre or paraphrase anything. It was what it was, exact letters, archaic at best.

Many people had mistakenly believed that ASL was English conveyed through signs. Nate learned that ASL is not a form of

English, that it has its own distinct grammatical structure. It's obviously based on the visual, needing no auditory tones.

Nate climbed the stairs to the room where Hop did his work and knocked on the edge of the open door.

"Come in," Hop signed.

Nate stepped in. *"Hey, pardner, want to see an interesting letter?"* He signed.

"Sure. What do you have?"

"Come over here and pull up a chair," Hop gestured, turning the laptop so that Nate could read the screen.

The letter was from a college student who was heading up one of the groups Hop had encouraged several weeks ago. He knew from working with Stella that ASL had, for some time, become a quiet sort of underground hip thing to know. In fact, so many students had begun showing an interest in it back in the early 2000s, many of the colleges and universities had started offering classes, classes that qualified as a second language. Instead of taking French, Spanish, or German, many students were opting for American Sign Language.

Knowing that, Hop got the idea to enlist their help through his Blogs to begin teaching others, not only the language, but deaf culture, which was far more complicated than the language.

"This one is really interesting. Reminds me of some of the work that Stella is interested in, Emotion Recognition Software. Here read it," Hop signed.

"Dear Mr. Brody:

I think what you're doing is wonderful. Many of my friends, along with me, have pretty much stopped speaking to each other and now use primarily ASL, unless we're around a newbie.

"I am a communications major at Rice University. I'm only a freshman, but I am astounded at what I'm learning. For instance, what incredibly visual animals we are. Hearing is really far down the ladder when it comes to our consciousness. Just the fact that most of our brain tissue is dedicated to the analysis of images, says a lot.

"As opposed to a cat, for example, man's consciousness and ability to think are far more dominant. A cat's consciousness comes mostly from what it smells more than what it hears, and then what it sees—as do most other animals.

"People are just the opposite. We process most of our information through our sight, not our ears. So, guess what? How incredibly unimportant is hearing in the grand scheme of things?

"We have learned in communications that studying consciousness via sight is far superior than studying it via hearing. I just learned something you may already know, since you're a famous writer, but I'll tell you anyway. Man possesses something called 'theory of mind.' A part of a normal adult's consciousness is our understanding that others have goals, desires, and beliefs that are separate from our own.

"This separate consciousness to others is called theory of mind and it's all predicated on visual learning, or at least most of it. As you might guess, young children before the age of about four don't possess this consciousness yet and so they don't realize that others may think differently or want differently from them. In my opinion, that's one of the reasons it's so important to begin to teach children, almost from day one, the art and the beauty and the power of ASL, whether they can hear or not.

"At any rate, we all love you, man. Keep up the good work. We already have two ASL units going here after school and I hear many of the other colleges are doing the same. We might have something here after all and to think you started it all with a Blog. That is just too cool, man.

"Take care, Brian Hansen."

Nate laughed, then Hop joined in.

"Isn't that something, man?" Hop signed with an emphasis on the student's slang use of the word. *"He's light years ahead of me and he's only a freshman in college. I had no idea there even was such a thing as theory of mind."*

"Yeah, a little above my head as well. But his comments on consciousness tied to seeing are really interesting," Nate replied. He also noticed

as he spoke the words as well, that he was having more and more trouble hearing his own voice, which was slowly becoming a jumble of vibrations more than words.

He paused for a second, as Hop turned back to his computer. *God has such an incredible way of handling things,* he thought. *Here I am with all these wonderful, caring people, all because I lost my hearing. I might never have met Hop or Gracie and Bradshaw. But I also think of the mysteries of life, that God has chosen to pace me. He didn't take away my voice until I understood this all and he didn't take it until I could communicate without it. I'm very lucky; very lucky indeed.*

Hop glanced over at Nate and recognized that he was having an epiphany. He decided to let him continue in his thoughts.

Nate got up slowly and went downstairs. No one was in the living room and a chill had descended on the room. He bent over, picked up two spruce logs from the firewood box, threw them on the grate, and lit a fire. Then he walked over to the large easy chair next to one of the end tables, opened the drawer, and pulled out a pipe. Filling it with tobacco, he lit it, something he hadn't done in years, but somehow it seemed appropriate. He settled into the soft chair and watched as the flames began to lick the back of the fireplace. Soon, a wonderful feeling began to sweep over him. It wasn't happiness, but more a feeling of contentment, almost one of fulfillment, as if he'd accomplished everything he set out to do in life.

The fire soon began to warm his arms, but he was already warmed up on the inside with a sense of tranquility, something he hadn't felt since he graduated from college.

Just then Stella walked into the room and sat on the hearth. He smiled at her; she smiled back but with far more expression. He'd already become adept at reading those subtle looks and he almost knew what was coming when she held up her hands and with three swift, but very precise and elegant movements of her hands and arms, she said, *"I love you more than life itself."*

In that moment, he knew he could have died and been quite content with everything he would leave here on earth. Then he moved closer to her, put his arms around her, and kissed her gently, but deeply. Pulling back slightly, he signed the word *"Ditto."*

Though it was only one word, she knew that he meant far more than that. They were closer now than they had been in years and she reached out and pulled her to him. Stroking the side of his face, she knew he had arrived—he finally got it—all of it, life, love, family, the family of man—all of it.

As Stella caressed her husband, Jennifer appeared in her pajamas in the kitchen doorway. She smiled and signed to her father, "*I love you, too, Dad,*" then turned and went back to bed.

Nate felt more peace of mind than he could ever remember. He was actually beginning to enjoy the silence. He could think more clearly than he ever had as he learned to rely on his visual consciousness.

He likened it to the peeling of an onion, like the first thick layer had been pulled from his eyes weeks ago, then more recently thinner layers that blocked his "seeing" were slowly peeled away. A new meaning to everything that had eluded him before was becoming as clear as his beloved Montana skies.

At first, when he began to learn various words and terms, he thought he'd been given the keys to communication. It wasn't until just recently that—along with his ever-expanding consciousness through the visual world—he understood that there was a complex world of syntax, parts of speech, verbs, tense agreement, and moods involved in ASL.

Still, those intricacies of language paled to him in relation to his new spiritual awareness. He wondered if those who had been born deaf always had this awareness. Were the deaf always more intuitive, more compassionate than those who could hear?

Finally, before he snuffed out his pipe to join Stella in bed, he thought about another joyous aspect of his "disability." He laughed to himself thinking of that word. Making love with his wife had become a complete new experience. Though their lovemaking had always been good for them both, now it was quite literally a thing of magic. His sense of touch and his internal closeness to her allowed him to reach heights of pure ecstasy, feelings he'd never experienced before—and he knew the feelings were reciprocal.

*N*early ten months after the first signs of the disease showed up in Troy, and five and a half months after the first visitors had been transported to the camps, very little official headway had been made toward educating the deaf, or even dealing with the residue of the disease.

There were still towns in quarantine, the government was fractious and ineffective, and the Hearing Habitat's governing board of directors who oversaw all two hundred camps was becoming known as a chronic underachiever.

The board of fifty members, mostly ex-government appointments, posts, or cabinet members had been reduced to nothing more than a debating society. Perhaps most ludicrous was the fact that only three of the members were either deaf, or had a family member who was, Halley Weber being one of them.

The bureaucracy was calcified almost from the first week with decisions being based more on patronage than merit. The interests were so polarized that consensus on anything was impossible.

There were members like Weber who argued for more time, to continue the status quo—hearing aids, appliances, and rhetoric, hoping to buy time for her friend, Rohrbacher, and herself. "I'm convinced we can teach them to speak," she would tell the body of directors. "We just need time."

There were members who vehemently fought to make S.E.E. the defacto language, though it wasn't even a language. Some members favored developing the language that the "visitors" themselves were creating. Some just said, "Let's train interpreters and let them all go. Enough is enough."

Air traffic was still limited to military flights, but restricted train and subway traffic was offered in some of the larger cities.

The American economy was in a shambles. The stock markets were only allowed to trade one day a week, and the ensuing economic fallout—including closed factories, banks that were only open on Mondays, and the turmoil in international markets' rush to sell treasury securities—caused a tsunami effect across the global economy.

Millions of jobs disappeared, millions of people were wandering homeless, gas stations were only open three days a week, and no one was allowed to purchase more than three gallons at a time—not that they could afford more at the twenty-five-dollar per gallon prices.

It was as if The Great Depression had collided with Katrina and the Dust Bowl drought of the '20s all in one cataclysmic event that affected every living soul in the country and beyond.

The fall of America's once powerful economy proved beyond a doubt that it had truly been the world's economic engine. The dollar's plummet created a domino affect in every region of the world. Trading partners withdrew from each other and took a circle-the-wagons approach to their own economies. Each country in the world was isolated; dependent upon whatever national resources they had within their borders.

Ultimately, those who had contracted the disease, those who were now just referred to as the "deafies," were blamed.

By April, many others were coming down with the bacteria. It had not yet gone through its own natural cycle of infection, though it had slowed, and those who became ill, just stayed indoors, or otherwise kept to themselves. No one wanted to be labeled, so the country became even quieter.

Nevertheless, there were bright spots. So many people now having to rely solely on sight, they became dependent upon things like the Internet, where everyone is deaf.

One of the driving forces to this new movement had been Hop's Blogs. His daily missives, insights, and calls to action became a rallying point for the deaf and for those who were adept at ASL.

The colleges and universities that had offered ASL as a second language were the first to encourage their students to form groups where they could exchange their knowledge and ideas.

Every night the Internet was a flash point of activity. ASL Blogs sprouted all over the country. Hop's Blog was getting more than half a million hits a day. Some visited momentarily out of curiosity, while others stayed and wrote beautiful essays or offered new insights either from their existing ASL training or through their own deafness.

The other industry, one of the few that was actually prospering, was the cell phone or handheld industry—SatCom in particular who had become the primary provider for text-enabled devices.

By April of 2011, they'd sold more than 200 million units, and texting messages had reached an astounding 10 trillion a month. Between the Internet and the texting devices, people were forging a new way of communicating that didn't rely on sound. This was particularly true for the young.

People were learning, one way or another, to talk with their hands and their bodies. Aden Bartholomew had become extremely wealthy, despite the economy. Not only had he sold ungodly numbers of texting devices, he'd also invented a new high tech sign language, most of it based on American Sign Language. It was being used to replace the traditional computer mouse. The technology was called, G-Speak, and it was allowing users to interact with computers using hand gestures.

That night, among the hundreds of daily hits on his Blog, Hop received this message:

"Dear Mr. Brody:
I am a student at Cal Tech and I belong to one of the largest ASL groups in the country. We have 200 members. Recently, we have been working with the new G-Speak technology. I don't know if you've heard about it, but it will certainly help further our cause.

"Like most of the students here, I am an engineer. My field is computer technology. SatCom, who has been selling so many texting devices, has nearly perfected this new technology. In its simplest form, it is a better mouse.

"I don't know if you ever saw the movie 'Minority Report' with Tom Cruise where he gestures to a large translucent screen with gloved hands navigating and manipulating crime scene information. The movie was a bomb, but the technology was fascinating and now it's real.

"According to the press release online by Bartholomew, he said, 'It seems to us that manipulating things with our hands is a fundamental way to interact with the world.' Can you believe that? I couldn't have said it any better myself. I wonder if he's deaf?

"You can go online yourself to see a streaming presentation. It's fantastic! Check it out.

"Sincerely, Matt Hogan, Cal Tech Sophomore"

Hop immediately typed in the site and watched in amazement as two unidentified black-gloved hands were gesturing to a screen with pictures and typography. A voice in the background called it, "Gestural technology," hence the G-Speak name.

The man then came forward into the picture still facing the screen and held his hands out like a child holding an imaginary six-shooter. As he pointed at an object, he pinched his thumb down against his forefinger and grabbed the object, moving it to another place on the screen.

Once again, the voice said, "As you can see, gestures are a far more nuanced way to interact with images." He then drew a circle with his left hand and the text automatically wrapped into a circle.

Next, the man pointed to a small picture in the corner of the screen, snapped his fingers, and the picture instantly enlarged to fill the entire screen. Then he pointed at the far left of the picture and gestured to his right, and was able to pan the entire part of the photo hidden off the screen.

Likewise, another simple gesture, pushing his hand toward the screen, brought the center part of the scene up into close focus.

The voice was obviously that of a marketing person who now began to tout the many possible uses of the technology.

"Ladies and gentlemen, think of it. The uses are practically endless: film editing, the video game industry, computer-aided design, medical imaging, air traffic control, shipping logistics, and even homeland security.

"This isn't some far off pipedream. It's real and it's today. Even the deaf can use it. In fact, this would be perfect. You don't need to hear a thing to not only communicate quickly, but to perform just about any task. It can even be taught ASL."

With that last statement, the screen returned to the homepage and Hop sat trying to catch his breath. He'd never seen anything like it. He couldn't wait to write tonight's Blog, to thank Matt Hogan, and to start passing the word. Within days, the entire country would be aware of this technology.

It seemed to Hop that a new paradigm was about to take place. He could feel an energy welling up like a snowball perched at the top of a very steep mountain. Before he signed off, he thought, "Every cloud has a silver lining."

56

April 30, 2011

"My God, you've done it. You've actually done it," Segar said as he danced around the diminutive scientist like a twelve-year-old who had just won the national spelling bee.

Dr. Revchenko smiled.

The two men, along with several other scientists, sat at the large teak conference table at BioGem. It was nearly midnight and all but Segar looked worn out. They'd been working nearly twenty hours a day ever since Revchenko had devised the mouth spray delivery device and the personalized nano-vehicle, smaller than a water molecule.

For the last four months, he'd been trying to perfect the vaccine. It was only by accident that he discovered the only way to reach and attack deadly meningitis bacterium in the brain was to create a molecule small enough to penetrate the brain barrier. As luck would have it, he discovered the most direct route was through the auditory canal and then the auditory nerves, the same way the bacteria originally managed to reach the brain in the first place.

Now he had the aerosol, the nano-submarine, and the passage-way. He could attack the disease on a molecular level without damaging any surrounding brain tissue. The vaccine would only attach itself to the bacteria cells.

"This means a huge bonus to all of you," Segar said. His face lit up like a child's on Christmas morning. His mind was racing at the thought of the millions upon millions he would reap, not to mention the fact that enough time had now transpired so that he was fully vested in all his stock options. *Billions was more like it!*

254

"I don't know how you did it, Dr. Revchenko, but you have broken through a barrier that was impenetrable. Unbelievable. Unfucking believable. God, I'll be the richest man on the planet."

Each of the scientists was smiling and patting each other on the back.

"My God, Dr. Revchenko, you'll go down in history alongside Albert Schweitzer and Mother Theresa."

"Well, it was a bit of luck, gentlemen, as you know," the doctor said as he scanned the faces of the other scientists at the table.

"We didn't set out to work with the auditory nerve or the deafness. It just turned out, once we'd come up with the vaccine and the delivery device, that it made sense to figure out how best to penetrate the normal brain defenses.

"Like so many things in science, it was a pleasant discovery."

Segar was nearly beside himself. His mind was racing off in a thousand different directions. He was already trying to figure out how much further he could capitalize on his discovery. Yes, he would have to pay a very large sum of money to the government and the FDA as a licensing fee, even though his company had done all the work, but that had been part of the agreement to limit the work to just his company.

He could single-handedly bring the country and the world back from the brink of total economic collapse.

Tonight, he would consult with his people on how best to capture it all. He knew the government would probably just force his hand, perhaps even renege on their deal and just nationalize the entire discovery. For tonight, however, he was going to celebrate.

Tomorrow, he would set up an online press conference to tell the world, to let them know *he* was the one responsible and to take immediate control. Then, after twenty-four hours had passed, he would contact the NORAD administration.

57

May 3, 2011

"*Y*ou *don't know what the hell you're talking about,*" the short blonde student signed to the husky letterman who hadn't a clue what the boy was signing.

"I'm sorry, I thought we were in America, where people use English to communicate," the jock sneered.

This time, the diminutive student, Josh Abrams, spat out the words as he signed them once again. "I said, you don't know what the hell you're talking about!" His face had turned bright red and a nervous sweat was beginning to bead up on his forehead.

"Yeah? And who appointed you ambassador to the deaf?" the muscular student said, jabbing a finger in the blonde boy's chest. "You and your flailing stupid sign language. Try living with ninety percent hearing loss before you judge me for having cochlear implants, okay?"

The short student did not back off, even at the finger jabbing. He took a deep breath, held his chin out, pushed back at the football player, and said verbally, "You just don't get it, do you? You're deaf, and you believe deaf people should be forced to hear and speak English. Someone else says they should at least be *signing* English, while still others say they should just use ASL because it's the easiest and quickest to learn."

"So, what's your point?" the confused student asked.

"*Aw, forget it,*" the boy signed. "*You're too stupid to understand.*"

After the football player left, scratching his head, the blonde continued to sign to six other students under the shade of a large oak tree in the central quad area at UCLA. All of them were in the school's ASL program.

"Before both the hearing and the non-hearing can really come together," he signed to the others who were underclassmen, *"the deaf community has got to get its shit together.*

"I mean, how are you going to get the average, hearing citizen to make an effort to communicate with the deaf, if you can't even get a majority of deaf people to agree on how they should converse with one another?"

"What do you mean, Josh?" one of the other students signed.

"I mean, there are too many competing factions out there. Even some of the faculty and students at Gallaudet are bitching about the new president there, saying she isn't deaf enough. Can you imagine?

"And then there's that other stupid organization that has their own rules and agendas—oralists to the bitter end. They want every deaf person to learn to speak. 'Oh, and by the way, we'll help you if you need a hearing aid—better yet, you should get cochlear implants.'"

The blonde boy was obviously agitated and passionate about the subject matter. He had the other students, sitting in a semicircle, enraptured with what he was signing.

"For everybody else who's deaf, you're either mainstreamed into hearing classrooms, or special classes, or you go to a deaf school, or you learn to sign. Even then, what are you taught? ASL, signed English, cued speech, finger spelling? Or do you just use lip reading? And if so, should you be going to speech therapy, too?"

The students were riveted. *How did he know all this?*

As if he had heard their thoughts, the young man continued, *"My father is deaf. He went through hell growing up and, let me tell you, things haven't changed that much over the years.*

"My grandmother insisted on hooking him up to every hearing aid known to man to try and get him to hear. Insisted that he learn to talk. She was mortified that he'd been born deaf, and to this day she is still embarrassed for him because he signs.

"My grandfather fought every step of the way against making my dad become oral. But my grandmother was a very strong, opinionated woman. She spent all her time trying to teach my father to talk, and you know what happened?"

The other students were all leaning forward on the concrete bench surrounding the young man—their eyes fixed on him.

"I'll tell you what happened. He didn't learn a damn thing. Think about it. How in the hell can you teach a child to talk if they can't hear? It's nearly impossible.

"Babies and children learn by mimicking what they hear and see. If a baby can't hear, he or she cannot mimic sounds. And if they can't mimic sounds, they can't exchange ideas using the spoken word.

"Doesn't it make sense to teach a child using the senses he or she does have, rather than wait for the acquisition of a sense they might have in the future?

"Of course, since my father didn't learn how to learn, by the time they sent him to kindergarten, he was years behind the others ... and he still couldn't talk anyway!"

The young man had run out of wind. Drained, he sat down, knowing that he had expressed his thoughts clearly enough to at least be worthy of his friends' consideration.

And he knew he wasn't alone. Across the country, ASL groups were meeting daily and these kinds of discussions were becoming more and more commonplace.

One of the students sitting there pondering Josh's ideas, a beautiful redheaded girl with deep brown eyes, had indeed been stirred by his words. Her name was Karen Winegarden, and she had transferred to UCLA from NYU to study deaf education. Sitting there cross-legged on the grass, she let her mind embrace the thought as it slowly came to her. *"I've got an idea,"* she finally signed to the group.

Josh nodded her way with a smile. *"Yeah? What is it?"*

The girl stood up, tugging the hem of her short skirt down over her shapely legs. *"Well, we all know that they're trying to help people learn sign language in those Hearing Habitats, right?"*

"Yeah, so?" another interjected.

"So don't you imagine that they're probably way understaffed? I mean, look how hard it is to get enough teachers to teach the hard-of-hearing kids in our public schools. Do you really think the government just magically

came up with enough educators to help a couple of million people over-night?"

The wheels in Josh's brain were beginning to turn as well. *"Are you saying what I think you're saying?"*

"I'm saying that I think we should put together a group of ASL signers and visit the nearest Habitat to help. I know there's supposed to be a vaccine coming that'll restore their hearing, but what if that takes longer than they're saying? Or what if it never comes? Those people are going to need a way to communicate."

Josh could hardly contain his excitement. *"Karen, that is an awesome idea! My dad's got this big RV that he'd let me use, and spring break's just around the corner. We could get a group together and head to New Mexico then. Anybody here want to go?"*

Another boy in the group answered by first forming the sign for *"road,"* then following it with the swooping gesture for the word *"trip."* Soon, every person in the group was laughing and repeating the signs over and over again.

Road trip, road trip, road trip!

58

May 10, 2011
NORAD
Presidential briefing

There were twenty-six people present at the morning meeting: the Joint Chiefs, all cabinet members and necessary officials; all those who had been there from the beginning. It had been seven months since they'd sequestered themselves—ten months since the first quarantine in Troy.

Robert Jordan had not given them an agenda. He preferred to surprise the entire group.

"Good morning, everyone. I'd like to start this meeting by being the messenger of great news. Yesterday, I received a call directly from BioGem's CEO, Daniel Segar."

Jordan waited. He wanted to relish the surprise on their faces. Every one of those in attendance fell silent, leaning forward and hanging on to Jordan's every word.

"And …?" one of them could not help but ask.

"And they've done it. They've synthesized a vaccine. Within thirty days, there will be enough of the antidote to treat every person who was infected. In less than three months, every man, woman, and child in the country will have access to an inoculation to prevent the virus from spreading."

Everyone around the table burst into cheers. Some stood up and gave high fives to those next to them. An ecstatic chorus of overlapping voices filled the room. "Fantastic. Yes! Thank God," could be heard amidst the din.

"Oh my God, that's wonderful," Halley Weber said and nearly started to cry. "Thank God," she kept repeating to herself. And while she was truly amazed by Jordan's news about the breakthrough, she was even more relieved that no more camps would have to be built. No more than three million people would have to be subjected to the government's less than stellar attempts at handling their needs.

No more than three million people would be added to the already formidable population of deaf people living in the United States.

The room was in pandemonium. Even the normally staid, elderly Joint Chiefs were nearly dancing around the table.

"People. People. Wait. Please sit down. I know you're all excited, but I have one more bit of news I know you'll truly relish."

The group sat down, almost in unison. *What*, they wondered, *could be even better than this news?*

"Friends and colleagues, it gives me great pleasure to announce that this administration is going home." The President once again paused for dramatic effect.

All those seated turned to one another, eyes wide open, unable to catch their breaths.

"By the end of the week, each of you will be given a shot from the first manufactured batch of the vaccine. After a two-day checkup for any adverse side effects, which I've been assured are quite minimal, you will all be allowed to leave and go back to your homes.

"General Brewer, your first order of business will be to have the National Guard stand down. I want all the units returning home within thirty days. And I'm leaving it up to you to set up a distribution system for the delivery of the vaccine. You can start by going to each of the camps. You'll have a captive audience there.

"Boggs, I want you to schedule a live press meeting from the Oval Office for next Monday. Starting next week, the media is to come back on line, and the banking industry and stock market need to reopen ASAP.

"And Halley," he said, his voice expressing only a hint of somberness, "I'll need you now more than ever as we push forward with a plan to mainstream the people who have gone deaf."

Amid all the positive reports and celebration, the President's omission of the fact that no treatment had been developed to restore the hearing in people stricken by the virus had gone all but unnoticed.

"I understand, sir. This issue will stay my top priority until I hear otherwise directly from you."

Jordan gave Weber a solid pat on her shoulder and turned to face the group once more. "That is all for now, people. May God bless you and this great nation," he said as he stood up and left the room.

59

The next day. May 11, 2011

"*O*h *shit!*" Hop signed to Nate, whose attention remained fully focused on the laptop in front of him.

Realizing his mistake, Hop ran over to Nate and tapped him on the shoulder, "*Pardner. They're coming,*" he signed.

Nate stopped typing and gestured back, "*Who? Who's coming?*"

"*The FBI. I could spot them a mile off. Those idiots always wear suits. Doesn't matter where or when.*"

Hop had been scanning the horizon beyond the forest high on the ridge where the cabin sat. He'd done that several times a day since they had arrived, using a very high-powered set of Panasonic binoculars with night vision capabilities.

As he suspected, they were coming at night. The binoculars were capable of seeing more than a mile even at night. In this case, the typical government Crown Victoria Ford was unmistakable. The heat given off by the engine and exhaust lit them up like it was high noon in July. He could see five agents—two in the front seat and three in the back. Each was carrying a shotgun—and Hop suspected a sidearm as well.

Hop could see the cloud of dust pluming behind the slow-moving vehicle. He guessed that they would stop soon, pull off the trail, and proceed on foot.

Hop still didn't know why they wanted Nate, but that was of little consequence. Now it was time to vacate quickly, formulate an exit strategy, and try to figure out another place to hide. He also had to make an immediate assessment of the bare essentials they needed to take with them because, at best, they only had five or ten minutes to get out of there.

"Nate, take down the satellite dish. We'll take that, the computer, and your short wave. I'll grab Jennifer and tell Stella and your parents to throw some canned goods in a plastic bag. We don't have much time," he signed hastily.

Nate fully understood. He'd gotten much better at signing in the last two months and now, though his vocabulary was still quite limited, it was second nature to him. Besides, it was just as fast to sign, maybe even faster, than speaking.

Hop looked around the cabin and sighed. He hated leaving. As his eyes darted around, he realized he also had two boxes full of files, replies to his Blogs, Internet addresses, copies of his columns—everything he'd been working on since they'd come up here.

He could only carry one at a time, so he grabbed one and then ran downstairs to wake everyone up.

"Honey," he whispered repeatedly to Jennifer, shaking her.

Her eyes opened slowly. "Uncle Hop. What are you doing?"

"Honey, it's time to go. Come on, get dressed. I'll tell you about it later. Your father is in danger and we've got to get out of here right away."

"Can I take my bear, Uncle Hop?" she gestured.

"Yes, sweetie. Take your bear, but that's all."

Hop then ran into the other room and told Gracie and Bradshaw not to worry. The Feds were only coming for Hop and Nate. They should just sit tight. They would be all right.

In a panic, Nate, Jennifer, Stella, and Nate's parents were herded with whatever belongings they could assemble in two minutes into the car.

"Everybody in?" Hop signed over his shoulder, though hearing all the doors slam, he had already jammed the car into gear and stomped on the gas. With a roar, the car careened down the dirt road toward the highway.

Looking out through his window, Nate saw the twin beams of the oncoming sedan approaching the house. He sighed a breath a relief when the car stopped and the men piled out and into the cabin.

At the same moment, Hop gasped as another government vehicle, identical in every way to the first, lurched out onto the road and blocked their way. As he skidded the car to a stop, four men, all dressed in dark suits, exited the car. In seconds, four guns were drawn and aimed at exactly the same place between his eyes.

"FBI," one of the men shouted. "Turn off your engine and step out of the car with your hands above your heads. All of you."

From the backseat, Stella, with her unblinking eyes frozen in terror, stifled the urge to scream. "FBI?" she asked. "Hop, what's going on? What do they want?"

Nate could read her lips easily in the glare of the car's headlights. *"I think we're about to find out,"* he signed before opening his door and stepping out into the night.

"Stop right there!" one of the agents shouted. "Are you Nathan Bannister?"

Nathan looked the man square in the eye and nodded.

"You are under arrest," was all the man said.

Hop eased himself out of the car with his open hands placed high above his head and said, "Under arrest? For what?"

"Acts of terrorism against the people of the United States," the man replied as another stepped forward and put a set of handcuffs on Nathan's wrists behind his back.

"Terrorism?" Stella gasped. "What are you talking about? Nate works for the government!"

"We're quite aware of that, ma'am. We have a complete record of correspondence between his office and the Iranian terrorists who released the virus in Troy."

An expression of bewilderment flashed across Nathan's face as he picked out every other word or so of the agent's incredible accusations. Nathan twisted his face and furrowed his brow, an expression that said, *"I have no idea what you're talking about!"*

One of the agents threw a briefcase onto the hood of the car, opened it, and rifled through a stack of papers. "Airborne dispersion patterns. Wind-driven contamination. Infection probabilities.

"I'm willing to bet that you know exactly what we're talking about, Mr. Bannister."

Nathan's memory was triggered immediately by the agent's recitation.

"But, but those were just ..." Nathan began to plead.

"Shut up, Nate!" Hop signed with wildly expressive gestures. *"You don't owe them an explanation. At least not without a lawyer to represent you."*

Another agent, who had until this point not said anything, lowered his gun. Watching the silent dialogue between Hop and Nathan, he leaned against the car while pulling a cigarette from his jacket pocket. Lighting the cigarette and taking a deep inhalation of smoke, he scratched his chin thoughtfully as he studied the two men.

Something wasn't making sense.

60

$\mathcal{B}$randy Jones couldn't sleep. Tossing and turning on his cot in the Portales Habitat, he pulled the cover away from his shivering body and rose up out of bed.

With his joints creaking in the cold, night air, he stepped into the fuzzy red slippers he had brought with him and shuffled out of the building with the intent of using the bathroom. On his way to the bank of portable toilets placed outside of each building, he stopped and marveled at the stars shining brightly overhead.

Standing there in the black silence, he was caught off-guard by the sight of a shadowy figure darting through the night air up ahead in the distance. Straining his eyes to see, he watched as the shadow ducked into an enclosed, shaded canopy, one of many that had been placed around the camp to provide shelter from the blistering sun during the day.

Not necessarily sneaking, but walking quietly nonetheless, he crept up on the canopy. He was less than ten feet away when the round, white beam of a flashlight hit the tent's sidewall closest to him. Stopping dead in his tracks and thinking that someone would be running out any minute to ask him what he was doing sneaking around the camp at night, he was relieved to see the silhouettes of children bounding through the circle of light on the wall.

Smiling to himself, he recollected how he used to make similar hand shadows at night when he was a kid. Only these weren't just hand shadows being projected against the wall—they were full-body shadows, shadows he could instantly recognize by the way each child posed in front of the light inside the tent.

To his delight, he watched the lumbering, spread-armed gait of a monkey or gorilla pass through the sphere of light. He smiled and even laughed out loud as the shadow-simian stopped and comically scratched at the sides of its stomach.

Before long, a kangaroo, or maybe a rabbit, hopped through the light, and Brandy hopped slightly to mimic the form on the wall. And once again he smiled, his teeth nearly glowing against his leathered dark brown skin.

And that's when he heard it—the laughter. It came to him so abruptly that it startled him, but far beyond just being surprised was the incredible joy he felt for being able to hear once again. It was a miracle, or the closest thing he'd ever felt to a miracle before in his life.

With the skin on his arm prickling with goose bumps and his heart skipping a beat inside his chest, he realized he must see first-hand the source of this incredible moment, of what he could only describe to himself as a rebirth of sorts. With newfound boldness, he walked up to the canopy and, just before throwing the canvas door wide open, he peered at the four children through a slit in the fabric.

As he knew already, the children were lined up behind one another, waiting to take turns in front of a beam coming from a flashlight resting on the ground on the other side of the canopy.

And also, just as he knew he would, he found them laughing and giggling with one another—their faces beaming as they strutted and pranced back and forth through the light.

But then the silence enveloped him once more, which was immediately followed by the realization that he had never actually heard them at all.

But how could that be? He thought, stumbling backwards away from the tent before dropping to his knees. *How could I have heard them so clearly?*

When the revelation hit him, he was more astounded than ever, for what he came to know about himself that night was that he could *feel* joy—feel it in a way that he never would have thought possible.

Feel it so completely that he knew just what it sounded like.

61

*T*he jail in downtown was as good a place as any to begin Nathan's interrogation.

Sitting alone in a featureless room, except for a lone wooden table, two chairs, a bare light bulb hanging from a socket, and a large mirror he assumed was two-way, Nathan placed his trembling hands on the table and waited. He could not be sure that it was because of his deafness, but he was sure that he had never noticed his heart beating so violently in his chest before.

He had lost track of how long he had been sitting there—one hour, two?—before anyone joined him in the room.

The cubicle's solid-steel door creaked open on rusting hinges, and one of the men who had captured them quietly stepped in and sat down in the other chair. His scowl was evident even behind his dark sunglasses.

"Good evening, Mr. Bannister," the agent said as he hoisted the same briefcase he had placed on the car's hood earlier that night. Opening it, he began rifling through a stack of papers more than an inch thick.

"It would appear we have a lot to talk about," the man said dryly.

Nathan had not had near enough time to become proficient at reading lips. *"I'm sorry, but I can't hear you,"* was all he signed after noticing that the man had finished talking.

The agent's finger tapped slowly on the stack of papers and he gave a vacant stare towards the mirror. Then, with agitated, jerking movements, he grabbed a tablet and a pen from the case and began to write.

You're deaf? was all it said.

Nathan nodded.

Not according to our records, you're not, he wrote.

Nathan shrugged and rolled his eyes, easily conveying the thought that someone would have to be living under a rock not to know that millions of people had gone deaf in the last few months.

Are you saying you went deaf after contracting the virus? the agent wrote and, after placing the pen down on the table, looked towards the mirror once again.

From the mirror's other side, Agent Tony Martinez was intently watching the exchange between the two men.

Nathan picked up the pen and wrote the word *yes.*

The agent sitting at the table leaned back in his chair and sighed in frustration. Then, staying behind Nathan's line of sight, he pulled a gun from his shoulder holster and held it just inches from the back of Nathan's head.

"I think you're lying, motherfucker. I think you wanted to get revenge on the government for making your life miserable after the whole Libby incident. I think you found a couple of small-time accomplices in Iran who could get their hands on a deadly virus, and I think you used your expertise in contaminant dispersal to assist them in releasing that virus.

"And you know what else, you piece of shit? I think I'm going to blow your fucking head off right now and save the country the expense of giving you a fair trial." With that, the agent moved his gun to within a half-inch of Nathan's head and cocked the hammer back. "I swear to God, I do not mind blowing your goddamn head off right here and now!" he nearly shouted.

Nathan did not move.

Seconds later, Agent Martinez was standing beside them in the room.

"That's enough," he said calmly to the other agent. "Why don't you go get yourself a glass of water and cool down a little bit? I'll take it from here."

Soon alone with Nathan, Martinez casually sat down and offered his hand. "Agent Martinez," he mouthed and then reached for the tablet and pen.

"*Do you have anything you'd like to tell me about your email correspondence to Iran last year?*"

"*I have never knowingly emailed anyone in Iran.*"

"*Ever?*"

"*Never.*"

"*Why would they email you?*"

Nathan shrugged. "*If their intent was to release an airborne virus, I would be the best person to contact for information. My name is attached to dozens of EPA airborne contamination studies, and my job is to disperse information to concerned residents of this country.*"

"*Of which they are not.*"

"*No, but how would I know that? Besides, any information I would have shared with them would not have been classified. If you've got copies of my email responses in that folder, I'm sure you already know this.*"

"*And you're really deaf?*"

"*100%.*"

"*I'm sorry.*"

Nathan stopped for a moment and looked around the perimeter of the room before writing, "*I'm not.*"

"*Why were you hiding out in that cabin?*"

"*Because I thought it was safer there for me and my family.*"

"*And what's the reporter's place in all this?*"

"*At first, it was just a great story. But he's got two deaf kids and it became personal. He's in touch daily with people all over the world who want to be a part of the solution to what's going on.*"

"*And how might they do that?*"

"*By volunteering at the Habitats. Some are already on their way.*"

"*Is that where he'd be going?*"

"*Probably. The one in New Mexico's closest, and he's already heard from some college students that are going there to help out.*"

"*Would you have joined him?*"

"*Yes. With my wife and daughter, and my parents.*"

Martinez took a moment to look directly into Nathan's eyes, and the two men stared at each other far longer than most men would feel comfortable doing.

"We know where you live. All of you," Martinez wrote.

"I'm sure you do," Nathan replied, then watched as the man got up, stuffed the papers back into the briefcase, and quietly left the room.

With a certain knowing intuition, Nathan was also quite sure that every agent had left the building, the parking lot, and the town. He was free to go.

Walking out into the cool night air, he noticed Hop's car parked at the curb in front of the building.

62

Monday, May 16, 2011
Portales, New Mexico

*W*ith high hopes and giddy excitement, Josh steered the large motor—home over the last rise leading to the Portales Hearing Habitat. He had driven the RV nonstop all night long so that he and his friends could arrive by morning.

He wasn't sure just what to expect when he got there, but he did know that a volunteer movement was underfoot—a movement that had been building momentum with each passing day. Through Hop's Blog, a virtual army of eager college students, retired deaf interpreters, teachers on vacation, and ASL signers from all walks of life had committed themselves to the cause of providing some immediate communication skills to the newly deaf amassed in Hearing Habitats throughout the country.

The volunteers were keenly aware that, even if the virus-afflicted people eventually regained their hearing, this was a golden opportunity to present ASL as a useful second language to learn.

The sight of hundreds of cars, trailers, motor-homes and buses parked outside the main entrance to the Portales Habitat caused Josh and his group to let out a collective gasp as he drove up and parked at the end of the long line of vehicles leading up to the guard gate.

"Would you look at that?" he signed. *"There must be thousands of people here waiting to get in! Don't they know that there's still a chance we could become infected?"*

Karen, relaxing in a pink velour sweat outfit while reclining in the large passenger seat of the RV, gazed out at the crowd for a moment before signing back. *"I'm sure they do, but since the only last-ing affect of the virus is deafness, I guess they figure they've got nothing to lose."*

"Good point," Josh replied.

Up at the guard gate, the security officer was pleading into his cell phone. "Sir, if we don't let these people through soon, I'm afraid we're going to have a real situation on our hands."

General Renkins' commanding voice was so loud that the officer had to hold the phone a few inches away from his ear. "I don't care how many people show up! These centers were not designed to accommodate visitors!"

The guard understood Renkins' underlying message clearly. There was no way that the general public would view the Habitats as anything other than third-world internment camps.

"Understood, sir, but I'm telling you, the people who have been sitting out here for days are not going to take it much longer. And no one's turning back."

Renkins paced back and forth in his office. Taking off his cap and rubbing his balding head, he realized his options were getting fewer by the minute as similar reports were coming from other hab-itats all across the country.

"What if we told them the virus had mutated—that the odds of death had gone from negligible to probable. Would that stop them?"

"I doubt it. They seem to know more than I do about what's going on here. I'm sure they'd see it as a smokescreen."

"Dammit," Renkins spat into the phone. "Who the hell would have figured on a bunch of bleeding-heart volunteers showing up! Don't you see how bad this is going to make our government look?"

"Yes I do, sir. But that doesn't change the reality of what's going on right now—namely that there are literally thousands of people here who are ready to storm this gate and go in. And I can tell you this, sir. I will not fire upon citizens of this country, deaf volunteers no less, to disperse them."

General Renkins sat down heavily in the leather chair behind his desk. Taking a moment to decide whether he should call the President or not, he realized that he did not want to be the one to ruin the President's moment of glory as he addressed the nation later that day from the White House.

"Well then, I'd say you've got a decision to make, officer. At this point, the only command I can give you is to maintain civil order to the best of your ability. Do you understand what I'm telling you?"

"Yes, sir, I do."

"Then carry on, soldier. I'm sure we'll be in contact with each other sooner than later."

*   *   *

The slow-rolling caravan, filled with people who could scarcely believe what they were seeing, was herded through the Habitat's dusty compound, and directed to Portales' main administration building.

"This can't be real," Karen signed with trembling hands. Watching the Habitat's residents shuffle like zombies through the portable buildings, she made no attempt to hide her disillusionment. *"This, this is the best our government could come up with?"*

Josh did not sign back as he pulled the motor home to a stop and prepared to rally his group for whatever experience was in store.

"Okay, people. I know this is not what we were expecting to find, but that doesn't change what we came here to do. Obviously, there doesn't seem to be any real structured learning going on—look at everybody just wandering around like they're lost—so I think the best we can do is just go out there and do our best.

"Pick a person, or see if you can form a group, and just start with the easy stuff. Show them, 'hello.' Teach them how to ask for necessary things like food and water. Take the time to make them feel comfortable signing back and forth with you."

Karen stood up, brushed her wavy red hair away from her face, and put on a brave smile for the group.

"Just make sure they know why you're here," she signed. *"Let them know what's going on in your heart, and I'm sure everyone will be fine."*

Josh nodded in agreement and opened the door to the motor home. Squinting out into the bright New Mexico sunlight, he stepped down and lent a hand to each person as they exited the coach.

"Good luck," he signed. *"When you get hungry or sleepy, just come back and make yourself at home. Other than that, I don't know what else there is to tell you. We're here for as long we want to be here—or until the food runs out."*

Karen stepped out of the RV and began the process of acclimating herself to her surroundings. Walking slowly through the group of Habitat residents that were beginning to form around her and the other volunteers, she smiled and signed *'hello'* to each one of them.

She did not know who or what specifically she was looking for, but, guided by her instincts, it did not take her long to zero in on the right person or, as it turned out, group of people, to approach.

They were an odd, eclectic bunch: two elderly women, four small children maybe eight or nine years old, and a sinewy African-American man who appeared to be in his late fifties or early sixties.

How in the world did these people end up together? She wondered as she walked up to the group and held out a hand in greeting.

"What is your name?" she moved her mouth slowly to ask each one, knowing that these four words were quite easy to lip-read.

"Edna," one of the two old ladies replied out loud.

In reply, Karen formed the letter "E" with her left hand and gestured for Edna to do the same while touching her chest.

"Jamie," one of the children chimed in, and was shown the letter "J."

"Brandy," the man volunteered.

"Brandy?" Karen mouthed and raised her hands in question.

Brandy nodded.

"Like the drink?" Karen relayed with a drinking motion before raising her hands into a question sign once more.

Brandy laughed, shook his head, and pointed to his skin. "No, like the color," he said.

Just like that, Karen was finding a way to carry on a basic conversation with each one of them, and together they walked slowly amongst the vehicles that had arrived that day. Meandering amongst people engaged in similar interactions with each other, they passed a luxurious motor home sporting every possible convenience and electronic gadget imaginable. Set up under the RV's exterior awning, a full-blown tiki bar and lounge—complete with fiberglass tiki gods and plastic pink flamingoes—had been assembled upon a bright green pad of Astro-turf.

Circling the bar was an assortment of folding lounge chairs, each aimed at a giant plasma-screen television, which hinged out from the side of the motor-home. On the screen, the President was just finishing up his address to the public.

"*Satellite?*" Karen signed to the RV's owner, a jovial man decked out in a straw hat and a loud, Hawaiian-print shirt.

The man nodded and conveyed to all his new guests that the bar was open and that they were more than welcome to sit a while and make themselves comfortable.

Karen read the open-captioned letterbox at the bottom of the screen while simultaneously signing to the man. "*So the President finally came up for air, huh? That must mean there's a vaccine.*"

"*That's right,*" the man signed back. "*Within the month, everyone here in the camp will receive the shot. Two weeks later they'll all be able to go home.*"

"*That's wonderful!*" she signed with a beaming smile.

But before she could even attempt to relay the good news to her group, the words scrolling on the bottom of the screen stopped her dead in her tracks.

"Unfortunately," the President said, his expression stoic as he stared directly into the camera, "at this point, we have not been able to develop any treatment regarding hearing loss. Though we will continue to pursue all avenues leading to the reversal of deafness incurred by more than three million of you, at this moment no such remedy exists. However, no new people will contract the virus. We will have contained that within the month.

"But let me assure you that this administration, at this very moment, is taking every step possible to mainstream these people back into society. We will not rest until every American is able to actively converse with their fellow countrymen."

The slackened jaws and wide-open eyes of every person in her group revealed their feelings about the news.

"What? We'll never hear again?" one of the children asked Karen, who had suddenly been thrust into the role of government liaison. "We're going to be deaf forever?"

Karen felt instantly overwhelmed. Frozen in place like a statue as she fumbled for what to say, she did not move as Brandy walked over to her side and put an arm around her shoulder.

Then, putting his hands up in the familiar position that conveyed the word "*stop*," he motioned for everyone to sit back down in their chairs.

Karen looked up into his soft brown eyes, recognizing a peace that she often noticed in the eyes of the deaf.

Standing there, Brandy did not look away from her as he slowly pointed to himself and mouthed the word "I'm," followed by the instantly recognizable "*OK*" sign.

After that, he looked up at the sky and searched for the simplest way to express what he wanted to say next.

Seconds later, he held up one finger and mouthed the word, "But …"

After that, he pointed to himself again. "*I …*"

He fumbled for a moment as he thought about the best way to convey the word "*need*." That he decided to open and close his hands in a brushing motion towards himself spoke volumes about the logic of ASL.

Finally he pointed at her. "*You.*"

"*I need you,*" he stated again.

Noticing that tears were beginning to well up in her eyes, he motioned out toward the two old women and children sitting there. "*We need you,*" he signed perfectly.

63

Wednesday, May 18, 2011

*H*alley Weber's face turned a purplish-bright red as she sat, holding the phone. After pounding her finger on the loudspeaker button, she lunged up and slammed the door to her office closed.

"They're what?" she nearly screamed.

General Renkins had faced the fury of commanding officers many times before, but this was a tirade like nothing he'd ever experienced.

"I said, there's a bunch of people who have been showing up at every Habitat, and they've been teaching the guests ASL. Look, I'm just reading the report as it was handed to me, okay?"

"No, it is absolutely not okay, General Renkins. From what I've been told, *you* are the person responsible for what takes place at those Habitats. You are the one who's been put in charge of the three million people living there."

Renkins was not one to back down. "Correction, Secretary Weber. I was put in charge of those people's safety. And when the situation became unsafe, I had to allow each officer on site to make the right call to maintain order."

"And the only way to maintain order was to let a bunch of deaf people in?" she screeched.

"Thousands of deaf people. At each Habitat," he clarified.

Nearly panting, she sat down and started scribbling some notes to herself. "You're telling me that, without a plan and nothing more that some guy's Blog to keep them informed, over a hundred thousand people just happened to show up and volunteer their services?"

"It would appear so."

"And they're teaching the guests American Sign Language?"

"That's what I'm told. And, just in case you're wondering, morale has improved at the camps dramatically ever since these people showed up."

Weber took her time in replying.

"General Renkins, of course I'm glad to hear that the people are happier there. But happiness is not what this is about. We are trying to make sure that these people are prepared to go out in the real world and function amongst hearing people. All ASL does is keep them cocooned in their own little culture of deaf people. We are not helping them by keeping them isolated!"

"Beg your pardon, ma'am, but whatever it was we were doing didn't seem to be helping much, either."

"Excuse me?"

"I said whatever it was …"

"I know what you said, General Renkins. And before we go any further, would you mind telling me just how much training you've had on the subject?"

"Well, like I said, I'm no expert."

"Exactly," she hissed. "Listen to me. ASL is a crutch. It's not something a hearing person can understand. What we need to do with these people is either figure out a way to restore their hearing, or create a working public interface so that they can go out and lead productive lives."

"Public interface?"

"Yes, like a text-messaging device."

"So you're saying that we either force them to hear, or we force them to sit face-to-face while they're having dinner and text-message each other? And, I'm sorry, but did you just imply that people who use ASL are not capable of leading productive lives?"

Renkins' incisive words caught Weber by surprise. "I did not say that."

"Oh, I'm afraid you did. Quite clearly, as a matter of fact."

"Well, what I meant to say was …"

This time it was Renkins' turn to interrupt. "I know damn well what you meant to say, Secretary Weber. You meant to say that deaf people should just stop being deaf."

With that, the speakerphone went dead.

64

Portales Habitat, New Mexico
May 19, 2011

*A*lthough he'd only been there three days, Nathan Bannister believed that he'd gotten a true sense of what the Hearing Habitats were really all about.

Sprawled out on a foam camping mattress inside his tent, with Stella and Jennifer fast asleep beside him, he pulled out a tablet, clicked on a small flashlight, and began to write:

Day three in the Habitat.

The initial shock of the President's announcement is starting to wear off, and I feel like this is really the place where my life as a deaf person begins. Before we pulled in here with Hop, there was the hope that I might get my hearing back. Now, there's only the reality that I won't.

I'd like to say that the government has managed this situation well, but that is not the case. And it's not the lousy food, or the backed-up toilets, or even the rudimentary housing that makes me say this. Truth is, on some levels I understand why people were brought here. This country was faced with a dilemma that offered no easy solutions. Amidst panic and confusion, difficult decisions had to be made and executed quickly.

It's the mentality behind the government's actions that has left me feeling so empty.

I'm deaf now. I know I will never hear words again. Or music. Or laughter.

But I am still a human being, and I will still experience those things. People will still communicate with me, and I with them. I will still dance when Stella asks me to dance. And I have already laughed more in these last few days than I had in the last few months that I had my hearing.

Life feels more precious, more valuable to me now. But I can tell that it has become officially less valuable to the people who run this country. I am now a burden to society. To communicate with me requires skills and time that people don't seem to want to invest. I'll learn to read lips—but they won't learn to sign.

I'll do whatever I have to do to provide for my family. I could go back to my job at the EPA tomorrow and perform it as well as I did before, probably better because I would have fewer distractions to contend with. But I won't be going back. My work now will involve helping deaf people be who they are. Being who WE are. He closed the cover on the tablet and turned off the flashlight. In minutes he was sound asleep, dreaming vivid dreams about the limitless blue sky back home in Montana.

*   *   *

A beam of sunlight streamed in through an open flap in the tent and caressed his face. It would have been a perfect morning to wake up slowly, but Jennifer would have none of that.

"*Daddy,*" she signed after tapping his shoulder and seeing him open one eye. "*Daddy, get up. Hop wants to talk to you.*"

Moving slowly, he eased himself up off the foam mattress pad, slipped on a fresh T-shirt and some shorts, and headed out into the bright morning sun.

"*Good morning,*" Hop signed before raising a large coffee mug to his lips.

"*Morning,*" Nathan signed back. "*What's going on?*"

"*I just wanted you to meet some new friends of mine before they headed back to LA. They're trying to get out of here before it gets too hot.*"

Standing beside Hop, Josh Abrams and Karen Winegarden stepped forward and shook Nate's hand.

"*Pleased to meet you,*" Nate signed with a smile.

"*The pleasure's ours,*" Josh replied. "*We've been reading Hop's articles and Blog almost from the first day. Sounds like you two have been through a lot over these last few months.*"

"*That we have,*" Nathan confirmed with a slow nod. "*It feels like it's all been some kind of bad dream, but then I look around and see that I'm still in it.*"

"*I know what you mean,*" Josh replied. "*But at least everyone will be able to leave here before too long.*"

Nate gave a shrug and looked out towards the rising sun. "*Yeah,*" he signed half-heartedly. "*But what happens after that?*"

Hop stepped into the conversation. "*Nate, I've been doing a lot of networking since we've been here, and you know what? There are more people than you might think who are ready, willing, and able to assist in the assimilation of those who became deaf after contracting the virus. Josh and Karen are just two wonderful examples of the kinds of people I've been meeting here at the Habitat.*"

"*That's nice to know. And you're both deaf?*"

They nodded in unison.

"*I guess the real test will be seeing how many hearing people feel like getting involved.*"

Karen held her closed mouth in a way that said she didn't fully agree with Nate's assessment. "*Yes and no,*" she signed. "*I was born deaf, and I've never waited a day in my life for anybody to do something that I thought might make my life easier. And you know what? I'm a better person because of it.*"

Nate was taken slightly aback by her bold testimony. "*Really? It hasn't been hard for you to make it in a world where hearing is normal and deafness is … abnormal?*"

"*I didn't say that. Of course it's been hard. But through it all, I never lost the feeling that somehow this 'abnormality'*" she signed with her fingers making quotation marks, "*has given me an advantage. Sure, I can't just strike up a conversation with anyone I please, but how many hearing people take the time to really listen to what a person's saying, anyway? What I want to know about a person is what's in their heart and, for me, that happens in the blink of an eye.*

"*And all the noise! Not that I've ever heard it, but I can just imagine the sound of jets and traffic and televisions and cell phones filling my head all the time. No thanks. I'll take the quiet over that any day.*"

Nate had not yet fully embraced the peacefulness that had taken over his life since losing his hearing. *"You know what? You're right. It's hard to explain, but I feel closer to my wife and daughter than I ever have. But why should I have to lose my hearing for that to happen?"*

"You don't have to lose your hearing, it just makes it easier.

"Nate, from this day forward, consider yourself as a unique human being that can sense things in ways most others can't. Your vision, your sense of smell, taste, touch, your intuition ... All of these things will just keep getting more and more acute as you adjust to your deafness. You won't talk, but you'll have more meaningful conversations than ever. You won't hear music, but you'll dance whenever the mood strikes you. You won't hear laughter, but you'll know the true meaning of happiness."

Nate gave her a smile that he knew conveyed everything he was feeling inside.

"Thank you," he signed and gave her a hug. *"Thank you so much for everything you've done here."*

Karen held him at arm's length, looked deep into his eyes and smiled. *"You're welcome. And if you or your family ever need anything, Hop knows how to get in touch with us."* After signing this, she looked over at Josh. *"Guess we better get on the road, huh?"*

Nate, after taking in a deep breath and letting it out slowly, turned to face the dawn of a brand new day.

"You know what, Hop? I think it's time for us to go home, too."

Author's Epilogue

We human beings are such fragile creatures. We crave companionship and the membership of the "normal," and yet we don't want our clubs to become too big or very diverse.

From the time that we are children, we ache at the thought of "standing apart" from our peers, and yet we crave the thought of being our own persons—individuals—with our own good ideas and inventions.

Essentially, we are pegs with round tops and square bottoms trying to find matching holes.

We want to be unique, yet fit the general consensus. We want to help the less fortunate, but not so much that they move in next door.

Does any group exist that isn't protective and prejudicial against some or even many other groups?

Today, the ruling party is comprised of white, Christian bourgeois, healthy, educated males. (No disabilities please. It's all right to be agnostic, but not Muslim or Jewish. Hindus and Buddhists are a novelty and, so, don't pose much of a threat.)

We were cruising down California Highway 101, known locally as Pacific Coast Highway, near Big Sur. It was a marvelous day, brilliant rays of sunshine just beginning to peek through the awesome sight that are the Great Redwoods, tall as buildings and as majestic as mountains.

There were four of us in the 1965 Mustang and we had the top down, of course. We were all singing loudly to the tune that was blasting out of the CD player—an old Beatles tune.

My friend was sitting in front with me and as the tune ended, I glanced over and noticed how happy he looked, a smile pulled way up to the corners of his eyes. As soon as the last note drained out of the speaker, he reached over and hit replay.

My friend is also deaf.

He couldn't really hear the notes, but he knew the tune was over by the lack of vibrations in the dash of the car. It didn't matter what had been playing, he was just enjoying the summer sun and our company.

He is amazing. He is far more intuitive than I am, far more in tune with other people's emotions. It's as if his visually-oriented world has opened his brain to possibilities most people don't ever dream. All of his being is focused through what he sees—and he sees everything!

People who are deaf, particularly those that use ASL, don't miss anything. You cannot lie to my friend and get away with it. He picks up on every little twitch, lift of an eyebrow, the gleam in an eye, even all the subtle body movements we all use unknowingly. You cannot lie to my friends about your emotions, your desires, and your prejudices.

Another well-meaning friend once told me how sorry he was to hear that we were deaf—that we were born with this disability. He said, "Boy, it must be tough living with someone who's at that kind of disadvantage."

In that moment years ago, my eyes were opened and I began to realize just how many people in the world feel the same way. Many believe that my entire family experiences less of the world because of me—that essentially, in some ways, we (my father, mother, and sister) are all at a disadvantage.

I answered my friend as I do everyone else with the same misguided thoughts: How can we be at a disadvantage? We expect Bryan to do everything the rest of us do. He gets no slack in our house. My God, he's hiked the Grand Canyon, played in a semi-pro basketball league, was a star on his Little League team, is even an accomplished master diver.

Having a friend like Bryan is not a burden to hearing people—it's a blessing. He's as normal as anyone I know (actually more so than most I know). We all agree, including Bryan, that if we could magically bring our hearing back, we wouldn't. We would not have life be any other way.

My friend Bryan often feels sorry for those who have hearing, but cannot see past their preconceived and ill-conceived prejudices, though he would never tell anyone that. He loves everyone for exactly who they are.

So, don't feel sorry for Bryan, or us. Celebrate him. He isn't sick. My life could not be happier.

The next time you meet a deaf person, remember that he or she has a great deal to share with you, so listen. Listen with your eyes if you can. Learn the language of ASL—you'll be a better person for it.

Just then, the Beatles tune was ending for the fourth time. My other two hearing friends were sick of it, but Bryan had a huge smile still pasted across his face as he reached over and pushed the replay button, sighed, and took a long last gaze at those incredible Redwoods.

Author's Notes

How We View It ...
By Stella Egbert

My father, John, the author of this book, has been walking around with a dream in his head and a passion in his heart for more than twenty years. He has always wanted to focus a very bright light on the misunderstood, shadowy world of the deaf. His idea was to write a novel, filled with intrigue, that would not only entertain, but bring to life the many complicated facets he has experienced as a deaf person.

Then, about a year ago, he read Malcolm Gladwell's book, *The Tipping Point*, and a fire was lit. Once he understood how tipping points worked, he realized his book, if he could write it, might act as one of those points. It could start an avalanche of understanding and action. It might even bring so many of the disparate factions in the deaf world together—for it is a complex and controversial world.

I am his daughter and, like him, I have been deaf from birth. When I was young, I attended public school with interpreters and later transferred to a deaf school where I received my diploma. Shortly thereafter, I attended Gallaudet University, the only liberal arts university for deaf individuals. At Gallaudet, I majored in English/Writing. Later, I taught international deaf adults in southern California, and began working toward my master's in linguistics. I currently work with educators for the deaf.

My father and I are not unique in our family. None of us has ever let the inability to hear stand in our way. In fact, sometimes we forget we can't hear; we forget that most of the world doesn't use ASL. My father was successful in the things he committed to, was the rock in our family, and was always an advocate for my brother and me when we received our education.

I am so honored that he would ask me to write what would normally be *his own* notes about his dream. I think that I have expressed his feelings as well as my own.

Everything I've learned and accomplished, I owe to his passion and his undying yearning to educate those individuals in both the hearing and deaf world.

At Gallaudet, my father, at age 18, was introduced to and understood the world of American Sign Language (ASL)—the wonderful symphony of tones and sounds that are transmitted through subtle gestures and expressions; a true language all its own. He also realized he was bilingual in terms of possessing English skills as a language as well. This was an avenue that allowed him and other deaf children, even at the youngest ages, to understand complex ideas, to form word pictures and later, words, and thus to begin to learn to read a written language—English.

Before he attended Gallaudet, he knew nothing about ASL, and that was a travesty. Like my grandparents, most parents are devastated when their child is born deaf; they panic.

These are the parents who are most likely to want their children to learn to speak, even before they learn how to learn. They want their children to appear to be like them; they want them to appear to be "normal." They certainly don't want to send their children out into an "unfamiliar" world. My grandparents chose that avenue and my father lived his childhood the way they understood it best.

So many parents spend countless hours trying to get their children to speak and in the course of these misguided efforts, the child loses valuable learning time—learning deferred is language delayed, or in some cases, lost entirely. In many cases, when these children do arrive at their first year of school, they are light years behind the rest of the class. And this is a crucial point—the more you delay the inevitable, the harder it is to close the gaps.

My father was lucky, though—his curious nature brought him outside his home for most of his childhood, and he learned about life on his own; and eventually, he discovered the world of ASL.

This, of course, is one of the many controversies dealt with in this book. Oftentimes, deaf children are put into rigorous speech therapy as soon as they are old enough. They may be taught Signing Exact English (S.E.E.), which is a rudimentary mode of communication at best and doesn't allow for a sense of fluidity, or of shared communications with other deaf individuals. S.E.E. is a system invented to compensate for failures in our public education system. It's not natural. It is not a language.

For deaf individuals, it is the use of two languages that is paramount; one that is visual that has linguistic properties, and is a shared language within a community—ASL and English in its printed form. This is bilingualism, the true fiber of a deaf person in America where ASL and English are the two languages to convey thoughts and to act as a bridge, one to the other. My father was finally given the means to bridge the two languages while he was at Gallaudet. I often imagine how marvelous it would have been had he been exposed to ASL from birth.

The choice of what deaf children will go through rests with their parents, for they all share a common belief that they are doing the best for their children. "The best" can include choosing assistive devices such as hearing aids. Although we are not against hearing aids or other assistive devices for those that can benefit, we are opposed to irreversible, invasive cochlear implant surgeries on very young, deaf children without the exposure of ASL. Several organizations that claim to represent the deaf espouse these remedies along with stressing that speech is fundamental to language and encouraging the least usage of ASL. However, when they don't work effectively, as is at times the case, not only there is no way to regain the natural hearing prior to implanting, there is also no way we can regain the time lost to incomprehensible input of speech and the opportunity of language.

Most audiologists agree that implanted children remain "severely hearing-impaired" and again, time spent trying to magically get a deaf child to hear and/or speak only *is time forever lost to true learning.*

Also, there are cognitive and linguistic penalties for delayed language acquisition. If implanting is decided, which is truly up to the parents and the child, in which is not wrong, we fervently encourage parents to expose the child to a visual language-in this case, ASL. In other words, in our opinion, it is inexcusable for a parent to leave a child without a whole language for years on end, because ensuring ASL will ensure not only an aspect to communicate, but a cognitive development that goes hand in hand when language are used with purpose.

It is necessary for the parents to become advocates of both languages. The parents must immerse themselves in the languages and their schools, and foster the sense of communication within the family and beyond.

The educational system is also an important discussion topic. The essential prime movers in language proficiency in ASL and English in addition to the parents are *those who are teaching deaf children to be bilingual.* Unfortunately, this isn't always the case. Not all mainstream programs provide deaf individuals with quality educational interpreters who are fluent in both languages. Some programs are even still mired in the 1970s.

The remedy isn't surgery, oralism only, or seeking a S.E.E. imperative. In fact, the solution is a natural process of becoming an individual who thrives on both languages (ASL and written English). A truly bilingual individual thinks in both languages and is capable of using both proficiently. Instead of countless hours wasted in rote activities, readily available and acquired paths to language acquisition and learning rests on these two languages.

Yes, the deaf child faces many challenges, but the lack of communication at home, inferior education in school, discrimination in employment, are obstacles that are continually *placed* there by "well-intentioned" hearing people, who, if they really understood, could readily remove those barriers.

Because there are many choices available, we get confused, so it is important that we become well informed. We should not feel pressured to decide upon what certain individuals feel, but what would be best for the deaf child. Instead of listening to only ourselves, or so-called experts, we should listen to the child, pay attention to the child, and see what s/he really needs. Oftentimes, we realize that the child has been telling us exactly what s/he needs and all we need to do is listen, with our *eyes.*

I hope that the dramatics and the excitement that this fictional story have offered have been successful in opening *your eyes* to the non-fictional challenges I've just discussed. It is far more instructive to paint with color and brush, than pen and black ink; hence, a novel versus a lecture.

My father's dream is that his book will be a *Tipping Point*, a way to foster a real and honest dialogue for hearing *and* deaf people— the small wave that grew into a tsunami of understanding throughout the world.

What follows is a complete resource section. If you are truly interested in this subject, then avail yourself with some very exciting books, articles, Web sites, and miscellaneous information that will help make "informed decisions."

Sincerely,

Stella and John Egbert

Resources

The titles listed below are recommended items to begin exploring the world of deaf people and the language they use. The Web sites listed are two good starting points to where you can locate more titles and resources.

Online Material Ordering and Information Resources
Dawn Sign Press
www.dawnsign.com

Gallaudet University Press
www.gupress.gallaudet.edu

Deaf Culture
"Deaf in America: Voices from a Culture," Carol Padden & Tom Humpries

"Inside Deaf Culture," Carol Padden

"A Journey into the Deaf World," Harlan Lane, Robert Hoffmeister, & Ben Bahan

"Understanding Deaf Culture," Paddy Ladd

"People of the Eye: Stories from the Deaf World," Rachel McKee

American Sign Language
"Signing Naturally," Ella Mae Lentz, Ken Mikos, & Cheri Smith

"ASL Handshape Game Cards," Frank Allen Paul & Ben Bahan

"100 Signs for ...," Dawn Sign Press

"The Gallaudet Dictionary of American Sign Language," Clayton Valli

ASL Literature
"ASL Literature Series," Ben Bahan & Sam Suppalla

ASL Linguistics
"Linguistics of American Sign Language, 4th Ed.," Clayton Valli, Ceil Lucas, & Kristin J. Mulrooney

"Language in Hand: Why Sign Came Before Speech," William C. Stokoe

Deaf Experience
"Alone in the Mainstreamed: A Deaf Woman Remembers," Gina A. Oliva

"The Deaf Experience: Classics in Language and Education," Harlan Lane & Franklin Philip